The Secret

Of

The Eternal Dragon

A STORY BY

BRUCE KILBY AND KEN JOHNSON

A SEQUEL TO THE LEGEND OF THE TOOTH FAIRY

ILLUSTRATIONS BY

JISOO SHIN

Abby
Enjoy Dragon Rider!
Bruce Kilby

The Secret

OF

The Eternal Dragon

A STORY BY

BRUCE KILBY AND KEN JOHNSON

A SEQUEL TO THE LEGEND OF THE TOOTH
FAIRY

Published by Fireside Stories Publishing

#8-5662, 208th Street,
Langley, B.C., Canada
V3A 8G1

www.firesidestoriespublishing.com

Editing, Interior Design and Cover Design:
Wendy Dewar Hughes, Summer Bay Press

ISBN: 978-0-9920742-4-1
Digital ISBN: 978-0-9920742-5-8

Readers can download the chapter plates for youngsters to colour from the website at Firesidestoriespublishing.com.

DEDICATIONS

BRUCE KILBY

To those who serve as First Responders

KEN JOHNSON

To my partner, Janice Brown, and my children, Stacey, Holly, and Connor Johnson. I would be remiss not to mention all the fans of our first book The Legend of the Tooth Fairy, who have been patiently waiting for and asking Bruce and me when is the sequel coming out? Well, here it is, for your enjoyment, to all my family and friends, you know who you are.

Acknowledgements

Bruce Kilby

A story rarely gets completely written without the suggestions and ideas of friends when the subject comes up in casual conversation. This book is no exception. I have to thank Murray Campbell, Colton Platzner, and my son Ryan for some comic relief and ideas that I included in the book.

Thanks also to Ken and Jan for some of the brilliant characters introduced into this sequel.

I'm thankful for the encouragement from my wife, Michelle, who often gave me the time to finish thoughts and offer sound ideas.

Finally, I wish to thank Wendy Dewar Hughes of Summer Bay Press for her continued support and assistance.

Ken Johnson

Again, I would like to thank Bruce Kilby for the pleasure of working with him on this latest project. We've spent many late nights creating this book and many days at events promoting our first book. We've had a lot of laughs and met so many wonderful people. I look forward to meeting the new and welcoming back our past clients.

Thank you, Jisoo Shin, for your commitment to undertaking this project and creating the artwork for this book in record time. We appreciate all your efforts and professionalism, while going through the busiest year of your life. You've managed to keep the magic alive.

Thanks to Janice Brown for promoting and selling our books at her store, The Changing Room, in Langley, British Columbia. Thanks for your love, support, and constant belief. You're still the #1 promoter of my endeavours.

Thanks to all of you, who fuelled our fire, by supporting our first book and encouraging us to keep moving forward with *The Secret of the Eternal Dragon*.

CHAPTER ONE
The Awakening

In the late afternoon, the southerly cool winds picked up, bending the long blades of grass that blanketed the treeless plains north of the Goblin desert. Bataar, a young Gumgolian goat herder, faced away from the breeze and turned up the collar of his summer deel, the traditional Gumgolian summer long coat his mother hand made to look just like the one his aav, or father, wears and his ovoo, or grandfather, wore before him.

The ten-year-old scanned the horizon and saw the first snows painting the tips of the distant Hanging Mountains in the far north. He knew this was the time of year when the sun started to set earlier and the cool evening air would nip at his nose and ears, especially during the autumn winds. He knew that by the time he got back to his village he would be thankful he had put his deel on. Bataar was thankful he had listened to his mother who had insisted he pack his padded long coat in the pouch slung over the back of Kushi, his reindeer friend.

Kushi and the boy had been born around the same time and had played together every day since they were young. As a baby, Bataar climbed all over Kushi and later on, they chased each other in the fields, playing their own game of tag. Kushi would sneak up from behind and nudge Bataar in the back, sending Bataar flying. Bataar would jump out from hiding in the hay and startle Kushi. And so it went as their great friendship began. He felt lucky to have Kushi as only a few boys had reindeer as friends and even fewer could ride one.

Most animals are stubborn and get annoyed when petted, especially when looking for wives. But not Kushi. He was always kind and gentle with Bataar as if he was one of his own kind. When Kushi's great antlers grew, Bataar was able to hold on to them while learning to herd goats in the grass plains. Kushi tolerated it and never grew irritated with his best friend.

Now Kushi nuzzled Bataar in the back to push him in the direction of home.

"Okay, okay, I get it Kushi. It's time to head home," he said, trying to keep his balance. He rubbed Kushi's snout lovingly, "Enough of this blustery wind. I know the sand it carries bothers your eyes, my friend, so let's be off."

The herd of goats also sensed the time of day and turned instinctively toward the Allrain Mountains foothills where the young boy's tosgon, or village, was nestled. Bataar tugged down the fur-lined flaps of his traditional pointed Gumgolian Toortsog hat to protect his ears for the long trek back. He knew darkness would soon set in so he grabbed Kushi's reins and started the craggy descent back to his family's yurt, a sturdy round tent.

The rumble in his tummy brought thoughts of supper and sitting by a warm fire. He could already almost taste his mother's steamed dough pockets stuffed with onions, minced beef, and vegetables, called Buuz, and, of course, some warm milk tea.

To protect them from the winds, his family's yurt and the other nomadic homes of the Noman people nestled in the low hills of the Allrain Mountains. Bataar knew that his father Chuluun and the other elders would decide to move the entire village soon to winter in a warmer climate. Bataar led Kushi down the difficult climb to the summer village.

Bataar did not notice the flock of lapwings and several sheldrakes that took flight, or the grey geese already heading away from the hills toward the plains. But he did notice that the goats seemed fidgety and bleated nervously.

"What is wrong, little ones?" Suddenly, resisting the direction the herder guided them, they bolted toward the plains in full charge. "Hey, where are you going?" Bataar shouted after them. His faithful friend, Kushi, reared in fright, pulled the reigns from the boy's grip, and plunged after the goats.

"Hey! What's going on? Now where are you going?" he called after his friend. "Come back! Come baaaaack," he pleaded. It was like his calls fell on deaf ears of the fleeing animals, *Strange,* he thought. *The last time they ran like that was during a lightning storm at the last leaf fall.* He scanned the sky and saw only the first evening star, and not one cloud in the sky. He looked around to see what else could have spooked the animals but saw nothing unusual. With on last valiant cry, he called after them, "Kushi, little ones, come baaaaack!"

As he watched his herd disappear in the distance, he felt the first tremor under foot. Startled, he tried to steady himself but the vibration only grew as the ground shook beneath him. He dropped to his hands and knees. He had never felt the ground shake like this before. His father had told stories of earthquakes years ago but he could not imagine what one actually felt like. Now he realized why the animals had taken off so fast. They must have sensed the quake coming and left

Bataar to ride it out alone. He wished that he too had run with the herd but it was too late.

The earth quivered and heaved violently. He could not even stand up, let alone run. Frightened for his life, he firmly dug his fingers into dry clumps of grass and held on. He looked up to see rocks fall from the nearby steep cliffs, bounce, then roll down the hill toward him. Great slabs of rock separated from the face of the mountains and smashed to the ground. The thunderous rumble was deafening.

There was nothing he could do but hold on and hope that none of the tumbling boulders hit and crushed him. Lying flat, he clung to the ground as massive rocks narrowly missed him. Then he curled sideways and covered his head with his arms as showers of small rocks, gravel, and dirt rained upon him.

Peering between his fingers, his eyes widened as he saw a great crack form in the ground before of him. The cavernous, jagged trench headed north, directly toward his village. He shut his eyes and prayed for his sister, Bolormaa, his parents, and his friends in the village. His thoughts then turned to his pet reindeer, Kushi, and his herd of goats. He prayed they would be all right.

Seconds seemed like an eternity, but gradually the rumbling eased and eventually came to a tentative stop. Bataar was covered in a layer of soil and debris. If someone had come upon him he would be unrecognizable as a human. He looked like a mound, simply part of the new landscape. The only indication he was even there was the point of his Toorsog hat poking out of the ground with an uprooted flower stuck on its tip.

Slowly, his fingers poked through the crumbling sand, then his hand pushed up the earth. His arm, then his whole body broke through and he sat up. Covered

5

in dust, he coughed, wobbling unsteadily to his feet. Beating the dust and the flower off his hat, he put it back on. Then he brushed off the dirt clinging to him and checked to see if he was hurt.

"Wha...what is that?" he squealed. He felt something squirm and wriggle inside his tunic.

At first, it tickled and made him giggle nervously but then his smile disappeared. These parts were known for vipers or rat snakes they called Mogoi, or slender racers. Now he panicked. He danced and twisted, trying to grab the creature as it raced around his body trying to escape his eager grasp. Finally, he tore open the front of his deel and out popped a pygmy gecko that leapt to the ground and scurried away.

Relieved, Bataar watched the gecko scamper off to find a home in the cracks of the newly scattered rocks. Now that his panic had subsided, he scanned the countryside to see if any recognizable landmark, person, or animal had survived the quake. Nothing looked familiar except the Fangai Mountains off in the distance. As far as he could see the terrain looked desolate, barren, and inhospitable. He saw no sign of his goats or Kushi and for the first time in his life, he felt utterly alone. He slumped down on a nearby rock and rested his chin in his hands.

His father had taught him that the herd always came first. His job was to protect the herd, so his first thought was that he should head south to round them up and hopefully find his friend Kushi. Instead, frightened, he longed for his mother, his sister, and his father. He wanted to know if they were all right. Perhaps he was now an orphan out here in the wild plains of the Allrain Mountains. In a moment he had made his decision. He stood up and turned toward the north.

Bataar trudged over the heaving landscape following the newly formed chasm that stretched toward his village. He could not track his normal worn goat path, as it no longer existed. Even the path along the stream had changed; the river's new direction now made its way around and over the rocks and debris that blocked its course. Forced, he climbed the steep hills, wearily making his way until finally cresting the ridge of the valley where his village below should have been. When he looked into the sheltered dale he flopped to the ground, stunned at what he saw. All of the tent-like structures were flattened or simply no longer existed. The crevice had gone straight through the village, dividing it in half and shredding all in its path. He saw no movement except for canvas remnants flapping in the wind. It was as if his worst fears had come true.

A tear trickled down his cheek. He knew he had to go and see if his family, or anybody of the clan, was still alive. With grave uncertainty, he stood up and descended into the village. As he climbed down the steep slope, he thought this must be the most awful day of his short life. In one instant his whole life had changed. This morning he was cheerful boy when he had said goodbye to his mother and shared a smile with his father as he left to tend the herd in the nearby grassy plains.

He had lost all his goats and his dear friend Kushi. He did not know if anyone of his family was still alive, or if he was now an orphan. His need of proof drove him numbly toward his village.

As he approached, he scanned for any evidence of human life but found none. Not only did he not see signs of human life, he saw not one living creature. No chickens, no cows, no horses—not even a wild bird. The village was eerily desolate. He went to the edge of the chasm and looked down into the abyss to see if the earthquake had swallowed everyone up but all he saw was darkness.

"Hello? Anyone here?" Bataar called, and then listened for answering voices. Nothing but his echo replied. His family's yurt had somehow survived the quake and had only partially collapsed. He pulled back the canvas flap to see only strewn belongings, over-turned pots, and scattered boxes. He picked it up his sister's doll. *What has happened to her?* He held the doll in his hands. His sister and the rest of his family were gone. That's when he sat down and sobbed.

Bataar woke the next morning as the sun peeked over the eastern hills. In his sleepy state, he thought that everything he had seen the day before was perhaps all a dream. Leaping to his feet, he looked around, but nothing had changed. The tumbledown village looked just as he left it before the hours of darkness had settled on him. During the night he had felt two small after-tremors that had startled him awake, but all seemed calm this morning.

He started a fire and put on a pot of water to make some tea. After his small breakfast, he started to pick up the debris to rebuild the yurt. He knew he needed to start putting things back together as autumn would soon change to winter.

With a growing sense of despair, he searched the other gars hoping to gather things he might need and perhaps find a survivor buried beneath the debris or anything that might tell him where everyone had gone. Once again, he found nothing, not even a pet. Strangely, it was if everyone had vanished off the face of the earth—or perhaps into the depths of the earth itself. He gathered what food he could find and started erecting the poles that would rebuild his home.

He attached the latticework to the upright poles to form the round outside walls of the yurt. Being small, he struggled to put up the roof poles and was trying to lift one up when he heard a voice behind him.

8

"You are a little small for building yurts, I think."

Startled, Bataar spun around. His father, Chuluun, sat majestically on his horse, wearing the traditional nomadic Gumgolian dress.

"Father!" he shouted. "You're alive!"

"Why would I not be?"

"But, but the earthquake?" Bataar noticed all the village people now returning from the hills. "I thought it had swallowed the entire village!"

His father laughed, "Ah, my son, I told you stories of earthquakes did I not?"

"Yes, father but..."

"We learned what to do the last time the earthquakes came."

The look on Bataar's face told his father that he had not. "But..."

"We know that as soon as you see all the birds fly and the animals flee suddenly, we need to go also," his father interrupted.

"I am so glad to see you, father."

Wrapping his arms around his son, Chuluun said, "I am proud of you, my brave son."

The village people set about rebuilding the yurts and putting the camp back together. As nomadic people, it did not take long before the village started to look like it had before the quake.

"Father, I lost Kushi and the goats," Bataar said sadly. "I could not hold them back when they started to run."

"Do not worry, my son. We will go after them once we get set back up again."

Everyone in the village worked hard all morning to re-build the broken down structures and it was not until early afternoon when Bataar heard a familiar noise in the distance. He looked up but saw nothing.

"What is it, my son?" his father asked.

"I thought I heard...oh, it's nothing, Father. It must be the wind trying to fool me."

"I have heard the wind whispers many times my son."

Then he heard the sound again. This time he recognized the familiar wavering cry of a goat. Not just any goat but one he knew well. He looked up to the south ridge and saw the old goat Bat, leader of his herd, silhouetted on the crest. Bataar's heart raced when he saw another goat, then another appear. The whole herd had returned. Finally he saw Kushi following up the rear. Bataar jumped for joy!

"You found your way home!" he yelled, running up the hill to greet them. "Father, they came home!"

"Yes I see, son. Go meet them."

Out of breath from running, Bataar flung his arms around Kushi's neck and hugged him hard. "I knew you would bring them back; I knew it. I am so glad you came back to me." The reindeer nodded his head and snorted, as he too was happy to see his friend. The goats on the other hand, were more interested in grazing than meeting Bataar. But to him, that was okay. They had all come home safely.

In his joy, he nearly stepped on a round shape poking out of the ground. The large, smooth oval looked unlike any rock he had ever seen before. Bataar shooed a couple of goats away and used his hands to scrape away the dirt from around the orb. As he dug, he saw another, and another. *What kind of rock is this?* he wondered. *The shaking ground must have raised these from their rest.*

Picking up one of the beautiful spheres he lifted it up into the sky. It felt lighter than a rock and peculiar translucent colours appeared when held up toward the sun. In fact, it wasn't like a rock at all. It was more like...a giant egg.

Far, far away in a dark chasm deep inside a volcano, Fangor, the last dragon of Fairyland, opened one red eye. He sensed something. He sniffed toward the east, past the town of Bicuspid, and roared.

Chapter Two

The Invitation

"Here is the latest news," the smartly dressed female newscaster reported on the television. "Today in Bicuspid, rather strange, larger than normal bat-like creatures, have steadily gathered in local neighbourhoods as well as near the Root Canal. Although no one has been seriously hurt so far, there are several reports of people being attacked. The recent disappearances of several pets are also being blamed on these ugly creatures."

A twilight camera shot appeared on the screen showing several large bats with glaring yellow eyes hanging upside down in elm trees, from lampposts, and from the eaves of many local buildings.

"Experts believe these are a new species of bat but are not sure of their origin." The camera now switched to a male co-anchor. "As these bats appear only at night, townsfolk are being asked not to go out between dusk and dawn unless absolutely necessary. Do not leave children unattended, and travel in pairs. They are also advised to carry an umbrella to fend off aerial attacks. Keep all pets inside."

The camera moved back to the female anchor. "Now for some international news from Brushya. Brushyan palaeontologists report that a young Gumgolian goat herder has found what they believe to be new species of dinosaur in the foothills of the Allrain Mountains in the

13

remote area of Rainmen, Gumgolia." File footage showed the young goatherd waving at the camera on the Gumgolian grass plains then focussed on a group of prehistoric eggs.

"These eggs were first believed to be Velociraptor eggs similar to those found several years ago in the nearby area. Due to their large size and colouring, they now believe these eggs to be of a previously unknown species of dinosaur. Tests will be conducted to determine exactly what kind of dinosaur they belong to at the Brushyan Paleontology Museum in Mosjowl. We will be back with sports in two minutes."

"Wow, Dad! Dinosaurs! Can we go to Gumgolia?" Connor shouted as he looked up from playing with his toy tyrannosaurus, a birthday present for turning four today.

His dog, Snapper, jumped up and down trying to grab the toy dinosaur saying, *I want it, I want it, I want it*, with his eyes.

"I think those eggs are special, Daddy," Connor's big sister, Holly, said.

"I am sure they are, dear. It's always exciting when they find new things."

"Like my tyrannosaurus!" Connor shouted pushing Snapper away from his toys.

"I am more concerned about those bats, son. You never know what kind of diseases those things carry. We don't want some kind of plague or rabies going on around here should one of them bite someone. I would not want one of them to come down and carry you away for their supper," he joked.

"Awww, Daaaad!" Connor giggled. "Dat won't happen!"

"You're probably right son; you would only be a snack for those guys anyway. They like a bit of meat on the bones!"

"Daaaaad!" he protested again, returning his focus to the toy dinosaur. "I think they should call it Gumgolasaurus!" He held up his toy and roared.

"No, Dad, I think these eggs are really special. I can sense it," Holly said. She had already heard the news story from her stuffed bear, Taddy Boy, the night before.

"Maybe so, maybe so," he answered, his attention returning to is newspaper during the television commercials.

"Another tooth came out last night, Daddy. Now I can put it in my Tooth Fairy Tooth®. I will make the Tooth Fairy Call so the tooth fairy will come!"

"Yes dear, I'm sure he will."

"Or she," Holly corrected, walking away to find Taddy Boy.

High in the snow-covered mountains north of Bicuspid, in the protected glen where the one remaining enchanted Fairyland nestled, King Mo-lar and the other Fairyland kings were all abuzz. They had heard Fangor wake and roar from the dark belly of the secret cave.

This cave had been magically hidden and sealed centuries before on an agreement made between the dragon Fangor, the human king, King Overbite, and all the fairy kings from each of the hives from all around the world. It had been done to prevent dragons from causing mass destruction to humans ever again. Humans were terrified of dragons because they fed on their livestock, scorched their crops, but more hideously, snatched their young children for their baby teeth.

Unknown to humans, fairies also needed dragons. Dragons warmed their lands so that their giant toadstool homes grew and kept winter frost away. Their wings were made of dragon scales and, unlike the drooling gummies who used dragon scales for Nightmare Dust, their potion was used to make magic fairy dust and give sweet dreams.

Fangor kept the last Fairyland safe from intruders. The Drooling Gummies, goblins, evil witches, and warlocks all coveted the fairies' secrets to use for their own sinister ends.

The last Fairyland still had thousands upon thousands of fairies living there, even after the ancient dragon wars that had killed all but one dragon. Now it buzzed with concern. The fairies always became anxious when the one remaining dragon woke up unexpectedly.

They hovered in anticipation around the cave's entrance that led into the inner grottos of the volcano. Every fairy knew what happened the last time a young human named Garth woke Fangor from his sleep. He had become *furious* – as they tend to do. All the world's dragons arose and the dragon wars had been declared. A furious fight between the dragons and humans knights raged. Many knights proved their valour but many died fighting the fire breathers. The war lasted until each dragon was slain, all except one: Fangor.

Before the wars, hives of fairies gathered around a dragon who protected their hiding places, kept the land warm, and all living together in harmony but as each dragon died, its hive had to join an existing hive with another dragon. Gradually, as each dragon fell, the hives melded into one Fairyland on the side of the volcano north of Bicuspid, with King Mo-lar as its King and Fangor as its dragon.

The last time Fangor had been allowed out of his cave had been many centuries before, to defend Fairyland against an attack from an army of bat-like creatures they called the Drooling Gummies, led by Pyorrhea Pete the Pirate and his henchwoman, Ginger Vitas. With the help of Garth, a magician's apprentice, along with the fairies, a sea princess, and the human knights, they repelled the evil Gummies who wanted to destroy the fairies by turning them into human boys and girls. But most of all, they wanted to pluck fairy wings and steal dragon scales for their noxious Nightmare Dust.

Desperate to keep the last dragon alive, King Mo-lar made a new agreement with the human king, King Overbite, that the fairies would hide Fangor in a cave behind a magic door and promised that the dragon would never leave if the people would let him live.

Fangor knew this too and even though he had become a friend of Garth, to humans he was seen as too dangerous to be freed. In order to keep Fangor alive and keep his flame eternal, the fairies promised that they would come at night and collect children's baby teeth when they fell out, and leave a coin or two from the rainbow's pot of gold for the hopeful boy or girl. All the children had to do was to put the tooth in The Tooth Fairy Tooth® and say the Tooth Fairy Call:

Tooth Fairy, Tooth Fairy please come tonight,
Please take my tooth on your midnight flight,
Sprinkle some magic to chase my nightmares away
And leave a brand new coin that I might spend or save.

Even though humans may have forgotten why the Tooth Fairy came for children's teeth, for centuries the pact had been in place and the three partners have lived in peaceful harmony.

Now, Fangor had woken up. Not wanting another war, King Mo-lar, King of Fairyland, knew he had to investigate what the trouble was all about.

17

> "Oh dear, what can the matter be
> Fangor sounds like he wants to be free."

King Mo-lar waved his wand over the magic door covering the cave's entrance as he had done every day to bring Fangor the children's teeth from around the world. What appeared to be solid rock now disappeared and he flew into the cave's gaping dark entrance. Down he went, twisting and turning toward Fangor's lair hidden deep the volcano's belly. As he descended, his nose twitched at the smell of bitter sulphur and could feel the heat from the molten lava rising from the depths below.

Finally, he entered a vast cavern lit by the lava bubbling away below. He found Fangor settled on a ledge amid rising steam. The dragon's preferred perch kept his scales moist and skin soft. He was surrounded by sack upon sack filled with tiny teeth for his morning meal. Curled up but unquestionably awake, he lay flicking his tail in obvious agitation. Fangor snorted and smoke bellowed from his nostrils as he watched King Mo-lar descend and hover before him.

> "Fangor, my friend indeed
> We heard your roar and wondered
> Is there something that you need?"

Fangor lifted his head and spoke.

> "I am with heavy heart
> As I lay here in the dark,
> For I have sensed eggs of my kind have been found
> Dug up from underground.
> This you must believe
> To make them live I need to leave."

A frown came upon King Mo-lar's face.

"To let you leave would break your oath
To see you die would hurt me most,
Is there something I can do,
So the humans won't hurt you?"

Fangor growled in dismay and a burst of flame left his jaws.

**"To let my kind survive
And let fairies have new hives,
We must bring to life the eggs that were found
I wonder, is my friend Garth still around?
To convince the King to release me from my bond,
And to help my kind live with his magic wand?"**

Sweating from the heat, King Mo-lar pondered then replied,

"Ah my dear friend you forget
Humans are not eternal yet,
Their lives are very short indeed
As they do not have magic you see."

Fangor wondered out loud:

**"If Garth is no longer with us
Is there no human we can trust?"**

King Mo-lar thought for a while then snapped his fingers.

"I have an idea, my friend
My fairies I will send,
A descendant we will find
To see if they will help you with your kind."

Fangor roared with delight.

**"Yes, my friend indeed.
Find the one who can help me."**

19

With a nod and a smile, King Mo-lar wiped the sweat from his brow and raced off, up out of the cave and back to Fairyland. After resealing the door and thankful of the fresh air, he called for a gathering of the Fairy kings.

> "Gather one, gather all
> A royal meeting I do call."

The kings from the other realms came forth and sat on the royal circle toadstools in the middle of King Mo-lar's courtyard. King Wisdom from the Northern Upperfangs, King Toothhurty from the Eastern Palates, King Mungmouth from the Western Tonguies and finally, King Jeb from the Southern Backtooths gathered around King Mo-lar.

> "Please don't worry
> Fangor isn't mad
> But he wants to leave
> And that's a problem we do have."

Startled gasps came from the kings and all those in the public gallery surrounding the courtyard. King Wisdom blurted what the others were thinking:

> "But our promise to King Overbite will be broken.
> His escape will surely be noted.
> Why would he want to leave
> After all these centuries?"

King Mo-lar replied,

> "He has sensed the presence of others of his kind
> Far away Dragon eggs that he must now find,
> To bring back the dragons so they can roam
> Once more to find their homes.
> And if he can bring them back to life
> Once again we will all have our own fairy hives."

The kings began to talk all at once, excited at the prospect of having their own hives back. Others were

20

undecided as to what to do. To break the promise, or keep things as they were, was indeed a problem.

King Mungmouth stood up and stated,

> "Alive we stay
> If we keep things this way
> And Fangor at bay."

King Toothhurty replied,

> "But if dragons came back to the land
> We will once again have our own Fairylands."

King Jeb predicted doom.

> "If Fangor is slain we all fail
> We all become just fairytales."

King Mo-lar interrupted.

> "Please be calm, I have a notion
> To save us from all the commotion.
> We will get a human we can trust
> I'm sure a descendant of Garth will help us,
> I have kept an eye on all his heirs over time
> She will not be difficult to find."

King Wisdom commented,

> "She? A girl this must be.
> Does she have the magic she will need?"

King Mo-lar replied,

> "Why yes indeed, I believe she has
> Through all this time the magic has last
> She is wise, thoughtful, and strong—
> Maybe not afraid to help a dragon."

King Toothhurty spoke.

> "If this is our only chance
> To help our circumstance
> Send a fairy with a plea for help
> To come to the aid of the fairy elves."

21

King Mo-lar answered,

> "I have been told she has made a Fairy Call
> A message I will send after nightfall,
> With the coin for her tooth we'll leave
> And invite her to her destiny."

With nods of approval, the kings departed to await her reply.

As promised, when night fell, he sent a tooth fairy out to find the descendant of Garth with a note from the king.

CHAPTER THREE

The Adventure Begins

"I had such a strange dream last night, Taddy Boy. I was riding on the back of a dragon! Can you believe it?"

"Uh huh, been there, done that. Don't want to do it again," Taddy Boy replied with a yawn.

"You have got to be kidding! *That* would be so exciting! Could you imagine travelling the around the world..."

"No, I can't. Too old and too tired. The last time I did that I was stuffed in a backpack while my magician's apprentice buddy shot fireballs at bats!"

"But, but..."

"Why don't you see what the tooth fairy brought," Taddy Boy said, trying to change the subject.

Holly opened the Tooth Fairy Tooth® container sitting beside her bed and looked inside. "Wow, dude, there are five silver dollars in there!"

"Dude? What is a *dude?*"

"There's also something else."

"What do you mean, *DUDE?*"

"It's just a saying, Taddy Boy, nothing bad. Look, it's a tiny note on some old paper." Holly unfurled the piece of parchment and tried to read the message. "It sure is tiny."

"What does it say?"

"The writing is so tiny I need a magnifying glass."

Holly scurried off to the living room to find her dad's magnifying glass that he kept beside his chair to read the small print in the newspaper.

"Whadaya got there, Holly?" Connor yelled. He was eating his breakfast cereal at the kitchen table.

"Nothin'," she replied as she hurried back to her bedroom.

"Whadya get from the tooth fairy?" he yelled but got no reply except the slam of her door.

"I only asked!" he yelled after.

Holly flattened the paper on her white student desk and turned on the lamp. "Now let's see..." She held up the glass to her eye to focus on the writing, and then read the note out loud:

"Magician's apprentice, come as soon as you can.

We need your help to save Fairyland"

"Oh no, we can't do that. Uh, uh, too dangerous, soooo very dangerous," Taddy Boy declared.

Ignoring Taddy Boy and examining the piece of paper, Holly mused, "I wonder what it means."

"It means nothing, little one. Just throw the note away and let's plan to spend the money. I know you like chocolate."

"I wonder *who* they mean."

"Obviously not you, because you're no magician's apprentice...right? How about breakfast? Aren't you hungry?"

"But *you* said I was a long lost descendant of Garth and wasn't he a magician's apprentice?"

"I lied! Er, I mean, that was a mistake."

Raising her eyebrow, Holly replied, "And didn't *you* just tell me the story of how he helped the fairies a long time ago?"

"Doh...that was a mistake too."

"I think this note was for me."

"Oh no, here we go again," Taddy Boy said with a sigh.

"*Daaaaaaaad*," she yelled, "can you tell me what this means?" Holly ran down the hall to her parents' bedroom where they lay in bed trying to get their much-loved Saturday morning sleep-in.

"You're gonna get yourself in *big* trouble," Conner yelled from the kitchen as he slurped another spoonful of milk and cereal.

"Dad, Dad! Wake up," Holly shouted, tugging on his pyjama collar. "I got somethin' to show you."

Her father didn't even open an eye. "Not now, sweetie," he muttered. "Can't you see that your mother and I are trying to sleep in?"

"But Dad, this is important!"

"Later, sweetie. Please let us sleep." He squinted at the bed side clock, "It's only...*what?* Six AM!" He slumped back into his pillow with a sigh.

"I told ya. *Big* trouble." Connor now stood at the bedroom door with milk dribbling down the front of his sleeper pyjamas.

"Dad, Dad, this is important. Are you awake?" She pulled on his one exposed wrist dangling out from under the covers.

"I am *now!* What do you want?" he said opening his bleary eyes.

"Look at, look at what I got in my tooth container."

"Let me guess...money?"

"Yeah, I got five silver dollars but there was something else."

"That's nice, dear," he mumbled.

"But Dad, I think it's important. There was a note, see?"

"Maybe a Chinese fairy left you a fortune cookie," he mumbled. Holly's face showed no amusement. "Okay, okay, what does it say?"

26

"Look. It says, *Magician's apprentice, come as soon as you can. We need your help to save Fairyland.*"

Holly's father sat up and took the note and the magnifying glass from her. "It's all gibberish to me. I can't make out one word, or letter, for that matter. It looks like a foreign language to me."

"No look. It says, *Magician's apprentice, come as soon as you can. We need your help to save Fairyland.*"

"Well, I can't read it. Show your mother. Maybe she can figure it out."

Holly's mother rolled over. "Let me have a look, honey." After studying it closely she said, "Hmmm, I can't make it out either. These are strange letters I have never seen before. Hey, are you sure this was left with your money? Or is this one of your made up stories?"

"No, Mom, honest," she said, taking the note back. "I can read it."

"Well, I don't think it means much. Why don't you go off and play and let us sleep a little while longer. We'll have a look at it later, okay, sweetie?" She yawned and pulled the covers back over her head to block out the new day, curling up next to Holly's dad who was already sound asleep.

Why can't Mom and Dad read the message? Holly wondered as she left the room.

There was only one person who could give her answers—Taddy Boy. "Well, Taddy Boy, Mom and Dad couldn't even read it let alone tell me what it's all about."

"It's Elfin," her bear replied with a shrug.

"What is Elfin?"

"The language of the fairies."

"How come I can read it and they can't?"

"Because only those with magic within their hearts can read it. Your parents have long since left the world

27

of children, stopped believing in fairies, and therefore have forgotten the ancient language of the fairies."

"I have magic in my heart?"

"You *are* the descendant of Garth, the Magician of the Royal Court of Bicuspid. That is why you can hear me and no one else can."

"So the fairies need my help."

"It appears so, little one."

"I am not little," Holly snapped. "I may be young but I'm not little!"

"Of course, my lady," Taddy Boy replied, with a mock bow.

"Waddaya doin' Holly?" Connor stood in the doorway as their pet dog, Snapper, scampered into the room.

"Nothing," she said.

"I told ya before, dat ting don't talk!" He eyed Taddy Boy and snickered.

"Go away!" Holly commanded. "I told *you*, he talks to me!"

"I think ya gone cuckoo," he shouted, swirling his finger around next to his temple.

"I said, go away!"

She picked up a toy stuffed bunny and threw it at him, but a giggling Connor had already run down the hall. She could hear is mimicking voice. "I got magic in my heart! I got magic in my heart."

Snapper grabbed the bunny and shook it in his teeth. Then, seeming to realize the bunny was not real and didn't squeak, he turned his attention to Taddy Boy. Leaping onto Holly's bed he sniffed the bear.

"Get that fur ball with fangs away from me," Taddy Boy cried. "He's giving me the beady eye."

"Take your dog with you, Conner," Holly called, pushing the animal off the bed and out the door.

"Oh, wouldn't want to see Snapper rip your precious Taddy's head off, would ya?" Conner jeered.

"Connor!" Holly's father yelled from the bedroom down the hall. "Go watch cartoons on TV and leave Holly alone. And for heaven's sake, the both of you, stop all the noise and let us sleep!"

"That dog's got a problem," said Taddy Boy.

"He's after your squeaker," Holly giggled, closing her bedroom door.

"Squeaker? What's a squeaker?"

"Oh, don't worry about it. Stuffed toys for dogs all have them these days."

"How embarrassing," he replied.

Holly turned her attention to the note. "But I am not a magician's apprentice."

"Nor was Garth when he started out on his adventure. Not saying we should be going on any adventure, mind you."

"Oh, Taddy Boy, you are such a scaredy bear." She gave him a loving scratch behind his ear.

"That's what Garth said before we nearly got killed!"

"That was a long time ago. We are much braver these days."

"We are?"

"How would I become a magician's apprentice?"

"Well, Garth found a magician's shop in the old part of the city and was given a magic book by Whitey E. Namel, a magician of the First Level. Garth became the magician's apprentice of Tar Tar Goldcaps, the famous magician who put all the ogres to sleep."

"I remember the story you told me. His statue is in the city square but it was moved there many years ago. We could still look for the old shop."

"But the old city was destroyed by an earthquake a long, long time ago. The new city of Bicuspid was built on top of the old one. There is no way the magic shop of Whitey E. Namel would still exist today."

"Maybe it's just buried," Holly asserted. "We could go into the subway to find it."

"You don't give up do you? Just like Garth; he didn't either. Why don't we just plan to spend your five silver dollars?"

She ignored his suggestion. "Is there any other way?"

"Really? Oh, okay," Taddy Boy sighed. "How about the castle? Maybe we could go and ask the king. I am sure he would know where Garth had his magic workshop in the castle."

"There is no king anymore...or a castle, really. Only ruins are left."

"No king! What do you mean, no king?" Taddy Boy gaped at Holly.

"Dad says we have a republic so we no longer have a king."

"What about the promise?"

"What promise?"

"You know, the one I told you about in the story between the humans, fairies, and dragons?"

"Fangor has been hidden in the volcano for so long no one really thinks dragons exist anymore. Adults don't believe in fairies either. They have all forgotten."

"What about the tooth fairy, the Christmas elf, or, or Easter bunnies?"

"Yeah, my parents still believe in them, but I know a lot of adults who don't."

"They *have* to believe in them! They keep the balance between good and evil. The guardians of mother earth! Humans need magic!"

Holly shrugged. "Children still believe in them."

"Whew, thank goodness! There is still hope." He paused and thought for a moment. "What happened to the king?"

"The last king was King Overbite. We learned in school that after he married Princess Pearly White, they had a son they named Poseidon."

"Yes, I remember that day. What a day! They married after we had defeated the Drooling Gummies."

"What do you mean 'we'?"

"Well, I was there, wasn't I? I was in the backpack all the while the battle raged."

"As brave as you are today?" Holly gazed at him fondly.

"Well, I..." he stammered then changed the subject. "That's a good name they gave their son."

"Yes, but when he grew up he became the ruler of the seas, just like Princess Pearly White and King Neptune had done before him."

"And like Pearly White, he went back to the sea?"

"No one really knows," Holly explained. "Both Poseidon and Queen Pearly White disappeared and never returned. The king was so sad. He yearned for his son to return to take over the kingdom but when he didn't come back, the king died in grief. With no heir, the line of kings of Bicuspid ended."

"How very sad." Holly knew that if Taddy could cry, he would have had a tear in his eye.

"Now we have presidents."

"Maybe the president would know of the promise."

"I don't think so. It was agreed to so long ago."

"That is sad, too." Taddy Boy shook his head.

"Well, we have to do something. The fairies have called for help from a magician's apprentice."

"Do *we* have to?" Taddy raised one eyebrow.

"Yes, Taddy Boy, *we* have to. We will go to the castle ruins and see if we can find a map to Fairyland or anything that can help us."

"I can't wait," he said, rolling his eyes.

CHAPTER FOUR

The Castle's Secret

By the time Holly's parents read the note she had left, she was already halfway to the castle ruins, riding the bicycle she had got the Christmas before. Taddy Boy was once again, just as he had been with Garth, stuffed into her backpack with his head poking out of the top and looking over her shoulder.

Holly's father paced back and forth. "Where does she think she's going all alone!" he yelled.

"It says she is going to the castle to become a magician's apprentice. Not to worry, she will be home before the streetlights come on," her mother said, re-reading the note.

"I told her she would be in *big* trouble," Connor told them, still playing with his dinosaur on the floor. "I said, 'don't go' but she wouldn't listen! Oh no, not *my* older sister," he said adding emphasis with a satisfied smirk.

"Why didn't you wake us? You know she can't be out on the streets at her age!" his dad asked.

"But, you always tell us to act like grownups!" Connor replied, wondering why he was getting into trouble.

"Don't be smart, young man!" his mother snapped. "You should have woken us!"

"But Dad said not to make any noise."

Both parents looked at each other.

"Should we call the police, dear?" Conner could see his mother's worried expression.

"No, I'll go out and look for her myself and bring her back. Honey, where's my phone? It's not in the charger."

"She took it," Connor answered.

"What? Why didn't you say so?" his dad said.

"You didn't ask," Connor replied.

The sun had not quite risen when Holly had left the house and she could see the odd pair of glowing yellow eyes of the strange bats that still hung in the trees. She sped as fast as she could on her bicycle hoping not to be seen, but the ever-watchful eyes did indeed follow her. One hunter swooped down to attack but his long talons missed their target as Holly turned a corner. He retreated to a large elm tree.

"Did you see that?" Taddy Boy croaked.

"Yes, I saw him."

"We should go back. I told you, these things are *dangerous!*"

"I don't think so."

"What do you mean? 'I don't think so!' Don't you remember the story? They will eat you up in one second flat!"

Holly knew these were no ordinary bats. She knew these were the gummies Taddy Boy had told her about in the story. They were the huge, ugly beasts that snarled, had long teeth, and were led long ago by Pyorrhoea Pete the Pirate and his henchwoman, Ginger Vitas. These beasts could tear apart and devour an animal in seconds flat. She didn't know why yet, but for some reason they had returned to Bicuspid.

"I remember, but I don't think they will attack me."

"They, they just did!" he said in a quavering voice.

"They have more important things to worry about right now."

"Yeah, and what's that?"

"The sun."

One by one, the bats left their perches and headed for the western coast, away from the rising sun and toward the safety of their dark caves.

"No one likes a smarty pants," was all Holly heard coming from the backpack.

Just as the sun had edged above the horizon, Holly reached the front gates of the Bicuspid Castle only to find that the front gates were closed and would not open for public tours until 10:00 AM.

Happily relieved, Taddy Boy said, "Well, that's that. I guess we can go home now. Maybe we can stop by the candy store and spend some of your money?"

"I don't think so," she replied, testing the door handle.

"But Holly, the castle doesn't open for hours."

"There must be another way in," she said propping her bicycle next to a tree. Investigating, she started to walk around the outside castle walls that were, for the most part, still intact.

"Why did I know you were going to say that?" Taddy Boy grumbled.

She made her way around, following the path outside the wall that led down to the old castle docks on the Root Canal. Over time, a tangle of trees and shrubs had grown but none were large enough nor near enough to climb to get over the high wall. As she rounded a corner, she found a portion of the wall that had crumbled into rubble.

Pondering out loud, she said, "I wonder if this fell during the earthquake many years ago."

The wall was between two ruined guard towers that were once used to protect the inner castle from a seaborne attack.

"Now this is what we are looking for, Taddy Boy."

"It's an awfully *big* pile of rocks, Holly," he pointed out.

"Nothing ventured, nothing gained," she said and started to scale the first large block of granite.

"Hmmmph!" was the only sound she heard coming from behind her. She grinned and kept climbing.

Block by block, she climbed up the massive pile of fallen stones. Some of the huge blocks were her size or bigger, forcing her to reach for tiny crevasses to get a finger or toe hold as she slowly made her way up the heap. After an arduous struggle, she made it to the top, just below the old battlements. She looked over the edge and saw to her dismay that before her was a sheer drop the height of the church's steeple on the other side.

"How am I going to get down, Taddy?"

"I think jumping is out of the question," he said matter-of-factly.

She looked up and saw the castle's intact rampart just out of reach.

"It looks like I'll have to jump," she said eyeing at the gap between the pile of boulders where she stood and the rampart.

"I don't think..." was all Taddy was able to say when she took a run and made a giant leap toward the support beam of the rampart. "Noooooooooooo," he screamed in her ear as she soared through the air.

With her arms outstretched as far as she could reach, she barely managed to grasp with her fingertips the broken end of the wooden rafter jutting out of the floor. Desperately hanging on, she dangled and swung in mid-air.

"You know I am in the back of this bag, don't you?" Taddy Boy gasped. "It's my life you are playing with here."

Holly pulled herself up onto the battlement. "Don't be such a scaredy bear." Then she giggled. "Anyway, you *are* full of stuffing and if I fell, you would make a nice cushion to land on."

"Thank-you very much!" he sputtered. "Don't worry about me, your old tattered friend, your companion since you were a baby. Did I mention old? No, no, don't worry about me. I'll just sit here in my favourite position, in the back...scared squeak-less!"

"Oh, come on. You know I wouldn't let anything hurt you. You are my very best friend." She pulled him out of the pack and giving him a big hug.

As always, Taddy Boy's heart glowed with warmth. The more and harder she hugged the more his heart glowed. "I love hugs," he said, with a sigh.

After a moment of rest, Holly stuffed the bear back into her backpack. "Okay, let's get going."

"So soon?" he crooned. "I was enjoying that."

She ran along the wall, avoiding fallen debris and jumping over holes in the floor, making her way to the next guard tower that, from a distance, appeared mainly intact. The thick wooden door that once protected the keep had long ago rotted and now dangled open on just one hinge. Given the volume of cobwebs that draped every corner, it was quite clear that no one had been on the ramparts in a long, long time.

She slipped past the door and made her way down the stone stairs that circled the outer wall half lit by the early sunlight steaming through narrow arrow slits. When she reached the bottom, she pulled back the bolt and unlocked the heavy wooden door from the inside. It creaked in protest but, though unwilling, finally gave

38

way allowing her access to the outer courtyard of the castle. She stopped still, her mouth dropping open. The earthquake centuries ago had caused shocking widespread damage. Walls had cracked and fallen, sidewalks heaved, the roofs or outer buildings had caved in and many of the once proud entry arches had collapsed.

"Some earthquake!" Holly exclaimed.

"Not quite how I remember it," Taddy Boy said sadly. "Where are the guards? Where are all the people?"

"Long gone, I'm afraid. No one has lived here for a very long time."

Holly made her way along the restored and neatly maintained tourist paths to the castle keep entrance, but once again the main gate was closed and the portcullis down. A sign was nailed to the heavy crossbeams:

Danger!
Do Not Enter!
No public beyond this point!

"Ahhh, too bad. Now we do have to leave," Taddy Boy said, obviously relieved. "Coming?"

"Well, it looks like we have to find another way in," she replied.

"Why?!"

"Oh, Taddy Bear, you are such a chicken."

"I am? I thought I was a Teddy Bear."

Once again she started to walk around the inner perimeter walls looking for any means by which she could to get inside. She tried each handle of all the doors once used by the palace guards, servants, and delivery people, but all were locked. She even tried to squeeze through a crack in the wall but it was too small even for her. Finally, looking up above an arched doorway, she saw a pigeon fly into a small stain glass window that had been broken some time in the past. "There's a way but how am I going to get up there?"

"Well, I can't climb up there."

She inspected the wall for cracks or missing stones where she might climb but all seemed solid. "If only I had a rope."

"Ah, well, there you go. No rope, no hope. Let's go home."

As she continued to look around for something to climb on she heard a strange noise coming from a crevice in the wall. "Can you hear that?" she asked staring at the spot from which it came.

"Hear what?"

"That drum beat, you know, the beat box sound rappers make on a microphone."

"I thought it was some kid driving by outside with his music up way too loud."

"No, it's coming from right in front of me. Like, from the wall!"

"Are you sure? Do you think there's a rapper inside the castle?"

"No silly, its right here...somewhere," she said, leaning down to take a closer look.

She peered intently at the wall but could not see a thing. All of a sudden, a big lizard changed his skin colour to a bright shade of green and appeared right in front of her eyes.

Jumping back Holly cried out, "Whoa, you scared me."

"What *is* that!" screamed Taddy Boy.

The lizard's eyes moved in different directions and his throat swelled to the beat of the music coming from his throat. Around his neck he wore two gold chains. Diamonds and rubies studded his boney spine, and a toothpick hung from the side of his mouth.

"That thing is uglyyyy," Taddy said. "Don't touch. It might bite."

"How come I couldn't see you? Were you on the wall in front of me all the time?" Holly asked the lizard.

In the beat of his rap music the lizard replied,

"Yo, yo, my name is T-Pick,
Chameleon beatnik.
See my colour change slick,
I can make ya seasick, yo."

The chameleon's skin started to change colour to the rhythmic beat of his music coming from his throat.

"Wow, that's just like the laser lights I saw on that show. The singing competition show Mom and Dad always watch on television."

T-Pick moonwalked, spun around, and gangster posed. "Yo!"

"Wow, you're pretty cute, T-Pick."

"Are you talking to a reptile?" the familiar voice interrupted from the backpack.

"I talk to you, don't I?"

"Yo, yo, long ago
I was a magic man's sidekick
By the name of Mendrix
Zapped me with a speak trick
Ain't it sick, slick?

"Where did you learn to rap?" Holly wanted to know.

"Midnight moves
On the janitor's shift
If ya get my drift
Soothed me
Cruised me, mama
Wooed me
Yo, every night
'Til daylight
'Til I got it right
Had to sing it
Don't ya dig it? Yo."

"Connor would think you are sooooo cool!"

"Conner can't hear *me*, let alone a pigmy iguana!" Taddy Boy said.

"Yo, I can hear ya, bro
Tell me it ain't so.
I'm not talking to no boy
I'm talking to a fuzzy wuzzy toy!"

"Okay, that's it, buster. You like to rhyme? Take this: I'm rough and I'm tough, and I am Taddy Boy and that's enough!" he growled.

T-Pick changed his skin to bright red and flicked his long tongue out and smacked Taddy Boy on his nose.

"That's enough, you two. You are both cute so let's make friends," Holly said, intervening. "We have to find a way in here."

"Yo, yo believe it
I know the secret
To get the lock undone!
Wag the dragon's tongue
Go to the statuette
And turn the amulet. Yo, mama."

"T-Pick, you mean there's a secret door?"

"Now where would the dragon's tongue be?" Taddy Boy wondered aloud.

"I saw dragon's heads carved above each archway of the castle," Holly replied.

"That's a lot of tongues to be wagging," Taddy muttered.

"Yo, yo, no, no,
I gotta be a good friend
With hands to lend
Looks like a matchstick
Maybe a little plastic
But he's fantastic
Hip hop is my homey
Never phoney
I know he'll show me

From the shadows of the ivy covering the wall, a large praying mantis leapt out and in its gangly way began dancing to T-Pick's music. With long back legs he bounced around, spun, and finally did a back flip. His short front arms bent this way and that in a true hip hop fashion, and he landed on Holly's hand like G-Roy and Superman.

"Wow, Hip Hop, you are soooooo good. I wish I could dance like that," she exclaimed. "T-Pick said that you might help us find the latch that opens the secret door. Would you be so kind and show me which tongue to wag?"

"Are you talking to bugs now?" Taddy Boy asked.

"I can't think of a better idea. Can you?"

Only silence came from the backpack.

Hip Hop made some clicking noises that only T-Pick seemed to understand.

"Yo, yo, he says go behind the ivy
The ones I use to hide me,
Yo, find the dragon with one eye
Under the nest of magpies,
Don't try the door for goodness sake
That one is just a fake, yo."

"Thank-you, T-Pick. Would you and Hip Hop like to come along?" Holly asked.

"Noooooooo," came muffled cry from the backpack.

T-Pick hopped onto Holly's left shoulder away from Taddy Boy but when Hip Hop started his slow awkward climb up her arm, she cringed and it was all she could do not to squeal and fling him off. *You never know when Hip Hop might be able to help*, she thought, clenching her teeth.

Holly stared at the wall and the ivy that clung to it. It looked solid, without any gaps, especially for an entranceway. She made her way along the wall searching until presently she found a dark hole.

"Ah ha!" The ivy resisted her attempt to look in but sure enough, she found the hidden space T-Pick had told her about. She parted the vines and stepped into a long forgotten archway. She frantically waved cobwebs from her face. "Yuck!" she hollered. Once cleared, she saw that before her stood an old wooden door with a latch and lock. Anyone else finding this door would think this was a secret way in but thanks to T-Pick and Hip Hop, she now knew otherwise.

She looked up and in the middle of the archway saw the magpie nest sitting on top of the sculpted head of an angry, one-eyed dragon. Its jaw hung open and a long tongue stuck out from between the teeth. "How am I going to reach that?" she said out loud.

"Ask the reptile or the stick," Taddy Boy remarked.

"They are too small to reach it. Maybe if I threw something at it?" she pondered, "How about you, Taddy?"

"I *don't* think so," he said.

"I'm only kidding," she replied, looking around for a stone or a stick. "Maybe if I stood on someone's shoulders..."

"Don't even think about it," came the voice from the backpack.

Then another idea came to her. "I guess I'll just have to climb the ivy."

"Watch out for those magpies! They will peck your eyes out," Taddy Boy warned. "They're real ornery."

She scrabbled up the vines in spite of the magpies that screeched and squawked in protest. "I will, Taddy, now if I can just reach the lever." She tried reaching out to grab the tongue but suddenly a magpie flapped past her, squawking, and startled Holly. She slipped, but clung desperately to the vines. The bird circled and began pecking at Holly's hair and Taddy Boy's head to protect her nest of babies.

44

"Ow, ow, ow," Taddy yelped with each magpie peck.

"It's okay, mother magpie. I won't hurt your young ones."

"I don't think she believes you. Ow, ow, ow," Taddy continued to squeal as the bird persisted.

Skirting the nest as best she could, Holly reached forward and yanked hard on the dragon's tongue, wagging it from side to side. The moment it moved, she heard a deep scraping noise, as if stone was being dragged across the floor somewhere within the castle.

"Okay, something moved in there," she said then remembering what T-Pick had said. "Now we go for the statuette."

She climbed back down the ivy vines, happy to see the bird return to her nest, though the disturbed magpie continued to squawk loudly.

"What's that noise? Is someone in here?" a curious voice demanded from the direction of the entrance.

"Oh-oh," Taddy Boy said.

A custodian guard had called through the bars of the courtyard gate and was about to enter. Evidently, he wanted to check out why the birds had become so excited.

"Excuse me," another voice called. Holly knew right away it was the voice of her father.

"Have you seen a young girl? She's about this high," her father said. "She's tall for her age; she's blond, wearing jeans, a pink top, a red jacket, and pink sneakers?"

"I am sorry sir. I can't say that I have."

"She left a note saying she was coming here and I found her bike outside of the main entrance."

"Well, I haven't seen her or anyone else. I did hear a noise coming from the courtyard and was about to check it out when you came along. No one is supposed to be in here until ten o'clock."

"Do you mind if I come along?"

"By all means do, sir. I wouldn't want to see your daughter lost in here. Only parts of the castle have been restored and there are areas that are still quite dangerous."

"Dangerous?"

"Oh yes, the castle has been in ruins for centuries. Many parts have collapsed over time. Not only that, some say it's haunted."

"Haunted?"

"Yes, yes, many have heard moaning coming from the castle. They say the old king still roams the halls."

"We had better get a move on then."

Holly heard the key unlatch the gate and knew she didn't have much time. "*I'd* better get a move on," she whispered and turned to look for the statuette.

"Yo, yo, beg your pardon
Look in the palace garden
Past the carved white marble
Of a palace guardsman, yo."

Using the courtyard statues and neatly trimmed hedges to hide behind, Holly hurried unseen down the path toward the garden. Her father and the custodian were searching the ivy where they had heard the magpies squawking. A twinge of guilt pricked her as she slipped through the archway guarded by the marble statue of a palace guardsman and into the palace garden. She could hear her father calling out for her and didn't like deliberately avoiding him but she felt something stronger was pulling her forward. She could sense she had an important date with destiny.

Holly continued on until she could see the fountain. Standing in the centre was a statue she recognized from the pictures in her school history book. The figurine was of Princess Pearly White risen from the sea and casting a spell. It was from the time when she helped the fairies rid Bicuspid of the drooling gummies so long ago.

As she approached, the details of the statue became clear. *Oh dear, what happened?* Holly was shocked and saddened to see the state of her heroine from so long ago.

The fountain had long since stopped working from years of neglect, and the moss-covered statue was in sorry shape. Cracks had appeared in several places and pieces of marble had fallen off, including an ear and one arm.

"I hope that's not the arm with the amulet," Taddy Boy said, gazing down at the arm that lay shattered in the fountain's dry pool.

Holly examined the other outstretched arm pointing a wand. "Well," she said, "we'll soon find out." Above the statue's wrist she could see the once gilded amulet, pitted by time. She could make out a weathered trident etched on it and scrollwork that looked like waves around its rim.

She checked to see if the castle custodian and her father were coming and seeing no one, she reached for the amulet. "Here goes," she said. To her delight, it moved. She listened and waited but nothing happened. Frustrated, she turned it again the other way. Still nothing happened.

"Well, I can't see anyone in here. Let's check the gardens," said the voices coming from the courtyard.

Holly ducked behind the statue. She could see the two men coming down the steps into the garden and, sure enough, one was her father.

"Hey, that's your dad. Maybe he would like to come along," Taddy Boy suggested.

"I don't think so. He wants to take me home."

"Not such a bad idea. I'm good with that. Get back to that cozy bed of yours," Taddy Boy hinted.

The two men were making their way down the path toward the fountain.

"Oh-oh. Well, I guess we're done for," Holly said with a sigh.

"That's too bad, but I'm over it already," Taddy Boy whispered.

Holly was about to run to escape notice when she heard a low rumble close by. She watched as a large stone slab at her feet slid back and revealed a set of stairs leading downward beneath fountain.

"Just my luck," Taddy Boy moaned.

CHAPTER FIVE

King Overbite's Ghost

Holly darted down the worn sandstone steps hoping she had not been seen. Again, she felt bad that she was hiding from her father but the fairies had called on her for help and she felt bound to do something in the name of her long ago ancestor, Garth.

At the bottom of the stairs, a long narrow passageway, covered in a thick layer of dust and grime, opened up to her. Small creepy crawling things scattered from the light suddenly beaming down the stairwell for the first time in centuries. Centipedes, cockroaches, bugs, spiders, and rats all ran for the safety of the dark shadows.

Holly walked straight into a huge sticky cobweb blocking her path. "Yuck!" she hollered frantically swatting the tacky web from her hair and face.

"Don't forget me!" Taddy howled. "I hate cobwebs!"

"You're such a wuss," she muttered, brushing him off.

T-Pick took care of the approaching spider with a snap of his long tongue.

"Thank-you T-Pick," Holly said.

"Yo, tongue like a lasso
Tasted like a cashew
Glad to help you
But gotta get a move on

50

Get caught before too long
That would be a sad song, yo."

Beside her Holly noticed an unlit torch stuck in the wall with a striker and a piece of flint in a pouch hanging next to it. It took her a few minutes to figure out how to use it then she lit the torch and the moment she took it out of its holder, the slab above closed behind her.

"I'll call my Dad later." She sighed, knowing she might be in a little trouble for dashing off without permission.

With Taddy Boy peering over her right shoulder and with T-Pick and Hip Hop on her left, she slowly made her way down the dark, damp, and musty-smelling passage, burning the enormous cobwebs as she went.

"Well, this is disturbing," Taddy Boy said. "Such a nice place you've brought us. I wouldn't exactly call it the Hilton Hotel."

"Oh hush, Taddy Boy. We had to get in somehow."

"Yes, thanks to the two misfits on your other shoulder. Right now I could be catching a well-deserved nap on your big soft bed."

"They were only trying to help."

Holly lit the torches that hung on the stone walls as she made her way down the narrow corridor. She could now see that roots from the trees in the garden had found their way through the cracks and several slabs of stone had fallen in making passage more difficult. Her torchlight continued to light the way sending a lot more creepy crawlies scattering for the cover of darkness and sending chills through Holly's young body. She really didn't like bugs and hated the sticky feel of the cobwebs as they brushed her face and hands but she bravely pushed forward while T-Pick zapped more scrumptious insect meals.

When she reached the end of the passage, she noticed that a large stone wall section had recently slid open. "Now I know why we wagged the tongue of the dragon," she said to her small companions.

"What a racquet that was," Taddy complained.

This second door must be security for the castle in case invaders, she presumed, had they found the secret door at the fountain. With both doors closed, attackers would have been trapped inside the tunnel.

Holly poked her torch into the cavity behind the sliding door before she entered and, to no surprise, discovered more rats scurrying across the floor of a long unused storeroom. Untouched for the centuries, empty sacks of flour and grain lay around, and wooden keg stools and tables, along with kitchen pots, were strewn where they had been abandoned when the earthquake hit. Long ago, rats had eaten every scrap of any food that had been left but one could easily tell it was a room for storing the castle's supplies. She presumed she was in the cellars as there was a barred doorway with no windows and she had not climbed any stairs.

"Now what?" Taddy Boy asked looking at a sturdy iron gate blocking the way out into another hallway.

Holly tried turning the iron handle and shaking the gate. "There must be a hidden key or another secret passage," she surmised out loud. Looking around, she began checking for hidden spaces and along the walls for any sign of a door.

"It could be another trap," Taddy said nervously. "We can always go back the way we came. Maybe your Dad has gone and we could sneak home before he does?"

"There must be a way," she murmured.

"Or not," Taddy muttered, resigned.

As she neared a shelving unit, Taddy Boy noticed her torch flame flicker. "Hey look, there's wind coming from somewhere."

"Yes, I see it too. Good for you, Taddy Boy. It appears to come from behind these shelves." She passed the torch along its edges and watched the flames waver with a puff of breeze. "Look," she said, glancing down, "there are scrape marks on the floor. There must be a passageway behind it."

"Of course there is," Taddy said. "Can't be just a doorway. No, there is always a secret passageway or something."

Ignoring Taddy Boy, Holly continued, "This storage shelf must open." She tugged on it but could not budge the unit. "Well, it has to open somehow."

She searched the walls for a handle or lever by pressing on each stone, on shelves, and on the furniture looking for anything that might seem out of place, and pulled on anything that dangled—all with no success. Then from the corner of her eye, she saw a mirror hanging on the wall. "Strange. Now why would a mirror be in a storeroom?" Examining it more closely, she saw the face of a dragon carved into its frame. "This must be it!"

"I'm not so sure," replied her reluctant adventurer friend.

She touched, pushed, and prodded the dragon and the scrolls that decorated the ornate frame, and then lifted the mirror to look behind it, and still she saw nothing unusual. Even peering into the mirror gave her no clues; she saw nothing but her own image. "Well, it did look strange," she said, her shoulders sagging. Taddy Boy and the chameleon stared back at her reflection as she murmured, "Who puts a mirror in the storeroom?"

"Yo, believe me,
Keep looking deeply
Deep as you can see
Something hides

53

Something in the dragon eyes, yo."

Again Holly stared into the mirror. Then, looking past her own reflection she saw a face with eyes that for only a moment, appeared to glimmer. She spun around and there behind her, a dragon was carved into each side of the stone pillar in the center of the room supporting the roof.

"Aha!" she cried, running to examine the carvings. She looked again for the glimmer she thought she had seen but it had faded away. She peered into each of the dragons' eyes on the other sides of the column but again saw nothing. "Was it my imagination?" She reached up and tried wagging the tongues of each of the fanged mouths but nothing happened. "Darn it!" she said, peeved. "I thought for sure that was it. I thought the mirror was showing me the way."

"Now what?" Taddy Boy said.

"I'm not sure," Holly moaned. "Give me a moment. I have to think about it." She took off her backpack and casually hung it on the nose of the dragon's head facing the mirror, grabbed a stool and slumped unhappily down. As she pondered what to do next, T-Pick hopped off Holly's shoulder and jumped onto the dangling shoulder strap of her hanging backpack to catch more flies. With those few ounces of extra weight, the dragon's head started to slowly tilt downward and, unnoticed by Holly, its eyes started glowing red.

"Hey, we're slipping here," Taddy Boy yelled as the pack started to slide down the nose of the dragon's great head.

"I'll save you!" Holly jumped up and grabbed the backpack. As she pulled on it, the shoulder strap got hung up on the dragon's tooth and, realizing it was stuck, she gave it a harder tug. Finally, it gave way causing her to stumble backward, trip, and fall.

"Oops," she giggled.

54

"Do you mind?" said a muffled voice from under her.

"Oh, I'm so very sorry, Taddy Boy." She picked up the pack and checked Taddy Boy. "Are you okay? Do you hurt anywhere?"

"Yeah, just my pride."

As she re-fluffed the flattened Taddy, a low hum began to rumble from behind her. Holly spun around.

"Yo, yo look at the eyes
They tell no lies
Galvanize
Hypnotize..."

The chameleon was falling into a trance.

"Don't look into the beam!" Holly yelled, grabbing T-Pick away.

"What's with the eyes?" Taddy Boy asked.

When she looked back she saw that the eyes of the dragon on the pillar were now in line with the head of the dragon carved into the mirror frame. The eyes in each of the heads glowed an ominous and pulsating red. Suddenly, a massive pulse of energy shot out from both of them hitting in the exact spot where Holly had, only moments before, stood in front of the mirror. Where the blast had torched the stone floor at their feet, a curl of smoke now drifted upward.

"Whew! That was close. Anyone standing there would have been fried," Taddy Boy exclaimed.

"I think it was a magic trap!" Holly said.

"Why?"

"I think it was to stop those who don't know the secret switch."

"Like us, you mean..."

"Well, kind of, but..."

"No, I don't want to hear it," Taddy Boy interrupted. "I'm getting hungry. How about we head home for lunch?"

"You don't eat."

"Well, I was thinking of you."

"There has to be a way in," she cried, more determined than ever to find the secret switch.

"I am getting too old for this," the stuffed bear in the backpack said with a sigh.

Holly slumped back down onto the stool and stared blankly at the bookshelf, her eyes searching for any clue to open it.

"It's no use," Taddy declared. "You tried your best. Time to go home."

As she stared, she saw something she had not noticed before. The symbols carved into the two top corners looked familiar. She got up and moved closer then studied them again. Engraved into the wood were symbols of a dragon surrounding a pearl.

"Hey, that looks like your..."

"Amulet," she finished.

She pulled out the ancient pendant hanging from a chain around her neck and, sure enough, it looked exactly the same.

The amulet had been a gift from her great grandmother, who had worn it every time Holly went to visit her. When Holly had asked about it, her great grandmother had told her that it was very precious as her own grandmother had given it to her many years before and *her* mother before that. She had said that it was supposed to have belonged to a magician long ago but to her it was her good luck charm and that one day she would pass it down to Holly. For Holly, it was one of her most prized possessions and she now wore it every day in loving memory of her grandmother.

She positioned the amulet onto the carving relief and it fit exactly. Almost instantly and in a wisp of smoke, the dragon began to move in a circle around the pearl. The pearl spun in the opposite direction. From behind the wall, she heard the sound of mechanisms clanking and squealing in protest after countless years of idleness and, with a begrudging groan, the shelving unit swung open to reveal a set of stairs leading upward out of the basement.

"Wow, who would have thought?"

"Yeah, who would have?" replied Taddy Boy sarcastically.

Holly lit another torch and began her ascent with her companions clinging onto her.

She hadn't climbed far when she heard an eerie voice from up ahead moan.

"*Ooooooooooooh!*"

"What was that!?" demanded a trembling Taddy Boy.

Holly froze. "I, I'm not sure," she answered.

"Time to run! Feet do their duty!" Taddy Boy ordered.

"*Ooooooooooooh!*"

"There it is again! We're all gonna die!" Taddy Boy squealed.

"Yo, Yo what's your hurry?

Ya got no worries

It's just a ghost

The castle host

Searching the night

For Pearly White

Yo, yo, it's King Overbite," T-Pick rapped.

"King Overbite! I remember King Overbite. He's Garth's friend! Why is he moaning?" Taddy Boy asked. "Is he the ghost?"

"King Overbite died a long time ago. Humans do not have the lifespan of fairies and the enchanted," Holly explained.

"Oh, yeah. I forgot. That's so sad."

"Well, let's get going," she said and started climbing the stairs.

"What do you mean *going?*" Taddy gasped. "You don't want to meet some ghoul who can walk through walls, do ya?"

"Maybe, if he talks to us. Maybe he can help us find a way."

"But, but...really?" He realized his complaints were falling on deaf ears. "Oh, never mind, fearless leader. Lead the way."

Holly found her way up the stairs that opened up into the castle's kitchen. Although covered in dust from the ages, this part of the castle was relatively intact but had been sealed off after the earthquake. As if stopped in time, the preparation tables, bowls, ladles, and pots were all in place awaiting the arrival of the Royal Chef. The large fireplace with the spit, dormant of fire, was ready to be lit to roast chickens, a succulent pig, or a flank of beef. She found a lantern and lit the candle giving her better light than the torch and the natural rays steaming through the narrow windows. She carried on up the twisting servant stairs that led up to the main banquet hall.

The dining room was a huge, long room with pointed medieval archways that had been unable to support a major portion of the roof, which had caved in. With daylight steaming in through the gaping hole in the roof, she could see the tattered remnants of tapestries, and flags of the knights still hanging on the walls. A long banquet table stood in the center of the room, broken in three places, with the king's chair still at one end and the queen's at the other. The chairs in between were strewn about along with plates, cutlery, and goblets, which lay broken and scattered on the floor. Curiously though, some pieces still stood in place on the table as though the company had just walked away. However, it was obvious that pigeons and other animals had made this their homes here for a very long time.

"Wow, what a place!" Holly exclaimed.

"What a mess!" Taddy Boy added.

"It must have been grand at one time."

"I remember the banquet for the wedding between King Overbite and Princess Pearly White. It was majestic in here. All the kings from all the realms, the lords and ladies, dukes and duchesses, and nobles came from around the world. There was feasting, music, and dancing for a week! Now, that was grand!"

"Wow, it sounds like quite a party."

"Yo, getting down

Down town

Rappin' with the hounds

Losin' it

To the music

Groovin' it

Schmoozin' it

Break dancin'

Romancin'

Outstanding, yo," T-Pick chanted while Hip Hop strutted his stuff.

"Not *that* kind of music, Gecko Boy!" Taddy Boy replied sharply. "I mean really nice-to-the-ears music."

"He's a chameleon, not a gecko," Holly corrected.

"You mean a comedian."

"No, chameleon!"

"Yeah, whatever..."

"Now, stop being impolite, Taddy Boy. You know T-Pick loves his music."

"Is that what you call it?"

"Taddy Boy..."

"Okay, okay."

"Did my great, great, great, times ten grandfather eat here?"

"Garth ate here many times. Sometimes he would bring me when he was still a boy. But now the place looks…well, terrible." The bear looked around the room.

"So where do we go from here, Taddy Boy?"

"Well, it has been a while but I think the reception rooms are beyond those doors across the room. That's where people waited to meet the king and queen."

"Do you think the king might be there?"

"He's probably in the throne room past the doors behind his chair."

"*Oooooooooooh.*" The eerie sound repeated from the direction of the throne room.

"Well, I guess that confirms it," Holly declared, making her way through the debris to the large doors at the end of the room.

"Holly! What are you doing? Remember where you go, I go!"

"Scaredy bear."

"Okay, I admit it," he protested. "I'm okay with that. At least I'll live."

As she tugged on them, the heavy ornate doors creaked open and when she poked her head inside, a piercing scream nearly deafened her. Her eyes flew open wide and her hair was blown straight back from the force of the gust. She slammed the door closed. "Now, that was scary," she gasped, pressing her back to the door.

"Yup, my fur stood on end that time. Now is it time to go home?"

Holly heard voices coming from the direction of the reception rooms. "Well, Mr. Johnson, we've searched everywhere I can think of."

"What's in there?" Holly heard her father say.

"That's the royal banquet hall. It is in ruins. The roof fell in long ago and it has not been restored."

"Let's have a look, just in case."

As Holly heard the key clink into the lock, she whispered, "Well, it's now or never..." She quietly slipped into the throne room.

"*Ahhhhhhhhhhgggggg!*" the voice screamed. Holly froze. "*Where is my beloved Pearly? Where is my dearest son?*" The ghost of King Overbite's translucent figure wafted back and forth in front of the throne.

"Okay, let me get this straight," Taddy Boy whispered. "Your dad is in the room we came out of and you picked the one with the angry ghost?"

"No time for that. We have to hide."

"But, but..."

With one hand clamped around Taddy Boy's muzzle, Holly ducked behind the great ornate throne. A moment later, Holly's father rushed into the room. "What was that!?"

"I told you. That is the ghost of the last king of Bicuspid, King Overbite," the caretaker murmured as the spectre vanished.

"What?"

"Yes, the story goes that he roams these halls waiting for his true love, Pearly White, to return with his son, Poseidon."

"Well I...I don't think my little girl would, would, would be in here with, with THAT!" he stammered, backing up as fast as his feet could move, and slamming the door behind him.

"I can't breathe," Taddy Boy mumbled after they were gone.

Unclenching her hand from around his muzzle, Holly said, "Oh, I'm so sorry Taddy Boy. I thought you might say something and give us away."

"He can't hear me anyway," Taddy Boy snapped. "Only you, the lizard, and a lisping frog from a long time ago can hear me."

"Chameleon," T-Pick corrected.

"Chameleon, comedian; you're a lizard to me."

"Okay, okay, that's enough you two. Stop acting so jealous," she warned. "We need to talk to the king."

"And how do you propose we do that?" Taddy inquired. "Your father just scared him away. I know, let's call him. Here ghosty, ghosty, ghosty. Come out from where ever you are," Taddy Boy sneered.

"That's not gonna work. No ghost is going to come to a doggy call."

Holly looked slowly around the quiet room. Obviously, the throne room had been totally refurbished since the earthquake so the tourists could see what it had been like in medieval times. It was exactly how she imagined it. Splendid ornate columns highlighted in gold leaf supported stone arches carved with shields of flying dragons. Majestic tapestries depicting brave knights conquering dragons and large ugly bats hung on the walls. Stately tall-backed armchairs padded in red velvet lined the room, with ancient coats of arms above each one. Flags representing all the royal families hung suspended from the rafters, and a lush red carpet ran the entire length of the room to the waiting rooms. Towering candelabra lined the walkway leading up to the matching royal thrones.

Beginning with the floor to ceiling entry doors at one end of the room, one by one the candles in each candelabrum suddenly ignited flooding both sides of the room with light all the way up to the thrones. When the room was fully lit, Holly caught a movement from the corner of her eye. She turned to see that the spectre had returned and now stood directly behind her. She screamed and staggered back.

"Someone called?" the king asked.

"Ha! It did work." Taddy Boy boasted.

"You…you heard Taddy Boy call you?" Holly gasped.

"Why yes, I would know this scaredy bear's voice anywhere. This is Taddy Boy. A little more tattered and out of shape but I know that voice."

"Huh? Out of shape! With this figure?" Taddy boy objected. "I am…perfectly round, er, Your Majesty,"

"Many, many years ago, my court magician, Garth, allowed me and Queen Pearly White to hear Taddy Boy for ourselves. At the time, I thought Garth may have been going nutty because he always appeared to be talking to himself."

"You certainly do know him," Holly said, laughing. "He truly is a scaredy bear *and* he can drive you a little crazy."

"You too, Holly?" Taddy sniffed. "Now I know who my friends are."

"Welcome back to my court, little furry one. It is nice to see you have not changed." Then turning to Holly he added, "And you are…?"

"My name is Holly Johnson, sir."

"That's Your Majesty, or my lord," Taddy Boy whispered in her ear.

"Er, I mean Your Majesty my lord. Taddy Bear says I am Garth's great, great, great, great, great granddaughter. Or something like that."

"It's nice to meet you. I see you have other friends as well."

"Yes, my lord. This is T-Pick, the rapping chameleon, and his friend Hip Hop, the dancing praying mantis."

"Nice to meet you all."

T-Pick and Hip Hop bowed in awe of the apparition.

"Nobody comes to see me anymore. This palace was so full of life but now, they just run away."

"Are you in pain, my lord?"

"I wait. Oh, I wait for my love to return. *Ahhhhhhghh!*" the apparition screeched in torment.

Quaking, Holly shut her eyes, held her palms to her ears, and cringed.

"Did I frighten you?" the spectre asked. "I did not mean to frighten you but the torment runs so very deeply."

"I will try to help you find them, my lord. I don't know how and I don't know when, but somehow I will."

"You will?"

"If I can."

"You are so kind. I cannot thank-you enough." The spirit appeared to calm then and to smile for the first time in what may have been centuries. He whisked into the air then settled in his throne as he had done so many years ago.

"Your Majesty, I have come to seek advice," Holly said, bowing slightly.

"Pray tell. How can I be of assistance?"

"I received a note from the fairies in my Tooth Fairy's Tooth®." Holly fetched the note from her pocket and handed it to the King.

"This is Elvin language, I think. I am sorry but cannot read it."

"My parents couldn't either. It says:

"Magician's apprentice, come as soon as you can.

We need your help to save Fairyland."

"Oh, now that does sound important, but you did not say you are a magician's apprentice."

"As far as I know, I am not."

"The fairies think you are."

"That is why I came to you, my lord. I thought that you, having made the pact with the fairy king, would know what they might mean and how to get hold of them. Do you have their cell number?"

"I have not placed the fairy king in prison!"

"No, no, I mean their telephone number."

"Tele…what?"

"There were no cell phones in those days," Taddy Boy whispered.

"Oh. I'm sorry, my lord. Do you know how I could get hold of them?"

"I am sorry, but only Garth knew the way. He made sure of that to protect Fairyland from intruders and evil beings seeking their magic. You see, when the dragon wars started, the dragons liked to take our children. We thought they were eating them but they really only wanted their teeth. We hunted them down one by one, not knowing the fairies also needed them for what, I know not."

"I see. So how did it end?"

"One night, the fairy king visited me in my sleep and asked if when all the children were saved, could we save the last dragon if they kept him locked away in the mountain. I agreed, and they promised to collect children's teeth in trade for a coin or two from the rainbow's pot-of-gold to keep his eternal flame alive."

"Yes, now I remember. That was nice of you, my lord."

"Then the bats came. I remember those ugly, mean things quite vividly. They were giving my people nightmares and attacking the fairies, so we sent our armies to turn away those Drooling Gummies. The bond between us has been strong and we have been friends ever since. What do you mean 'now I remember'?"

"Taddy Boy told me the story. I was just hoping you could help me find a way."

"Ah, yes. Taddy would have told you of our adventure. I am afraid I cannot help you find the way and I also cannot go with you. You see, I can never leave these walls, for I wait for my true love to return."

The king then pondered for a moment. "I do have an idea! Perhaps Garth left a clue in his workshop."

"His workshop?"

"Yes. He used to work on his spells and potions in his workshop. He became a wizard of the ninth level before he disappeared."

"Disappeared? Taddy Boy, you never told me that he had disappeared."

"You never asked. By then he had given me to his son, Palate, to play with. He was a rough kid. Not the kind who liked cuddly bears. I lost so much stuffing with him."

Holly turned her attention back to the king. "Where would I find his workshop, my lord?"

"The top three floors of the west tower were where he spent most of his time. It still stands but the passageways to it collapsed many years ago. You have to go through the reception rooms down the Hall of Heroes, left at the grand staircase, past many Chancellor, Marshall, and Senate offices to the entrance of the west tower."

"Your father may still be out there with the security dude," Taddy Boy whispered.

The king overheard him and continued, "But I do know of another way. There's a secret passage."

"Wow! A secret passage?"

"Yes. It allowed him to come and go on royal business without being seen."

"Not the one in the basement storeroom," Holly said.

"You found my secret passage? No one knows of the passage from the garden except Garth."

"T-Pick told me about it," she answered, pointing to the chameleon.

"Yo, I bet you're wonderin' how I knew
Mendrix planned to make you blue

66

With another guy you knew before
But between the two of you guys
You know Garth loved you more
It took you by surprise, I say
But Garth sent him away
Don't you know that I heard it through the
grapevine
Through the grapevine
Yes, I heard it through the grapevine.
Yo, yo, through the grapevine."

"Mendrix! I never did trust him but I have never known of his treachery," the King growled.

Taddy Boy explained: "Garth found out that he was using his magic for his own profit at the annual meeting of Magicians of the Plantagenet Order. He was cast out of the order and he slowly slipped into the dark arts."

"Yo, I had to leave him
and I had to hide
on these castle walls,
in the cracks along the halls.
He turned all nasty and mean
Not like any friends you've ever seen," T-Pick added.

"It sounds like Garth looked after it so you did not have to worry. Maybe to protect you while you grieve," Holly suggested.

"He was indeed, my friend. That is why only he and I had a key. By the way, it looks exactly like the one you have around your neck, I see."

"Er, my grandmother gave it me. I thought..."

"Don't you worry, my little friend. You have it for a reason and somehow; I am not sure how but I get the sense Garth may be connected to this. No, you do not have to go back to the basement. Find the dragon and the pearl symbol on one of the shelves on the west wall in the great library."

"And that is in which direction, Your Majesty?" Holly glanced around the room.

"Go through the Hall of Heroes and reception rooms down the hall, turn left..."

"But, my lord, my father may still be out there looking for me. If he sees me I know he'll take me home. Is there another way?" Holly asked.

"We wouldn't want that now would we?" said the sarcastic little voice from behind Holly's left ear. "An adult to help us. Noooo."

"Hush, Taddy Boy," Holly said. "Listen to the king."

"Yes, I forget easily these days. The secret way. I am not sure I like deceiving your father but it seems your quest is dire. You may go through the doors behind me. Pass through my royal chambers and into my private passage. Make your way down the hall until you reach the outside wall and the entrance to the great library will be on your left. You cannot miss it. It's easy."

"How come whenever anyone says that, it never is?" asked Taddy Boy.

After Holly and her friends had left the throne room through the King's private entrance, another apparition appeared next to the king.

"Your prediction was correct, my court magician," said the king. "It seems Taddy Boy did his job perfectly."

"Yes, my Lord, I knew she was the one. I could sense it just like Tar Tar Goldcaps did with me those many years ago," said the ghost. Dressed in a tenth level wizard robe, the kindly old man had a long gray beard and wore the same style of chain and dragon pendant that Holly wore. "My old friend, Taddy Boy, has told her the story and now she is on the quest." He leaned on a wooden staff the tip of which glowed through blue metallic crystals.

"Garth, my friend, are you sure? She seems rather young to help the fairies on *this* adventure."

"If she is to prove herself she must do this on her own. I was not much older than she when we fought Pyorrhoea Pete the Pirate and the Drooling Gummies before. Now I am too old to keep our bond with the fairies."

"Can you help her?" the king asked.

"Only in spirit, my lord." Garth's ghost suddenly vanished, leaving the king to sit on his throne and ponder.

"I wish her Godspeed." Then he too vanished.

70

Chapter Six

The West Tower

"There, that was easy wasn't it?" Holly said to her disgruntled Taddy Boy when they reached the castle library door.

"I must admit; it was pretty easy."

The creak of door hinges sent echoes down the stone hallways. As she entered what was left of the once impressive library, a flock of pigeons took flight, startled by the noise. To her dismay, it looked nothing like what she thought a library should look like. All of the shelving units had toppled, ancient books and tomes lay strewn about and the roof had collapsed in the corner, blocking the main entrance.

"AHA!" said the voice behind her.

"Oh hush, Taddy Boy. Okay, I agree, it's not going to be as easy as I thought."

Holly picked her way down the stone steps and waded into the rubble. She stepped on huge stacks of books and climbed over scrolls, shelving units, desks, and stools that were all covered in dust and mud. After stepping through the back of a toppled shelf, she tripped and fell forward flinging out her arms to stop her fall.

"Ugh! What is that!" Her hand slipped into something slimy.

"I think it's what pigeons are famous for," Taddy Boy replied drily.

"Disgusting!" She glared up at several pigeons cooing in the nearby shelf as she swiped her soiled palm on an old scroll.

"Yo, pigeon poop
Double scoop..." started T-Pick with a rap beat as Hip Hop started to dance.

"Stoooooooop!" yelled Holly. "I don't want to hear it." She glowered at T-Pick. "Really?"

"Yo, just tryin' to lighten the mood
Get you in a groove.
Keepin' it smooth. Yo."

"Thanks, but no thanks."

"Yo." T-Pick glanced at Hip Hop but said not more.

Holly climbed upon one of the shelves. From that vantage point she could clearly the librarian's desk standing next to the entrance. A faded sign, which read, Miss A. Noid, was still attached. Next to it stood the empty perch. She recalled Taddy Boy's story of her ancestor's adventure here getting his ancient book about dragons so many years ago. "That perch must have been for Einstein Featherbrain, Miss A. Noid's pet owl," she said. "I wonder what happened to Theo and Quietessa?"

"Yeah, they were nice," Taddy mused. "I think they lived a long time."

She stumbled into the old west side of the library and found still-standing shelves against a wall. She presumed they were attached somehow but their contents lay scattered over the floor. She looked around for the dragon and pearl symbol and found it at one end of the room.

"This is where Garth found the ancient book, *The Legends of Fairyland*," Taddy Boy remarked.

"I should have guessed." She un-slung her backpack and began clearing the heavy debris away from the front of the shelving unit.

"What are you doing?"

"We have to make way for the shelf to swing out." She puffed as she strained to lift the heavy volumes and re-stack them away from the shelves. It was hard work for a young girl, but slowly the path began to clear where she thought the secret door might roll toward her.

"I wish I could have helped," Taddy Boy said. "But as you can see, I am only a talking teddy bear. Maybe you might cast a walk spell on me when you become a magician's apprentice."

"Garth never saw the need."

"That was his mistake."

"Perhaps he didn't *want* you to walk. I can only imagine the trouble you could get yourself into...or should I say, run away from?"

"But, but..."

"Maybe I should cast a silence spell on you? That would surely bring some peace and quiet."

"Humph!" was the only reply.

Holly inserted the medallion into the relief and heard an immediate click. Gliding easily on its own, the door gently swung *inward*.

"*Don't* you dare laugh. Don't you dare!"

The sound of stifled giggles came from behind her.

"I can hear you snickering," she said suppressing a smile. She was certainly not going to let Taddy see it and give the judgmental stuffed teddy bear grounds to gloat.

Spiralling stairs led up the tower and being small forced Holly to have to jump from one slippery moss-covered stair to another. She climbed the individual rocks protruding in from the outside wall.

Even in the dimly lit stairwell she could see that beautiful butterflies of all kinds filled the air or nestled gently on the walls and ledges.

"Oh, how beautiful!" She gazed at the assortment of colours as daylight streamed over the fanning wings. One bravely landed on her shoulder but took flight once Hip Hop noticed it. He was about to snap out his long tongue for a mid-morning snack.

When she looked past the stunning array of nature's gentlest creatures, she could see that farther up parts of the outside wall had collapsed, indicating a perilous climb ahead. Gusting wind whistled through cracks between stones. She shivered with cold and trepidation.

"I told ya this wouldn't be easy," Taddy boy said, confirming her thoughts.

Putting on a brave face, she spoke with assurance. "We'll make it, Taddy Boy. Have a little faith."

"Gonna need a *whole* bunch, I think."

Judging by the grime and dust covering every ledge, she knew she was the first to climb these slippery stairs since the quake. When she reached the part of the collapse, several stairs had fallen in. As she considered her next move, a gust of wind caught and she teetered, slipping on the top stone step. Grappling with her fingers, she caught herself and clung to the wall. Hugging the stones with a firm, steady grip, she noticed all of Bicuspid displayed below. She gasped.

"Don't look down!" warned Taddy Boy.

She hadn't realized how high she had climbed but the view was breathtaking. "Wow! I can almost see my house from here."

"Okay, young lady. Let's get back inside before you hurt yourself, or more importantly…me," Taddy Boy said uneasily.

"Scaredy bear," she said quietly.

"I only have one best friend," he replied.

She turned back to see how she could cross the open gap to the remaining steps above the collapsed section. On her left, several of the large wooden beams that supported a long since caved-in floor had wedged themselves between the curved walls and the stairs above the collapse. It was quite the jump but she knew if she was ever going to make it to her great ancestor's magician's laboratory, she had to try.

Taddy Boy sensed her thoughts. "Wha...what do you think you are doing?"

"I am going to jump." And she leapt.

"No, not again. Whoaaaaaa!"

She hurtled across the open space to the jammed beam, blindly trusting that it would support her weight. As before, on the ramparts, she caught the beam with her outstretched arms and hung on as her feet swung perilously below. The beam dropped from the sudden weight but then stuck and held. A bead of sweat trickled down Holly's forehead and dribbled into her eyes. She peered down into the darkness as the droplet of sweat fell and disappeared into nothingness.

"We're gonna die," whimpered Taddy Boy.

Just then she heard a familiar sound buzzing from her backpack. Someone was calling the cell phone.

"You've got to be kidding," she groaned. As it continued to ring she pulled herself up with all her strength until she could get her foot up on top of the beam. Lying astride the beam she searched for the phone with her hand. "Please Dad, not now."

The phone kept up its relentless ringing.

"Are you going to answer it?"

"No. There's nothing to say. I'll call him later."

"I think you should."

She paused to think about what she should do. "Okay." She pulled out the phone and answered, "Hello."

"This is Daddy. Holly where are you?"

"I'm kind of up in the air right now, Dad," she said now sitting astride the beam high up in the tower.

"I have been looking for you but only found your bike at the castle. Are you at the castle?"

"I am okay," she said as convincingly as she could.

"You just sit tight and I'll come and pick you up right away," he commanded.

"Really, I am fine," she said ignoring his order. "I am on an adventure, Dad, and I'll be home real soon."

"*Adventure?*" he shouted. "The only adventure you'll have is sitting in your room for a month! Now young lady, you get yourself home *right* now."

"I can't, Dad. I have to help the fairies."

"The fairies! Does this have to do with that gibberish written on that note you had this morning?" he demanded, his voice starting to rise again.

"Yup. I met the ghost of King Overbite and..."

"Ghost! You get home nooooow!" he bellowed. Evidently realizing he was losing his cool, he paused and spoke in a softer, much kinder, voice. "Your mother and I are very worried about you. We don't want you out alone at your age."

"Truly Dad, I'll be home soon. Love you, say hi to Mom." And she ended the call.

"Are you in trouble?" Taddy Boy asked, stating the obvious.

"Yup."

"A lot of trouble?"

"Yup."

"Okay then. Let's move on."

She shimmied along the beam on her belly, clutching it with her arms and legs until she reached the other end. Once again the butterflies swirled around her. She sensed somehow they had a reason to be there. One beautiful Monarch landed gently on her nose as calmly as if it knew her.

"Beautiful," she said with a sigh, "but why are you here?"

76

T-Pick was once again getting ready to lash out his long tongue and snatch the resting insect.

"Don't even think about it!" Holly commanded.

"Yo, mama
Thinking just one
Just for fun
Not a whole bunch
Just for lunch
A little crunchy
Got the munchies, yo."

"No. Please don't. I think these butterflies are special. I don't know why; I just get the feeling that they are. Try for a fly, a mosquito, or a beetle if you have to but leave the butterflies alone."

As if they knew they were in safe hands, several more beautiful butterflies landed on Holly as she continued her climb. She felt a sense of joy come over her, as if she knew everything would be all right. The higher she went the more she could see that the room at the top of the tower was perched precariously on the remaining part of the wall. But when at last she reached the top and stepped onto the wooden landing floor, she was amazed that, as if by magic, the floorboards felt as sturdy as rock. She breathed a great sigh of relief when she had finally reached the door of her long ago ancestor's workshop.

"Well, that was fun wasn't it?" Taddy mocked.

"Yeah, I don't want to think how we are going to get down."

"Really? You haven't thought about that?"

Several signs were posted on the door. In the center of the door one read, "Wizards Lair!" and another, "Garth's Hearth". The other posters were more ominous: Keep Out! No Admittance! This Means YOU! Spell Caster at Work! And, You have been WARNED!

"I don't suppose you might think they mean you?" Taddy Boy asked.

"Maybe..."

"I didn't think so." He sighed in disbelief. "But really, you haven't thought about how we're going to get down from here? Holly? Holly?"

To her surprise, the latch of the heavy wooden door opened easily and the loud creak of the old hinges echoed down through the West Tower. Stepping into the room, she stared in awe. Light streamed in through the high arched windows. She gazed around at the wondrous display of scrolls, books of all sorts and sizes, jars with frogs, newts, and other strange creatures in them, laboratory tubes, and shelves covered in strange curiosities.

"Taddy Boy, look at all this strange stuff."

"Been there, done that," he answered.

"Oh yeah. I keep forgetting you were here."

"Now about us getting down from here?" he crabbed.

"Oh hush, Taddy Boy. Look at all this stuff!"

Hanging in one corner were stuffed owls, a crow, and a huge bat with yellow eyes just like the ones she had seen on the news and on her bike ride over to the castle. Under a heavy layer of dust in the middle of the room a long, well-used table stood covered in papers, wax-draped candlesticks, and a strangely coloured quill resting in an inkwell. Next to it sat a comfy armchair draped with a purple robe. A wizard's pointed hat hung on one backrest post. On one wall hung what she thought was a brilliant painting of a dragon.

"Wow, what a room!" Holly went to the desk, unslung her backpack, and looked to see if there was anything that could help her on her quest. As she blew the heavy layer of dust off some of the scrolls, she wondered if she really was the one chosen to be a magician's apprentice or if the note had been delivered to her by mistake. "Am I the one to help the fairies?" she whispered.

"Yes, you are Holly Johnson," said a deep voice reverberating behind her.

"Who's there?" she demanded spinning around. She saw nothing except the dragon painting on the wall.

T-Pick started his rhythmic beat with Hip Hop grooving,

"Yo, don't go fainting
Look at the painting
Needs explaining, yo."

"Now that you say that, T-Pick, I thought I saw it move," she said, studying the picture. "Ever so slightly, but I'm sure it moved."

"That's creepy," Taddy Boy said with a shudder.

Creeping closer, she reached out to touch the image. Suddenly, the whole painting took flight and the room was filled with thousands upon thousands of butterflies. Where the picture of the dragon had been, now revealed a large cloudy mirror in the gilded frame.

"Wow!" she exclaimed. "The butterflies arranged their colourful wings to look exactly like a painting."

"Like Fangor," Taddy Boy added.

Holly stared as a smoky image slowly appeared in the cloudy mirror.

"Hello, Holly Johnson. I am Garth."

Startled, Holly stepped back as the ghostly, bearded face formed in the mirror.

"Don't be afraid, Holly. Taddy Boy knows me well. Hello, Taddy Boy, my old friend. It looks like you haven't changed at all. Well…perhaps you're a little more raggedy and out of shape but you are still my old Taddy Boy."

"Raggedy? Out of shape!" he huffed. "What do you expect of a stuffed bear who is eight hundred years old? You don't look so good either!"

"Well, perhaps so, but as Charles Dickens put it, I'm deader than a doornail and have been these many, many years."

"Okay then, you may have an itsy, teeny weenie excuse but I have been manhandled, girl handled, mauled, sewn, and re-sewn and that's not including you burning me, nearly drowning me and, and..."

"The same old Taddy Boy, I see. I guess you do look rather good for someone your age."

"It's good to see you too, Garth. It has been a while."

"Hello, Grandpa Garth," Holly interrupted. "I am your great, great, great, great..."

"Granddaughter. Yes, I know. 'Grandpa,' how sweet. It has been a long time since I was called grandpa."

"What's with all the butterflies, Grandpa?"

"They are my friends, and cousins to the fairies that came to the tower to protect my secrets."

"I'm sure glad they are friendly."

"You would not have made it up the tower if you were not who you are, Granddaughter. Meet King Dentin, the Monarch Butterfly, King of Butterflies."

Out of the throng of butterflies, a glorious orange, black-veined, and white-dotted butterfly gently landed in Holly's hand. It stood up on its hind legs so she could see that this was no ordinary butterfly. His face was almost human if not for his large eyes and two antennae protruding from his head. As symbols of his reign, he wore a tiny gold crown and a delicate gold chain around his neck.

From his position on Holly's shoulder, T-Pick couldn't resist his natural urge and lashed his long tongue out directly toward Dentin. Instead of connecting with the butterfly, it smacked into Holly's other hand that had flashed even faster between the two natural enemies. "I said, no!" she snapped.

T-Pick re-coiled his sore and swollen tongue and blushed a bright shade of pink.

"You heard Grandpa Garth. These are our friends, not lunch."

The stately monarch folded his front legs and glared at T-Pick, angrily tapping one of his feet.

"Yo, yo, so sorry, mister

Couldn't resist ya

Glad I missed ya

Happy to meet ya, yo," T-Pick beat boxed.

Then, endeavouring to remain gracious, the king nodded in polite acceptance of T-Pick's rhythmic apology.

"Hello, King Dentin. My name is Holly."

The butterfly rubbed his front legs but Holly could not make out what the king was doing or trying to say.

"He's says, 'Welcome, great ancestor to Garth'. He and his insect world are ready to serve you in your quest."

"My quest? How does he know?"

"All Fairyland knows the fairies have summoned you. They need your help," Garth explained.

"But why me?"

"You are the true heir to my powers, as I was to Tar Tar Goldcaps."

"But you are still here. Can you not help the fairies?" Holly wanted to know.

"I am here only in spirit. I can only influence from this side of the mirror as it has been many years since I walked these halls."

"He's a ghost that goes bump in the night!" Taddy Boy muttered. "You know, like the one you always think is in your closet."

"Something like that," Garth replied, with a chuckle. "You see, I vowed to protect the King and watch over Fairyland many centuries ago but now I am trapped within these walls. Just as King Overbite is as he awaits the return of Queen Pearly White and their son Poseidon. Until they do, we stay as apparitions and cannot enter the white light beyond. I was afraid the king's quest may be a lost cause and we are trapped here forever, but thankfully, you are here, Holly. Only you can help the fairies now."

"What do you think they want of me?"

"I am not sure but it must be dire. The last time was when the drooling gummies attacked Fairyland to pluck fairy wings for their nightmare dust and turn fairies into children. They hoped to rule Fairyland and, of course, the dragon."

Recalling Taddy Boy's story, Holly answered, "You mean, Fangor."

"Yes, the last remaining dragon. After the medieval dragon wars which, I am afraid..." he paused, embarrassed, "uh, I may have started."

"We do have a lot of bats in Bicuspid," Holly said, frowning.

"This certainly could be the problem, or at least part of it, but I sense something more. I sense something about my old friend Fangor. He is in pain."

"Well," she said, shrugging her shoulders, "I guess we should get started. How do I become a wizard?"

"Ho, ho, hold on there. Baby steps first. Let's try a magician's apprentice. You have a long road before becoming a full wizard."

"Here we go again," Taddy Boy groaned.

CHAPTER SEVEN

Evil Brews

As they had centuries ago, in the dark caves on the coastal cliffs northwest of Bicuspid, the minions of drooling gummies gathered, salivating and hissing cheers to their pirate emperor and queen.

"All hail Ruthless Toothless Brutus and Queen Hali Tosis!" The head hunter of the gummies announced over the sound of waves crashing in on the shores below.

"Hail Ruthless Toothless Brutus and Queen Hali Tosis!" the hoard spat in uproarious devotion.

With pomp and ceremony, Emperor Ruthless Toothless Brutus and his queen, Hali Tosis were each carried in by six large bat-like creatures. Their thrones mimicked those that Pyorrhoea Pete the Pirate and his queen, Ginger Vitas, had sat many years before in on their evil quest for Fairyland domination.

Slumped, and lazily eating grapes, a bored Brutus waved sluggishly at the cheering crowd. On the ends of each scrolled arm and on top of each back leg, his chair was adorned with skulls of multiple unfortunate creatures. He dressed regally in an 18th Century, long, blue seafarer's coat with deep, ornately embroidered cuffs and a high collar. Gold braid scrolled around his shoulders and the many buttons lining his chest. He wore a naval captain's hat, broad and trimmed in gold braid, like that seen in paintings of Admiral Nelson. His black boots reached up to his scrawny knees.

The queen followed him into the cave to an even more frenzied cheer, and she waved warmly and blew kisses at the crowd. She too wore a lavishly adorned, gold-trimmed coat but hers was bright red. A tri-corn hat decorated with ostrich plumes sat on her head, and she wore a white ruffled shirt and knee-high boots.

Once set down with his jewel encrusted wings spread out in a display of power, Ruthless Toothless Brutus hissed with satisfaction through his many missing teeth. "Well, Mateys," he wheezed, "after all these years of searching I think we are finally in the right place. We have found the last Fairyland! I am sure of it."

The crowd cheered even louder.

"The ancient maps of your ancestor seem to fit the lay of the land, my lord," said Queen Hali Tosis. Fairyland and the dragon have got to be close to this city they call Bicuspid." She grinned and sucked on her drool revealing an upper fang garlanded with a diamond-encrusted ring. Each talon glittered with rings and, like her husband, she wore many bracelets, broaches, and dangling necklaces that glimmered in the dim light of the caves.

"Aye, my queen, my hunters have been out scouting the area. They have had some skirmishes with the humans but nothing like the reported attack on our ancestors eight hundred years ago." He splattered drool and spittle over those hanging close enough to be in range.

From the dark shadows in the back of the cave creatures with bright yellow eyes quietly nodded in respect.

"The humans have become weak," he hissed. "The once mighty castle of Bicuspid is in ruins and appears abandoned with not one knight to be seen," he roared with glee.

"But the position of the castle and the Root Canal fits these lines on this ancient map of your forefathers," the queen spluttered. She raised an old and tattered map and pointed with a bejewelled claw. "Fairyland must be in these mountains to the north."

"True, but fairy lands are well hidden and enchanted with cloaking spells. Long ago our ancestors could follow the dragons to their lairs but none have been seen for a very long time. My hearties, we have to find another way," Brutus barked.

"Our nightmare dust has never been the same since we ran out of dragon scales and fairy wings," Hali Tosis added. "We need the fairies *and* the dragon.

"I could follow the fairies when they leave at night to get children's teeth then follow them back to their hive," came the voice of the head hunter from the shadows.

"Aye, a good plan, Head Hunter. Take some of your best hunters and follow the fairies on their nightly flights. We need to see where they go and especially, where they return."

"Yes, my lord." The head hunter bowed to each royal and backed away then waddled out of the chamber like a crow.

"My lord, what more did your ancestor Pyorrhoea Pete write in his war logs?" Queen Hali Tosis asked.

"My sweet, let me see." He pulled an ancient book from his drooping sleeve. Dragging a grimy claw across the page, he said, "The rag tag survivors barely made it back to the dark world of Plaque after the combined attack of the wizard known as Garth, the last dragon Fangor, Princess Pearly White, the sea princess wizard, the fairies, their insect friends, and of course, let us not forget the pesky nuisance of human archers. They used sleep and light spells on us, flaming arrows, and dragon's breath to wipe out our attacks."

A less confident collective groan rippled through the crowd.

"But now, my hearties, don't be discouraged. After all this time, it is our turn for glory; our time for *revenge!*"

The horde roared back to life.

"Our new armies are stronger and faster," he hissed to another roar. "And we are smarter." He winked at his queen. He had them under his control. The evil gummy horde hailed their emperor, waving and banging their clubs, spears, and swords.

"Yes, yes, my lord," Hali Tosis said, waving her wings to hush the crowd. "We must learn from this book before we attack again."

"How will we do that my queen?"

"We will have to shade our eyes from light. We can use these." She held up a pair of dark glasses. "Humans call them sunglasses and they wear them to cover up their eyes. Here, my lord, check them out." She handed a pair of aviator sunglasses to Brutus. "One of our diving hunter patrols has taken them from the top of an unsuspecting human's head."

"Ahh, these are deadly shades!" he hissed.

"We might even be able to fly in the daylight!"

The crowd grunted and snorted in awe at the spectacles darkening the eyes of their emperor.

"Well done, my queen," he praised. "Send out more drones to get more of these deadly nightshades. What else do you suggest my sweet?"

"Have all hunter patrols cover their mouths with bandanas to protect them from the sleep potions."

"Yes, yes, very good, my dear," he hissed. "From now on, all gummies patrols must wear scarves in case they confront the wizard," he ordered.

From the gloom, several sets of yellow eyes nodded, their owners bowed and left the room.

"We also need many fairy wings if we cannot get the dragon scales. Once plucked from the Elvin scamps, they will turn into human children and slaves to serve the gummy empire." The queen giggled with glee. "And we need to get our nightmare dust into full production if we ever want to control the human and animal worlds. I suggest, my Lord, that we set up some of our toothpick cages to capture the little imps."

Snickering with uncontrollable delight, the king cried, "Yes, yes! Cages, and lots of them! I will send out seek and capture patrols so the new slaves can start building the furnaces for the brew." He looked over to another large, yellow-eyed figure standing in the shadows. "When you capture some, see if they tell us where Fairyland and the dragon are. If they don't talk, we can still use them as slaves, but be careful, legend has it a great wizard who rides the dragon protects them."

The crowded streets of the fairyland hive were abuzz at the news of the dreaded drooling gummies sightings in the area.

"It cannot be.
It cannot be," wailed a shopkeeper.

"I heard it directly from the mouth
of one of the tooth fairies themselves.
They have seen more than one
of the bats from hell," answered another excitedly.

"I don't believe you.

We rid them from these lands centuries ago.

They can't be back. No, no no," stated an elderly moustached fairy.

"But they *are*.
I tell you no lie.
She said that she barely made it back alive!
We need to send up the arm,
call out the troops,
and get prepared for an attack!" said the old fairy veteran, drawing himself up.

"Time to put on the old uniform and kit." Then to himself he whispered, "If it fits."

"It was a close call all those years ago,
and we may not have Garth and Princess Pearly White
to help us now, you know," warned another, his tiny wings beating the air.

"Or the human knights,
to help us fight," cried another.
"Batten the hatches!
Lock your doors.
The gummies are coming;
the gummies are coming once more!" yelled the retired general, darting through the streets. He knew from the last attack that much needed to be done and there was no time to waste.

In the palace courtyard, King Mo-lar had gathered the Council of Kings and was pacing back and forth within the circle.

"My lords, my lords, I must confess,
Fairyland is in much distress.
The tooth fairies have returned from their midnight flights,
To report they saw drooling gummies in Bicuspid tonight."

89

A gasp was heard from all gathered. Questions murmured through the crowd.

"Were not these bats just fairytales
Told by bullies to make us wail?" asked one.

"Or old men after having too much ale?" asked another.

"Or parents using blackmail?" rhymed another.

King Mungmouth spoke up.

"It cannot be, it cannot be
Are they sure of what they see?
We drove them back,
Back to the land of Plaque."

King Mo-lar answered,

"Fairy eyes have perfect sight
They saw many yellow eyes in the dark of night
It appears that after all these years
They have come back against all our fears.
We can only imagine and trust,
That they want our wings and Fangor's scales for their nightmare dust."

The anxious buzz of wings rose from the attending crowd making it difficult to be heard.   King Jeb spoke out, holding his arms up to hush the crowd.

"We must prepare Fairyland to defend
Send out messengers to our insect friends
To keep an alert and watchful eye
For Hunters in the midnight sky."

King Toothhurty added,

"Double the enchantment spell that hides
All the entrances to our hive.
Warn the toads and frogs to croak
If ever they see them approach."

King Mo-lar replied,

> "We know if they find us their attacks will be
> relentless
> I only hope we can get help from our magician's
> apprentice
> But I will put all your ideas in motion
> With help from our friends we will drive the evil
> back to the ocean."

A cheer rose from the crowd but King Mo-lar hushed them quickly.

> "At night will be the most deadly of conditions
> To those who leave on their tooth gathering missions
> So be careful and don't forget
> Traps they will set
> To capture you and get
> Your wings to dissect."

A hush of concern rippled through all the young fairies, looking at each other in shock and disbelief. It appeared that all the scary stories their parents had told them were indeed true.

King Mo-lar then added,

> "Leave the hive each time through the secret
> woodland hollow.
> Come back a different way and make sure you are not
> followed."

CHAPTER EIGHT

Magician's Apprentice

"What is this, Great-grandpa Garth?" Holly asked staring at a twig bearing only five sparse leaves under a glass dome.

"That is a branch from the Tree of Knowledge," spoke the spectre image from the mirror.

"Tree of Knowledge?"

"Tree of Knowledge? Ha! No wonder I am so smart," Taddy Boy injected with sarcasm. "My head is full of sawdust so it must be from the tree of knowledge!"

"Your head is full of cotton wool and that is why you have a *stuffed* head," Holly informed him. "As you were saying before we got rudely interrupted, Great-grandpa?"

"Hmmmph!" was all she heard from the backpack.

"Yes. As you can tell by the lack of leaves, I have used it many times over my lifetime. That is why there are only five leaves remaining. You see, my sweet, every time you ask it a question you pluck a leaf and chew it. The tree will speak the answer you seek into your mind."

"Wow! Could I ask it where I could find a million, trillion dollars?"

"You could but it may not give you the answer you were hoping for. It might say, in the World Bank or give you a vision of sand dollars on the seashore. So you must be careful of what you ask for. You must be exact."

"I see. Do you think it might help me on my quest?"

"It may and you are more than welcome to have it. As you can see, I can hardly chew anymore. Just be careful when you ask it a question as once these leaves are gone there are no more."

"Unless we find the living tree," she replied.

"True, but that would be another adventure altogether and by the looks of my old friend, Taddy Boy, he is not contemplating more adventures."

"You can say that again!" the bear mumbled from the backpack.

"Holly, look behind you on the bookshelf and tell me what you see."

Holly turned around to see several cluttered bookshelves with numerous strange looking items interspersed between the books. The first thing that came to her eye was a rather large tooth. "What is this, Great-grandpa?"

"That is Wizzy, my wisdom tooth. He's a smart aleck. He likes to prove how smart he is using sayings, truths, historical facts, and quotes. I am not sure you want that. He can be rather annoying but after a while I found him…interesting, to say the least."

"Your wisdom tooth?"

"Well, not *my* wisdom tooth. It is too large for that. It is rumoured to have come from a magical giant panda from the land of Grin who gave it as a gift to the first Chin Emperor, Chinny Chin Chin."

"Grin. That sounds like a land of smiles."

"Sometimes yes, sometimes no."

94

"It was given to me by a tenth-level Chin magician by the name of Loos Fang centuries ago after I helped him with a plague of locusts. You may have it as well."

"Thank-you, Great-grandpa."

"You may regret that, my dear."

"Hello Wizzy. What can you tell me?"

A deep voice rumbled from the tooth. "A wise person sometimes changes her mind; fools never do."

"Well, I guess that's true," Holly replied, smiling.

"You should listen to the tooth, Holly," Taddy Boy said emphatically. "Maybe you should change your mind about going on this dumb adventure. I know — maybe we should go home and use your leaves to get a 'A' on your homework!"

"Not now, Taddy Boy. Not now." Holly waved a hand over her shoulder to shush him.

The tooth spoke again. "The most effective way to conceal ignorance is to listen and shake your head when asked for an opinion."

"Ah, a good lesson for you, Taddy Boy." Holly couldn't help but smirk.

"Quick, put the tooth away before it spouts another wise old adage. He won't stop until you do," Garth advised.

"A wise person will think without talking; fools reverse the order..."

Holly jammed the wisdom tooth deep into the bottom of her backpack, muffling the baritone voice. "I see your point, Great-grandpa."

"Holly, do you see a hat, a book, and a stick on one shelf?"

"Yes, Great-grandpa. A blue velvet cap like a French beret only this one has a headband with silver stars and a crescent moon embroidered on the top. There is also a book entitled *Beginners Magic* and some kind of a short stick."

95

"That's not a stick; that's Nova Cane! My original owner here used that thing to set me on fire!" Taddy Boy recalled with a shudder.

"Yes, my friend, you will never let me forget it, will you? I was just a boy at the time and for the thousandth time, I apologize...*again*."

Turning his attention back to Holly, Garth went on, "What you have there is a magician's apprentice cap, a beginner's wand and the starter book on magic. You'll need these objects to learn the basics before you may become an actual First Level Wizard of the Plantagenet Order."

"Wow! A magician's apprentice cap. Can I put it on?"

"You *may*, but it comes with an awful lot of responsibility. If you choose to wear it you automatically become a member of the Guild of Magicians, the ancient and honourable craft of Magician in the Plantagenet Order just like I, Tar Tar Goldcaps, and many other magicians listed in the book did many centuries ago."

"That's heavy."

"Heavy? What does heavy mean? Oh, never mind. As a member, you must follow all the rules or risk turning into a Black Wizard devoured with evil."

"Just like Mendrix?"

"Exactly."

Holly gulped. "Okay, then what?"

"Each year, on the summer solstice, all Wizards of the Plantagenet Order meet at the Stone Circle where you are tested for your next level of wizardry until you reach tenth level. It is not easy. You must be aware that your conduct is also judged by the elder magicians."

"That could be a problem for you, Holly," Taddy cautioned.

"Shush Taddy, I want to hear Great-grandpa."

"Your wand memory is checked to ensure your works throughout the year were true. If your acts are deemed false, you will be cast out of the order and thrown to the wills of the demons of the Dark Mouth. Like bad breath, a cruel existence awaits you when you serve their every whim."

Holly swallowed hard and asked nervously, "Wha...what are these rules Great-grandpa?"

"First, magic must only be used for the purposes of good or your spell will be reversed upon you and you will suffer the consequences. Second, you must never hide your identity as a magician. You must always wear your cap or, when you become qualified, the right colour robe and cone hat. Third, using your mind over matter to cast your spell, you must believe with all your might that the spell will work or it simply won't. You see, you call upon the power of Mother Nature and she requires *all* of your concentration. Finally, you must never use magic to gain power or riches."

"There go the million, trillion dollars," Taddy Boy sighed.

"I am afraid so."

"Well, if we're going to do this..."

"Or not!" Taddy Boy shouted a final plea.

As soon as Holly put the hat on, the dusty feather pen sitting in the inkwell on the desk shuddered and shook until all the dusty layers of time fell off, revealing a bright rainbow of colours as if from a once-magical bird.

"Ah, Quill has recognised you," Garth said.

"Oh yes, Quill your magical pen that was once Tar Tar Goldcap's?"

"That's right. Quill will write down all of your magic spells so you can remember them. Learn one per day and sleep on it and you will remember it forever. You only have to say the magic word."

97

"Please?"

"No, no, that's what your parents say is the magic word. I mean a real magician's word. For Quill it's..."

"Rat Rat!" Holly remembered it from Taddy Boy's story.

As soon as the words left her lips, the quill leaped up, spun, and wrote the following on a parchment paper lying on the desk. *"Hello Holly. My name is Quill and I am at your service."* Then it smartly somersaulted and flew up into the headband of her cap.

"As you know, Quill will write your spells in a language that only you can read. Remember, you can only learn magician's apprentice spells. Harder spells will come to you as you get promoted through the ten levels of magician. Your book, *Beginners Magic* will help you try your first spells just like I did."

"Use the lizard or the stick as your guinea pigs but leave me out of it!" Taddy Boy grumbled. "Been there, done that."

"Oh, I see the scaredy bear is back," Garth declared.

"Do you blame me? I was the one who was..."

"Yes, I know, put on fire. Once again, my dear friend, I am sorry about that. You will never let me forget, will you?"

Holly opened the book and noticed all the writing change into a language she could read. Just as Garth had experienced those many years ago, a plume of smoke containing the face of an old wizard appeared from out of the book.

"Welcome to the Guild of Magicians..." the voice boomed with authority then stopped and changed into a softer tone. "Oh, I see you have your elder wizard already here. Hello, Grand Magician Garth," said the apparition, acknowledging Garth's image in the mirror.

"Thank-you, Merlin. This is my great-granddaughter, Holly, so if you wouldn't mind I can look after this," Garth replied.

"No problem at all. It's nice to meet you, Holly. Call me if you need me." In a puff of smoke the image returned to the pages of the book.

"Before you learn to cast your first spell, you need your own secret word to activate your spell. You know, something snappy; something with pizzazz."

"Like abracadabra, presto, or shazam?"

"Yes, I thought of those as well when I was your age but those have been used by other magicians long ago. It must be your own word. Mine is Al-a-fangbite."

Holly tried to think of her own unique magic command word but nothing came to her. She picked up the pointed stick known as Nova Cane and twirled it like a baton, hoping it would inspire her. "Now what can I use?" she pondered.

"What do you like, Holly? Maybe that would help," suggested Garth.

"Now what do I like...Barbies, laptops. No, that won't do." She thought further and checked her pockets. She felt a round ball and pulled it out. "That's it!" she exclaimed. "My favourite candy!"

"Should I be afraid to ask?" said Taddy Boy.

"My command word is Jawbreaker!"

The wand in her hand started to vibrate and sparks flew from its tip.

"I was afraid of that," Taddy Boy nervously.

"Looks like Nova Cane is fond of your word," Garth observed. "All spells are easier to cast if the magic user chooses a staff or wand to focus the mystic energy. The more familiar a magician becomes with his or her wand, the more power it will gain. Nova Cane already knows you so he will help you as you go."

"Thank-you, Nova-Cane. It will be a pleasure to work with you."

"Don't you dare trust it. That thing can bite," yelled Taddy Boy. "It zapped me and set me on fire!"

"Oh hush, Taddy Boy. I'll be careful."

"To learn spells, a magician must read magic books and scrolls. Once read, a spell caster may cast the spell once but then must sleep on it to remember the spell forever. Remember, as this is important, only one spell can be memorized at one time or the magic user runs the risk of mixing the spells. A mixed spell will be lost forever in the mind of a magician causing the spell caster to slowly go insane," warned Garth.

"Good to know," Holly replied, suddenly more concerned.

"Now, look up a spell you would like to try," Garth suggested. "Don't expect too much, as the power of the spell depends of the level of the spell caster. As you gain experience, the power of the spell will increase and double for each level reached by the magician. As a beginner you should be safe."

"Speak for yourself," grumbled the voice from the backpack.

Ignoring Taddy Boy, Garth went on, "A spell caster may call on the 'elements of nature' to assist in their quests for good. Mother Nature gave this promise to our elders in ancient times:

'Fire, wind, lightning, ice, and rain will not desert the pure of heart.
Earth, rock, wood, and stone, may also be called upon to do their part.
But BEWARE, I will soon tell if the spell is cast for good or deeds of the dark.
So remember to use your spells wisely, as no one can hide from my eyes in the sun, moon, and stars.'"

"You never fool with Mother Nature, so they say," Holly recalled. She thumbed through the *Beginners Magic* book, flipping pages. "Now let me see...Sleep Spell, Waking Spell, Water Find, Stop Wind, Rain Maker...hmmm. I don't know which one to choose. Stone Cast, Freezing Spell, Can't Speak Spell. That looks interesting. I wonder..."

"Don't think about it," Taddy groaned.

Holly looked over to see King Dentin quietly basking in the sun with his wings stretched out. "I know, I'll cast a Speak Louder spell on King Dentin so I can understand him."

A gush of relief came from Taddy Boy. "Thank goodness! I thought you were looking at me."

"You are such a wuss!" she giggled. "Now let me see..." She then read, "*To make a person or thing speak louder or release a person or thing from a Speak Softer or Whisper Spell, an apprentice may use a magic potion of Pump Up Oil, Turn-it-up Magic Scroll, or point their wand or staff at the one they want to hear and read the following incantation followed by their secret command word.*"

"Okay, here goes." Holly pointed her wand at King Dentin, concentrated with all her might, and read the incantation.

> "You with your voice so low,
> Tell me what I need to know,
> Your thoughts and council without fear,
> In a voice that only we can hear."

Nothing happened.

"Remember your secret word and concentrate," Garth reminded her.

"Oh, yes." She pointed Nova-Cane and said her word, "Jawbreaker!"

The wand immediately shook and a bright white light glowed at its tip. Holly's eyes widened as the pulse of white lightning shot from the tip of the wand.

101

"Zaaaaaaap!" The crackling sound echoed in the room as the bolt left the wand and hit King Dentin, followed by a puff of blue smoke.

"Well, that was dramatic," Holly said.

"Did it work?" asked Taddy Boy.

Holding their breath, all eyes stared intently at King Dentin as he sat there, stunned and motionless.

Garth broke the silence. "That was much better than my first attempt. There's not a mark on him."

"I second that! At least he's not on fire," Taddy Boy added.

"Yo, lightning strikes
But got no bite,
She ain't no zapper
And she ain't no rapper
You got a lot to learn, girl.
In the magic world," T-Pick rapped to Hip Hop's dance.

"Is he alive?" Holly peered anxiously at King Denton, ignoring T-Pick. "He doesn't seem to be moving."

After a long pause, the butterfly flapped one wing then another. King Dentin lifted his head and spoke, "My lady, May I introduce myself? I am King Dentin, Lord of All Butterflies, Protector of All Moths and Flying Insects, and friend of elves, fairies, and gnome worlds."

"It's a pleasure to meet you, Your Majesty. My name is Holly Johnson." Holly breathed a sigh of relief.

"Well done," praised Garth. "Your first spell worked wonderfully. Once you sleep tonight you will remember the spell forever."

"Well, Great-grandfather, I came here to find my way to Fairyland because of the note the fairies sent me. They need my help."

"Yes, my sweet. They may need our help and I have seen the evil bats but I get the sense it may be something else. You need to go there as soon as you can."

"How do I get there, Great-grandfather?"

"Anytime you wish to go to Fairyland or come back to the castle, just call my friend, King Dentin, and his friends will help you. He helped me many times and it will save you three days travelling through the mountains. You will also avoid any unfortunate meetings with bears, mountain lions, and ogres and…you always take the risk of being followed."

"How do I do that, Great-grandpa?"

Just as the words left her mouth, the gathering of butterflies swirled around her en mass, completely covering her in fluttering wings. The throng slowly lifted off the ground with Holly, T-Pick, and Hip Hop, hidden inside. As the colourful multitude moved, Holly's arm reached out and grabbed her backpack, containing Taddy Boy, and pulling it into the swirl.

As the swarm left through the window, Garth heard Holly's voice call back, "Thank-you Great-grandpa. See you soon…I hope."

"Me too," added Taddy Boy.

CHAPTER NINE

Fangor's Request

Inside the swirling butterflies, Holly was amazed at how these small and delicate creatures carried her with such ease as they travelled toward the old volcano. Yet, a small niggle in the back of her mind made her unsure and she prayed they wouldn't let her fall.

Sitting on her shoulder under the ever-watchful eye of T-Pick, King Dentin, could sense that Holly was nervous. "Don't worry, Great-granddaughter of Garth, you are perfectly safe. We have carried Garth many times and he was much bigger than you."

"Many hands make light work," whispered the muffled voice of Wizzy the wisdom tooth from the bottom of the backpack.

"Thank-you, Wizzy," said a wide-eyed Holly, looking downward. "That's not very comforting at this moment."

"If he drops you, it's a long way down," chimed in Taddy Boy.

"I didn't need that either," she whimpered timidly.

"We will arrive in Fairyland by morning," King Dentin advised before Holly could ask. "You might want to get some shut eye so you will be fresh for your adventure."

"You won't drop me, will you? I have never gone to sleep this high up held up only by the little legs of thousands of butterflies."

"Of course not, my dear. It will be like sleeping on a white puffy cloud," King Dentin answered to comfort her.

"Very well. I am a little tired but before I do, I had better call home just to let them know I am okay."

"Your Pops isn't going to be happy," Taddy Boy said, stated the obvious. "You'd better hold the phone away from your ear."

Reaching for her phone in the backpack, she replied, "I know he'll be angry but I have to let them know or they will definitely worry about me."

"Take the wind out of an angry man's sails by staying calm," Wizzy suggested as she grabbed the phone next to where he lay.

"Thank-you, Wizzy. That's a good idea."

She took a deep breath and nervously dialled the number. One ring, two rings. *Maybe they're not home*, she hoped. Three rings, four, then the call clicked to the answering machine. "Yes!" she said in great relief and recorded her message. "Mom, Dad, I am going with the butterflies to Fairyland for a sleep over. Don't worry, I'll be home soon!" She clicked off before anyone could pick up.

"I am sure they'll be happy to hear that one!" Taddy Boy said.

"I know it sounds weird but I think it's always better to tell the truth."

"Truth is something hard to get people to listen to and harder for them to believe," Wizzy advised.

"Isn't that the truth?" Holly said settling down for a well-earned nap under the soft glow of fireflies flying along with them.

"And nothing but the truth!" Taddy Boy added.

In the forest below, several pairs of yellow eyes observed the mass of butterflies heading north.

"Do you see that? " asked one of the patrol hunters to the head hunter.

"Yes I do," he said, eyeing them suspiciously.

"Looks a little suspicious at this time of day."

"Very unusual. I thought Monarch butterflies migrated south this time of year."

"Shall we follow, Head Hunter?"

"No," he finally decided. "We weren't told to look out for these fluttering bugs and, they don't have enough meat on them to eat. Let's get back to the job at hand."

"Aye, aye," answered the hunter.

Knowing they had to feed the dragon, the head hunter was on the prowl for tooth fairies bringing money from the rainbow's end Pot-of-Gold to the human children's homes in exchange for their teeth. Fairies were what he wanted and fairies were what he was determined to get.

Back in the Johnson's home, Holly's mother found the phone and listened to the message left by her daughter. "Oh no! Holly left a message while you were in the shower. She says she's having a sleep over with the butterflies."

"A sleep over! She's only eight! That young lady had better get her butt back home and, and...who are the Butterflies anyway?" Mr. Johnson shouted from the steamy bathroom. "I don't recall meeting a family called Butterflies."

"You're right, dear. I don't recall any of her friends with that name," she said, now worried. "I'll call the number back and see if I can talk to her and the mother of the Butterflies."

"Hello?" Holly answered when the phone rang.

"Mom, here darling. Where are you? We are really worried about you."

"I, I..." Holly stuttered.

"And who are these Butterflies? We don't know these people. You never mentioned a friend with the name Butterfly. Your father and I think you are too young for sleepovers and want you to come home right away."

"Oh, I am okay, mom. There are lots of butterflies and they are my friends. You've seen them lots of times."

"I have?" she said, puzzled.

"Yes, they live on the way to the mountain. Would you like to speak to their, er...father?"

"Yes, put him on the phone."

Holly put the phone to King Dentin face. "Hello, Mrs. Johnson. How are you?"

"I'm fine. We don't think our daughter is old enough for a sleepover and I can't recall ever meeting you or Mrs. Butterfly at the school Parent-Teacher meetings."

"Oh, Mrs. Johnson, I have seen you many times in the gardens. You have blond hair and wear those beautiful floral summer dresses."

"That is true but I just can't recall..."

"Not to worry, Mrs. Johnson. Holly is quite safe with my family and I won't let anything happen to her. I'll make sure she gets home safely, too."

"That's very nice of you but I am not so sure..." Then she realized the phone had been hung up.

Mr. Johnson came into the kitchen wearing a fluffy white bathrobe. "Well, who are these people?"

With the distraction gone, Holly looked around the peaceful glade and noticed that not only were there no fairies but also no fairy homes or dragons either. "I thought we were coming to Fairyland?"

"It is very close by but Fairyland is a tight squeeze right now with all of the fairies from around the world cramming themselves into one fairy hive. Had we taken you there last night and you rolled over in your sleep, you could have crushed a few of their homes or even worse, a fairy."

"Oh, I wouldn't want to do that," Holly said.

"Garth liked to come here so as not to scare the younger fairies who might not have seen a human yet," explained King Dentin.

"I see. I guess they will show themselves when they decide to show themselves."

"In the meantime, it looks like they gave us breakfast," King Dentin said. A delectable assortment of apples, pears, grapes, sunflower seeds, honey, oranges juice, and milk had been laid out on a flat rock nearby.

"How sweet," Holly said, surveying the feast.

"I am not sure about that T-Pick fella. He's a chameleon and a predator to my kind. As King of the flying insects, I would not be pleased with him eating any of my subjects," King Dentin cautioned.

"Even nasty old flies and mosquitoes?" Taddy Boy asked.

"Even nasty old flies and mosquitoes."

"T-Pick can eat some fruit. Fruit is good for everyone, my lord," Holly replied.

As they ate, Holly read another chapter in her *Beginner's Magic* book. Having remembered her Speak Louder spell, she thought she should try another and found a Spell of Invisibility that piqued her interest.

"This could be useful in the days to come," she whispered. She concentrated as hard as she could then commanded:

111

"From all the eyes that can see
in shadow or in daylight be
Hide this object perfectly
with a cloak of invisibility.

She then pointed Nova-Cane toward an apple core and commanded her magic word: "Jawbreaker!"

The apple core disappeared instantly. "*Awe*some!" she said, amazed with herself and her wand. "I think I am getting the hang of this."

"Don't try the Fire Spell," Taddy Boy warned. "You don't want to learn the Fire Spell, or the Lightning Spell, or the Explosion Spell, or..."

"Oh, good thinking, Taddy Boy. I will probably need some of those to help us later but I promise not to try them out on you."

"I sure hope not! Fire and fur never go well together."

"Oh, you're such a scaredy bear," she said, giving his old head a rub then turned back to the apple core. "I wonder how long the spell will last?"

She read on. "'The time the spell will last will depend on the magician's level. For a magician's apprentice it could be a few minutes or a few hours, whereas for a tenth level magician it can last from a year to a thousand years. A scroll or Spell of Visibility will break the enchantment and return the person or thing into the world of sight.'" She closed the book. "I will learn that one tomorrow."

"By the looks of things, I can tell
You learn your lessons very well."

Startled, Holly spun around. Arrayed behind her were King Mo-lar, the other kings, and all of the fairies. The peaceful glen had been transformed into a wondrous Fairyland.

"My goodness!" Holly said, taken by surprise. "You gave me such a start. Have you been there all this time?"

"Sorry to cause you such alarm
But there are those who want to cause us harm,
So to keep us safe for certain
We hide behind this enchanted curtain," King Mo-lar said.

King Dentin bowed and with a graceful flutter of his wings announced, "King Mo-lar, Your Majesties from the Fairyland world, this is Holly, great-great-great-great-great-great-granddaughter of Garth."

"Thank-you for answering our plea, granddaughter of Garth.
You see we need your help with Fangor's yearning heart.
He knows ancient dragon's eggs have been found far, far away
And he wants them to live another day."

"But, but, I thought you wanted help with the drooling gummies?"

"They indeed will be trouble for us
To double the defences is a must
But if the Fairylands are to survive
We must rescue the eggs from where they hide."

"I see. So where are these dragon eggs?"

"Fangor knows where they are
In the land where ice and snow is never far
Once ruled by a terrible Tsar
With a place called Mosjowl is at its heart."

"That sounds like Brushya?"

"Brushya is on the other side of the world
And a long way for a young girl
You will need to be strong and brave
If these eggs you are to save,"

"Don't forget to *brush ya* teeth!" giggled Taddy Boy.

"That is a long way away," Holly said, concerned, ignoring Taddy.

"Yo, yo must ya
Go to Brushya
Mom and pops will bust ya
Might crush ya
Ground ya, yo," rapped T-Pick.

"The lizard's right, for once," Taddy Boy counselled. "I don't think your Mom and Dad had this in mind for your sleep over. Nope, not even a little bit."

"That may be true, Taddy, but this sounds important. I can only hope they don't find out. It's a good thing that they can't hear you or I would be in trouble for sure." With the decision made she asked, "How do we get there?"

"We? Why do *we* all have to go?" Taddy Boy moaned.

"Because."

"Because? What kind of answer is that?"

"Because you are my best friend." Holly gave Taddy Boy a big hug.

"Well...all right then," Taddy Boy said. He was always a sucker for a big hug.

Holly turned back to the fairies. "What do we do once we get these eggs?"

> "The guardian of dragons, we are told,
> Is the Emperor of Chin who was so bold.
> Once the ruler of the east
> He will know how to raise the beasts."

"Chin!" Taddy Boy cried. "That's another gazillion miles away! I don't think the butterflies can carry us that far. Holly, this could be dangerous and scary, and did I mention dangerous?"

"Well, I guess we should get started then." She shrugged, ignoring Taddy Boy. "And I think I need to speak with Fangor," Holly said hesitantly.

"Nothing to fear but fear itself," counselled Wizzy.

"That didn't help, Wizzy," Holly said.

> "I will take you down into the dragon's den
> But I warn, with great heat you must contend.
> He can be scary and mean, and his smell offends
> But you do not need to worry because he was Garth's great friend."

King Mo-lar waved his wand at the mountain and the rock wall disappeared to expose the dark hole of the cave entrance. Instantly, a rush of musty, heated, and foul-smelling air struck Holly's nostrils causing her to gag.

Covering her mouth and nose with the arm of her coat, Holly shouted, "Whoa, he's been down there for a long while."

"By the look on your face, this is one time I am glad I have a button for a nose," Taddy Boy said with a snicker.

"But it also means you can't smell yourself," Holly said and followed King Mo-lar into the darkness. As he flew, Holly started her climb down into the cave.

"Are you saying I am smelly?"

"Like any old stuffed animal that's eight hundred years old."

"But, but..."

"Don't worry, I love you all the same."

"But..."

"Maybe next time you won't give me such trouble when it's time for your bath."

"Smell or bath; I think I know which I prefer."

Holly chose for him. "Bath."

"Humph! I think not," was all she heard coming from the backpack until Wizzy spoke up.

"Nothing changes a bear's appearance as much as soap."

"Hey, I resemble that! I mean, I resent that!"

The descent took a lot longer than normal because, unlike fairies and dragons that can fly, Holly was on foot. The so-called path that had rarely been used became treacherous almost right away. At times, the path narrowed, forcing her to creep sideways and hug the walls, while the damp stones on other sections were so slippery she lost her footing and sent loose rocks and dirt cascading down into the chasm and the steamy molten lava boiling far below.

Holly knew they were close to the dragon when she heard a low guttural roar, felt a gush of wind, and heard the flap of wings coming up from below.

"What was that?" asked Taddy Boy.

Both T-Pick and Hip Hop darted into the backpack to hide. Neither liked the prospect of meeting a real live dragon. Holly kept a brave face when Fangor landed angrily on a ledge nearby. He roared and belched a fireball that sizzled past the stunned collection of would-be heroes.

"Not again!" yelled Taddy Boy. "I tried to tell ya, but no, got to be just like Grandpa Garth. Now we're all gonna die!"

Shaking with fright, Holly closed her eyes and did the only thing she could think of. She pulled out her wand. Concentrating as hard as she could she pointed the quivering Nova-Cane upward and whispered,

"From all the eyes that can see
it in shadow or daylight be
Hide this object perfectly
with a cloak of invisibility."

116

Then she yelled, "Jawbreaker!"

The point of the wand sparked, throwing lightning bolts in all directions around her and her companions. To Fangor's surprise the unwelcomed visitors vanished in front of his eyes.

"Who *dares* to enter my den?
I smell a human trying to descend,
Show yourself or you will burn
Never disturb a dragon, you must learn!"

With his voice echoing in the cavern, the tiny voice of King Mo-lar replied:

"No, no, Fangor my friend,
Do not take out your revenge.
This is Holly, great-granddaughter of Garth,
A friend to help upon the journey you wish to embark."

The red flare and the smoke from his nostrils drained from the dragon's face returning it to a brilliant green hue. Fangor, feeling a little embarrassed, spoke softly.

"Oh dear, big mistake.
I apologise for my haste to erase
A daughter of Garth's is a friend of mine
Now and forever until the end of time."

He hung his head with regret.

"Th, th, that's okay, Fangor," said Holly, knees knocking. The invisible image of Holly started to materialize back into view. "I am not sure how but I am here to help."

"But I have to break my vow
And travel to a place called Mosjowl.
Do you think the humans will mind?
If I make this journey to help my kind?"

"A broken promise is something that can never be mended," Wizzy's muffled voiced spoke from the depths of the backpack.

Holly rolled her eyes. "Thank-you, Wizzy. You're not helping."

**"Once we were strong and feared no one on this earth
But humans made me promise to hide in this mountain of dirt."**

"A pact made so long ago, Fangor," Holly said. "King Overbite is now a ghost so I believe your promise may no longer stand. Fangor, you have been gone for so long and, because no one has seen you in many lifetimes, no one believes in dragons anymore. For humans, dragons only exist in legends, myths, and mysteries."

**"After all this time
They must believe in the fairy kind?
For their teeth we give coins for them to find,"** King Mo-lar explained.

"Only kids believe in fairies, elves and such things now," Holly said.

**"So I must do what I must do
Even if a knight's lance runs me through."**

"Humans have much stronger weapons these days and if they see you fly, they would surely try to capture..."

"Or kill," interrupted Taddy Boy.

"Or kill you," Holly agreed reluctantly. "You see, adults would be afraid of you if they ever saw you fly."

**"If Fangor flies by day
Humans will see he's left
If Fangor flies by night
Gummies will know he can't protect,"** King Mo-lar observed.

"Yo danger, danger
Ain't no stranger
Two ways to go
One way to choose
One way to win
One way to lose," T-Pick rapped.

"Which way to go? That is the question. Shall we travel by day or by night?" Holly whispered as she thought aloud.

"A lady can't go anywhere while sitting on a fence," Wizzy said.

"I know, I know, Wizzy." She thought further. Finally, she announced, "We must go under the cover of night. Of the choices, this would be the least risky."

"We gotta get through those gnashing, bone-breaking, slobbering, bug-eyed monsters somehow," Taddy Boy warned remembering the last encounter he had with Garth. "We will have to disguise ourselves."

"Well, it's pretty hard to disguise a dragon the size of Fangor and I don't think I have the power yet to make a dragon disappear so..." She hesitated for a second. "King Dentin, may I ask for another of your tricks?"

"My kind would be happy to help my friend," replied King Dentin.

Holly nodded. "But for now we must rest and I should learn another spell." She thought for a moment then decided. "If Fangor has fire, I will have ice."

Chapter Ten

A Winter's Adventure

As dusk settled, Holly and the rest of the gang awoke, feeling fresh from their naps. She had learned the Ice Spell while she slept and planned on learning the Lightning Spell tonight. *Just in case of trouble,* she thought. While eating honey, berries, and an apple, she watched hundreds of fairies harnessing Fangor with reins and lifting a saddle with heavy pouches hanging from each side onto his back. Others held a bag full of children's discarded baby teeth for Fangor to get a good meal before departure.

The fairies knew they were safe from the prying eyes of the drooling gummies because the glade was still behind the enchanted curtain, but the fairy kings were no fools. They also knew the hideous bats would still be lurking out there, on the prowl for unsuspecting tooth fairies as one or two still had not returned from the previous night. The Council of Kings knew that they would need a distraction to make sure Fangor could leave undetected.

"Wow! He looks a whole lot larger than he did in the cave," Holly gasped.

"And uglier than I remembered," Taddy Boy added.

"I wonder what's in the bags?"

"Teeth. Thousands of them," Taddy Boy answered. "Fangor will need them to keep his eternal flame alive on our long journey."

"I hope they didn't forget about me," Holly said.

> "All preparations have been made
> So do not be afraid.
> Food to keep you fed,
> A blanket for your bed
> Clothes to keep you warm
> As you travel through the ice storms..."

Ice storms? What do you mean *ice storms?*" interrupted Taddy Boy.

"Shhh," Holly hushed. "Please go on, King Mo-lar?" King Mo-lar continued:

> "To help you on your voyage,
> A bag of fairy dust to help your courage,
> Enchant an enemy onto your team,
> Or give them a nap of sweet dreams."

King Mo-lar handed Holly a small bag of magical sparkles.

"Thank-you, King Mo-lar. We need all the help we can get."

> "We must leave with all haste.
> I must find this Mosjowl place.
> My ancestors have waited a long, long time,
> I have to get them before the stars align," Fangor

roared.

"Stars align?" Holly asked, puzzled.

> "Secrets in the moon and stars
> Even we don't know what they are.
> Dragons are from times ancient,
> You will discover all if you are patient."

Deep in the forest, several yellow eyes opened at the sound of a no-too-distant dragon roar. An enchanted curtain may hide them but a roar from a dragon was a different story. The head hunter sniffed the air and scanned the forest. "It won't be long now," he hissed. The gummies knew they were close.

"Ruthless Toothless Brutus must hear about this," whispered the head hunter. "Go tell His Imperial Majesty," he ordered to a younger drooling gummy prowler.

"I will send out the hornets, wasps, and bumble bees to clear any lurking eyes outside the curtain," said King Mo-lar.

"My butterflies will cover you as you leave but after that you are on your own," King Dentin added.

"Thank-you, King Dentin. Do you know which way to go to get to Mosjowl?" she asked looking from one king to another.

"Not really. I think it is somewhere in Brushya," King Dentin replied.

> "When we moved our hives to King Mo-lar's
> Fairyland
> Where the last dragon made his last stand,
> I have never been able to sit on my throne.
> Too far for one night travel, too dangerous to travel
> alone,
> Our land is many miles to the east and many miles to
> the west.

"Each way is too dangerous, would be my guess," said King Wisdom of the Upperfangs from the North.

> "Yo, Yo,
> I ain't been to no college
> But you got leaves from the Tree of Knowledge
> Maybe it knows
> How to show the way, incognito," T-Pick rapped to
> Hip Hop's Dance.

"I'll show *him* the way to go, *in-cog-nito,*" Taddy Boy grumbled.

"Taddy Boy, you really must stop being so mean to T-Pick. Unlike you, at least he's trying to help," Holly scolded.

Liking Hip Hop's idea, she reached into her bag and pulled out the jar holding the five leaves her great-grandpa Garth had given her and opened it. Just as Garth had told her to, she took one leaf, placed it in her mouth and chewed it. The bitter taste caused her to scrunch up her face and almost gag. "Yeeuck! That tastes awful!"

"Ask it a question before you lose the spell," Taddy Boy urged her.

"Leaf from the Tree of Knowledge, what is the safest way to get to Mosjowl undetected?" Holly said, still chewing.

Within moments, her eyes rolled up into her head and she went into a trance. When she began to speak, her voice was that of a wise and older woman speaking softly. "To keep from being detected, follow the north star into the land of ice and snow. Take rest at the red elf's house at the North Pole. Carry on over the Parents' Sea through to the White Sea and on to the land they call Brushya. Continue flying south, crossing Lake Omegski and Lake Belogski. Fly on until you find the Yoga River. Finally, follow the Mosjowl Canal until you see the bright lights of Mosjowl."

"Well, that sounds easy," said Taddy Boy.

Holly slumped and shook free from the effects of the enchanted leaf. "Are we going to see Santa?" she slurred.

King Mo-lar answered her.

"If you mean our friend Nicholas, it does appear so.

It means you will have a long, long way to go.
Once a year he travels the world.
I know he'll show the way to you, my girl."

"The sun is setting and we must fly
Time you said your good-byes," Fangor
growled impatiently.

The travellers climbed on Fangor's scaly back by a
rope ladder attached to the saddle. Grabbing Fangor's
reins, Holly felt a pang of guilt come over her knowing
what her parents would say if they saw her sitting on
the back of a dragon. They would definitely *not* want
her to go on this quest.

She reached into her backpack anyway and pulled
out the cell phone. She knew she had to let them know
what was going on but when she tried to turn it on, the
words 'No reception' appeared. She felt a wave of relief.

"Lucky you," Taddy said.

"Well, I guess what they don't know won't hurt
them," she said as she shrugged, hoping to convince
herself.

"Parents may doubt what you say but they will
always believe what you do," Wizzy advised, to ease
Holly's mind.

"Thank-you, Wizzy, but it's time to go." She put her
foot into the stirrups and nudged Fangor who instantly
took flight. "Good-bye, my friends," she called, waving
as they rose up into the sky.

In the bushes and trees nearby, the wasps, hornets,
and bees had indeed found their hidden targets. Stung
many times and with welts rising all over their bodies,
one by one the swollen hunter gummies retreated back
to the cliff caves. A strange premonition came over the
head hunter causing him to look back over his shoulder.
What looked to be millions of butterflies rose out of

nowhere, blotting out the pink sunset sky. "Twice in two days; now that is interesting," he slurped turning north to follow the suspicious throng.

With the thrill of freedom, Fangor flapped his huge wings and soared into the open sky. For too long he had been held captive in the mountain cave the humans called a volcano. Re-invigorated, he felt his dragon blood surge through his veins as he climbed into the dusk sky shielded by King Dentin and his butterflies.

With mingled fear and excitement, Holly found riding the back of a dragon exhilarating and could not help but smile. Hip Hop and T-Pick climbed deep into the backpack thinking it was better to listen to Wizzy than it was to look down to watch the earth below becoming ever smaller. Taddy Boy, who had vowed never again to go on a wild adventure, couldn't believe he was once again on an escapade with a magician's apprentice.

North they travelled toward the tree line and barren mountaintops covered in snow. It was not long before the butterflies struggled to keep up. Being gentle creatures, the air was getting too cold for their wings and they tired quickly, but bravely they carried on until they could no longer match the flap of Fangor's wings.

"This where we must leave you, Holly," said the gasping monarch. "We can travel with you no longer."

"Thank-you, King Dentin, for all of your help. Please let Great-grandpa Garth know that I will return," Holly called.

Just as the butterflies broke away, King Dentin saw the yellow eyes following them at a distance. "Look! A gummy has followed us!" he cried. "Regroup, regroup around Fangor!"

Holly quickly spoke the Spell of Invisibility:

> "From all the eyes that can see
> be it in shadow or daylight be.

Hide this object perfectly
with a cloak of invisibility."

Then she yelled, "Jawbreaker!"

In a blink of an eye, Fangor disappeared along with Holly and her friends leaving only the butterflies.

But their escape had been discovered and Holly saw the bat-like creature turn and head west to the coast.

"Do you think he saw us?" she asked.

"Oh yeah, there's no doubt. These guys have super night vision, and Fangor? Well, he's not the smallest guy on the block," Taddy Boy replied.

"I guess you're right. But at least he does not know where we're going."

"I will inform King Mo-lar," King Dentin said. "With Fangor gone, I am sure the drooling gummies will try to attack if they find Fairyland."

"We will get back as soon as we can and with any luck, we may have friends to help us," Holly said.

"Good luck, Holly," King Dentin said as he turned to head back home.

"Well, it's up to us now," Holly said, trying to smile.

"It always is; it always is," sighed Taddy Boy.

"What! You saw the dragon leave?" Ruthless Toothless Brutus screamed. "Did you follow him, matey?"

"Yes, my lord. I followed as far north as I could go before my wings started to freeze," the head hunter mumbled through the swollen lumps on his face inflicted by the wasp, hornet, and bee stings. "The butterflies saw me when they dropped their shield but I saw the dragon; I am sure it was a dragon. Then it just disappeared."

"Disappeared out of thin air? Very interesting," Queen Hali Tosis said, pondering.

"Aye, my dear, a very interesting situation indeed. They suddenly disappeared? I hope there is not a wizard involved. We know what happened the last time."

"Yes, my sweet. Why would a dragon head north?" asked the Queen. "There's nothing up there but ice and snow."

"Perhaps, my lord, so we could not follow," offered the head hunter.

"Or a distraction for us to follow him and leave the last Fairyland," replied the queen.

"My Lord, he may circle back and attack us from behind when we finally assault Fairyland," suggest the hunter.

"When we find this Fairyland!" The queen glared at the head hunter. Her disappointment in him could clearly be seen in her eyes. "The few captured fairies we have, have given us nothing," she hissed looking over to the tiny hanging toothpick cages each containing several tooth fairies. "If we pluck their wings they will certainly remember nothing as they will turn into human children."

"Aye, all true. Or perhaps there's something more — much more," the emperor brooded. "A quest perhaps?"

"Whatever it is they plan, we need to find out what it is," the queen insisted.

"Aye, my sweet," Ruthless Toothless Brutus said, nodding. "Send out scouts to all the bat colonies around the world to keep an eye out for this dragon. Even a dragon has to come out of the frozen wastelands sometime."

The head hunter nodded his agreement.

"He is a reptile and cannot hide in the ice shield for long. His blood will freeze just as much as ours," snarled the emperor.

"In the meantime, keep hunting for the last Fairyland," ordered the queen.

"Yes, Your Highness. All prowlers, hunters, and scouts have been sent." The head hunter bowed as he backed out of the cave.

"We are close, my dear, very close indeed." The emperor and the queen looked at each other and snickered in anticipation.

"I cannot wait, my dear husband."

Holly's spell did not last long and she and Fangor quickly rematerialized. As Fangor flew over the tree line and into the tundra, Holly had already pulled out the heavy cloak trimmed in eagle feathers the fairies had packed in her saddle bags and put it over her shoulders.

"Brrrrrrr, this air is cold!" she said to anyone listening but as soon as she put it on, she could feel the heat from the silk lining stuffed with eiderdown. Her shivering soon stopped.

"You ain't kidding. I can't feel my ears anymore. Or my nose for that matter," complained Taddy Boy.

"That's because you're stuffed," Holly replied.

"Oh."

"Cold it is and colder it will be
I feel my blood flowing slower in me.
I need heat before we get to where we are going,
Especially if this wind keeps blowing."

Fangor belched a weak ball of flame to ease the cold in front of him. Unlike with frost, Fangor knew his fire breath was no match for the arctic cold and bitter winds.

"Fangor, turn your head and I will feed you. That will help for now." Holly pulled on one of the dangling

129

sacks and opened the drawstring. When Fangor turned his long neck back to her she poured some baby teeth into his mouth.

Instantly, Fangor perked up and felt the rush of the eternal flame run through him once again. He flapped his wings much stronger and his fire burned hot and bright.

They continued traveling north into the dark tempest but it did not take long before Fangor once again grew sluggish and it took all he had in him to flap his wings. He had not flown any distance for a centuries and he now tired easily. Holly knew they had a long way to go and would not make Santa's house unless the storm eased up.

"This should last a short while but I will run out of teeth if we keep this up," she said feeding Fangor another bag of children's teeth.

> "I am afraid you are right
> It's been so long since I've taken flight,
> So long since I've worked my wings
> So hard against these terrible winds."

Holly thought of Quill. The magic pen was not only Garth's writer of spells but also the famous Tar Tar Goldcaps the ancient wizard that saved Bicuspid from the ogres. He knew magic much stronger than a mere magician's apprentice. *Maybe he could write a heat spell,* she thought.

"Quill, I need your help. Do you know a heat spell that would keep a dragon warm?" Holly asked then said the magic words, "Rat Rat".

Quill jumped out of the brim of her hat, somersaulted, and spun in mid-air, nodding frantically. But in this blizzard the rainbow coloured feather could not hold on against the wind. Holly reached out and grabbed Quill as he was about to fly past her.

130

"Whew, that was close!" she cried. "We nearly lost you."

"We're freezing back here. I've got bugs crawling between my legs!"

"Oh, Taddy Boy, that's T-Pick and Hip Hop. They're only trying to stay warm."

"Let them crawl between *your* legs then. Hey! That tickles!"

"Oh hush, Taddy Boy. We've got more important things to think of right now."

"You're not the one dealing with the bugs," he griped.

"Well, we nearly lost Quill so on to Plan B," she said as more snow swirled around them. She reached into her backpack past the snow-covered Taddy Boy and once again pulled out her *Beginners Magic* book. She had learned the Ice Spell before her nap and knew she could learn one new spell. The wind had now grown into a storm and flipping through the pages was difficult but she found the Stop Wind spell. "I hope I am strong enough for this," she yelled into the wind.

" Brrrrr, ditto that. My nose is blue, my ears are blue, and I can't see any more," said a shivering, frost-bitten Taddy Boy.

Holly read the incantation.

"Winds, winds, please die down
Go up, down, or all around
Give us rest from your biting chill
Leave this space calm and still."

Pointing Nova Cane she yelled into the storm with all her might, "Jawbreaker!"

Suddenly, a sleek invisible dome formed around her and Fangor diverting the driving wind around them. Inside the dome the air was still and although still cold, felt much warmer than when the wind chill bit at them. Fangor's breath was able to keep the space warm

131

enough for him not to freeze and allowed his riders to stay warm.

"That's much better," she said, brushing the snow off herself and Taddy Boy.

"As long as the razzle dazzle lasts," Taddy Boy added.

Holly hoped her spell would last a good long while but knew that when the spell did wear off they would have to land and rest Fangor.

They journeyed on. The terrain below them became more and more an icy desolation forcing them to huddle in behind Fangor's neck for any extra warmth. Holly felt quite pleased with herself that her spell lasted for about an hour. Her strength as a magician was growing with each spell she cast and she couldn't wait to tell her great-great-grandpa Garth when they got back. *If we get back,* she thought.

As the spell broke down and the biting wind once again nipped at her nose and ears, she knew it was time to rest. She guided Fangor to land on the lee side of a huge up-heaved chunk of ice where they could be out of the wind.

"How nice! How very ice-cy! A fine mess you've got us into," complained Taddy Boy.

"We have to rest Fangor. He cannot keep going without warming up."

"As good a place as any to freeze to death, I guess," sniffled Taddy Boy.

"At least there are stars to see. Look, I have never seen so many," Holly said trying to make light of the situation. The Aurora Borealis was in full splendour.

For one short moment, Fangor, Holly, Taddy Boy, and even T-Pick and Hip Hop were caught in the awe of the dancing green and pink lights and the spectacular sparkle of the trillions of stars.

What they hadn't seen were the three sets of black eyes peering suspiciously at them as they dropped down.

"Oh darling, I still can't get through on her phone. I am so worried about our little girl," Mrs. Johnson sobbed as they sat on the back porch under the starlight.

"I am too, my dear," said a dishevelled, red-eyed, and exhausted Mr. Johnson. He had had too little sleep.

"Me too," said Connor sadly.

"The police have been searching for her and there's no sign of her," Mrs. Johnson wailed.

"We have posters up and search parties out looking for her. I don't know what else we can do," Mr. Johnson said, wiping here eyes with a tissue. "There is no such family as the Butterflies anywhere in Bicuspid or any of the nearby counties."

From the corner of her eye, Mrs. Johnson noticed the flutter of wings. A butterfly landed on the rail in front of her. Then another landed on her arm, followed by yet another. In no time, several butterflies had landed all around the family, slowly fluttering their wings in unison.

"Where did all these butterflies come from?" asked Mr. Johnson.

After a thousand had landed, a Monarch butterfly settled in her palm, seemingly unafraid. Amazed, Mrs. Johnson carefully raised her hand so that the butterfly was at eye level so she could peer into the insect's tiny face. Although she heard nothing, its eyes seemed to speak to her and it brought a sense of peace and serenity to her. "Darling," she said softly in great relief, "I believe our little girl is okay."

"Really?"

"Yes. The butterflies are here. I think *these* are the butterflies Holly was speaking of and they're telling me she is okay."

"I, I think I feel it, too."

"Me too," Connor said.

It was Fangor who first noticed the three white faces with black eyes and black noses appear in the blur of the snowstorm. He roared and belched a ball of flame in the direction of the intruders who hastily backed out of range. The mother polar bear roared and stood on her hind legs to show her lack of fear and to protect her cubs. Learning from their mother, the cubs too snarled and stood but were not nearly the imposing and fearsome sight that mother bear presented, standing nine feet tall.

"Oh-oh. We've got company," Taddy Boy muttered.

"I can roast them black
Before they attack
I've never eaten polar bear before
And their teeth would be a nice reward,"
Fangor roared.

"No, no, Fangor. Please don't hurt them. They are as scared of us as we are of them." Holly stepped between the two predators.

"What are you doing, Holly?" Taddy Boy squealed. "Remember, I am right behind you."

"Many are so filled with fear that they go through life running from something that isn't chasing them," Wizzy's muffled voice came out from the depths of the backpack.

"I don't suggest running right now because this something *will* be chasing us," Taddy Boy cautioned.

"I may have a better idea." Holly reached into her backpack and pulled out the bag of fairy dust King Molar had given her prior to their departure. "Maybe they can help us."

"Help us? They're about to make us their frozen dinner!" Taddy Boy yelled.

With hunger driving them on, the mother bear began stalking the easier prey by circling and approach from the rear and, at the same time, keeping away from the searing heat of Fangor's flame.

Fangor arched his neck, ready to belch another fireball.

The mother bear raced toward them about to pounce and with a wave of her arm, Holly showered her with a spray of magical sparkles. To the amazement of those watching, the polar bear mother stopped in her tracks, gave a puzzled sniffle, and curled up beside her. Holly gave the giant bear a cuddle behind its ear and the bear moaned with pleasure. The two babies ran from their hiding place to check on their mother and they too were dusted with glitter.

The mother bear spoke first. "My name is Agalu. In your language it means tooth. These are my cubs, she is called Kunwaktok, meaning smiles, as she is always happy, and this is Agil meaning to yawn as he is always tired."

"Pleased to meet you, Agalu. My name is Holly, this is Fangor, and my teddy bear is called Taddy Boy."

"I'm your brown cousin," Taddy said proudly.

"What, another bear speaks? Does he know the red elf as well?"

"Don't pay attention to him; he's my stuffed toy that can talk. A little too much if you ask me," Holly said.

Agalu smiled a bear smile.

135

"We need your help, Agalu. I need to keep Fangor warm for a little while so we can continue on our journey to Santa's house."

"Nicholas' house at the North Pole?"

"Yes, we call him Santa Claus."

"We like Nicholas. He gives us sugar cookies!" squealed Agil.

"Yes, me too," echoed Kunwaktok.

"How can we help a friend of Nicholas, the red elf?" Agalu asked.

"I am a magician's apprentice and I am able to learn only one spell a day. I used that on our way here to stop the wind. Fangor needs heat to survive and I'm out of ideas. Can you help us?" Holly pleaded.

"I don't know anything about spells but we stay warm when we hibernate in our winter by going into a cave," Agula said.

"We don't have a cave to go into."

"You could always make one."

"How?"

"Your dragon's fire can make a hollow in the ice wall. He can make it warm inside while we use our thick fur to block the entrance,"

Once he ate another bag of baby teeth, it did not take long for Fangor to melt a hole in the wall of ice large enough for them to snuggle into. Over the next several hours, Fangor warmed up again, the snow melted off Taddy Boy, and Holly slept cuddled up with the baby polar bears.

Refreshed, Holly woke and thought about the next leg of their journey. As she watched the others snooze, she wondered if she could memorize a new spell after such a short sleep. It frightened her to think that if she learned another spell with too little sleep it could cause her to confuse the spells and go insane.

"What is the matter, Holly?" Taddy Boy asked.

"Oh, you startled me! I didn't realize you were awake."

"I am a stuffed bear, Holly, and I can't go to sleep. I like to watch over you when you sleep."

"Ahh, that's so sweet. No wonder I love you so much." She gave him a warm hug.

Taddy Boy's heart glowed. "That was so nice but I am still wondering what bothers you, little one?"

"We were in trouble coming this far north. We didn't realize how cold it is and I don't want to get stuck again."

"You are worried about Fangor."

"If we do not have heat for the rest of the journey, Fangor would surely die and if he dies, we will have no way of returning to Bicuspid. If we don't get back, all the fairies will die."

"We might be in a little trouble as well."

She decided she was willing to take the chance and immediately opened her *Beginner's Magic* book and searched for the Fire Spell. "Now let me see, Fire Spell, where is the Fire Spell?"

Quill, her magic feather, began to shake in the brim of her cap then sprang out, twirled, and stood in mid-air before Holly's face.

"Do you know the Fire Spell, Quill?" she asked.

"Tar Tar Goldcaps wrote one many years ago and Quill wrote it for Garth," Taddy Boy said. "If he writes it, you can use it without having to memorize it. Then you won't go cuckoo."

She grabbed a piece of parchment from her pack. "Okay, Quill, will you please write for me the Fire Spell? Rat Rat!"

As he had done before, Quill spun, did a loop-de-loop and began frantically scribbling the incantation down. When he was finished, he did another loop-de-loop and flew back into the headband of Holly's cap.

Holly read the spell.

"Element of fire with your flame and sparks
Bring your light to take away the dark
Where to go is of no concern
My wand will point the place to burn."

She pointed her wand and commanded, "Jawbreaker!"

A great bonfire instantly burst into life at the cavern entrance radiating a warm glow into the cave. Agula, Agil and Kunwaktok awoke, stretching, from the new warmth. Fangor woke sleepily but the cave was cramped and had little room for him to flap his wings or stretch his legs.

Once outside, they gathered around the fire. "How can we thank-you, Agula?" Holly asked.

"No thanks are needed. We would do anything for our fr...fr...friend, Nicholas." Agula eyes started changing colour, a snarl came upon her face, and she growled as the fairy dust enchantment started to lose its pleasant influence.

Realizing what was happening, Holly ordered, "We must go." She snatched up her backpack and jumped up on Fangor's back. "*Now!*"

Shaking off the last of the enchantment, Agula once again became her ferocious self, reared up on her hind legs, and roared as she took a swipe at the rising dragon. Her cubs ran for cover.

"Go in peace bear of white
Teach your cubs the ways of life.
Fangor will not forget you
Nor the legend of the tooth," Fangor promised as they disappeared into the night sky.

CHAPTER ELEVEN

Santa's House

"Are you kidding me?" yelled Taddy Boy. "You mean we were only ten minutes from Santa's house?"

"It looks that way," Holly sighed. "I used my fire spell just once and we are already here."

"We almost froze to death out there!"

"A grouch never goes where he's told until he dies," Wizzy mumbled from the backpack.

"I am not a grouch!" Taddy Boy protested.

"Okay, you two, that's enough. I wouldn't want Santa to see you fighting. You know what they say about being good."

"But..." Taddy Boy began then thought better of speaking and remained silent.

They had flown through the enchanted dome that shields the famous North Pole residence from prying eyes. Instantly, the air felt warm and calm; the snow glistened from the light of millions of stars, and soft, happy music could be heard coming from the snow-laden buildings up ahead.

"I can smell candy canes!" Holly said excitedly. "And hot chocolate, too!"

"Maybe he has cookies!" Taddy Boy exclaimed, hoping.

They could see the twinkling lights from a brightly decorated alpine house. An inviting light glowed from the shuttered lead glass windows. Attached to the main building stood a large barn plus several outbuildings that Holly assumed were the famous toy factories.

"Yo, yo, Father Christmas

St. Nicholas

This is ridiculous

White beard and moustache

Red suit and a black sash

First class

Comes once a year with his toy stash

'Cause he's Father Christmas," T-Pick sang as he emerged from the backpack and crawled onto Holly's shoulder.

Fangor landed in front of the red-painted, wooden front door of the house guarded by two wooden nutcracker soldiers. Candy cane coach lamps flashed on as Holly climbed the candy cane-lined stairs and onto the front porch. Holly lifted the silver reindeer doorknocker and rapped on the heavy door. Another toy soldier drummer started rat-tat-tatting on his drum to announce the visitors.

To Holly's surprise, a small door at her waist level opened and a tiny face topped by a green pointed hat appeared.

"Who comes?" asked the small voice.

"Hello, my name is Holly, Holly Johnson and I am hoping to see Santa Claus."

"Hello. My name is Peppermint. This may not be the best time to visit. I'm afraid Nicholas is very busy in the mailroom."

"We were hoping to do our Christmas hinting early," Taddy Boy said.

"That's not true, Peppermint. We need some rest after travelling so far. We are on our way to Mosjowl in Brushya."

"Brushya! Well that is a long way from here. Maybe you could stay in the reindeer barn as long as that

141

dragon...Hey, what are you doing with a dragon? I have not seen one in a very, very long time."

"It's a long story..."

"Who sent you anyway? "

"King Mo-lar, King of the Fairies, sent me."

"Cousin Mo-lar! Why didn't you say so?"

The big wooden door opened and there stood a short elf wearing a white shirt and purple vest, green pants and purple, pointed shoes.

"Come in, come in."

"What about Fangor? He'll freeze out here."

"Oh, don't you worry about that. Jingles here will sprinkle some of Nicholas' magic dust and he'll shrink to the size of your hand."

"That's how he does it!" Taddy Boy shouted. "Very tricky; very tricky indeed. I wondered how he got into the home."

"Oh, Nicholas has many ways to get into houses on Christmas Eve. Not everyone has a chimney these days."

Moments later, a miniature Fangor scampered into the room and leaped up into Holly's arms.

"Wow," Holly exclaimed as she cuddled her friend.

"And who do we have here?" said a pleasant voice behind her.

Holly spun around and there in the doorway, stood a gentle-faced lady with white hair, dressed in a burgundy coloured dress and a white apron. She was smiling as she stirred cookie dough in a bowl.

"Mrs. Claus!" Holly gasped.

"Oh, please, around here I am just Carol."

"I'm Holly. Holly Johnson."

"Is that the Holly Johnson who lives on Loosetooth Street in Bicuspid, on the Root Canal?" asked a deep soft voice from another doorway.

"Why yes, it is..." Holly turned and there, answering the question on the lips of every child once and for all, stood a white-bearded, jolly-looking man wearing spectacles, a silver trimmed red vest, an old fashioned white shirt, red trousers, and a pair of worn slippers. He was large but slimmer than the pictures or the shopping mall Santas Holly had seen.

"Santa!" Holly said, her eyes lighting up. It was all she could do to stop herself from running to him and throwing herself into his big arms.

"Ho ho," he chuckled, never tiring of a child's excitement. It was a rare occasion when a child got to see him.

"How did you know it was me?"

"Santa knows many things, my dear." He winked and grinned a broad smile. "Remember, I get your letters every year, I come to your house every Christmas Eve, and I would know that dog-eared teddy bear anywhere," he said with a chuckle. "That old fellow has been around for a long, long time."

"Hey, what does he mean by that?" Taddy protested. "I can't help it that I can't see my ears."

"Nothing, Taddy Boy. You are still my very best friend," Holly cooed.

"At least I have one friend."

"Oh, my little Taddy Boy, I meant no offence. I will leave you something special this year if it makes you feel better."

"Don't be fooled, Santa. He's playing you," Holly implored.

"Ah, I see," Santa said, a smile crinkling the corners of his eyes.

"I have always wondered about your house, Santa," she said, dismissing Taddy Boy. "I have only seen it in a snow globe. May we have a peek?"

143

"Ho, ho. Why yes, of course, Holly, I'll be happy to show you," Santa beckoned her to follow him.

The first room they entered was the mailroom. Stacks of unsorted letters sat on desks and tables. Many more envelopes filled slots on a wall indicating which country they had come from while even more continued to float in down a delivery chute and pile on the floor.

"Wow, you've got mail!"

Santa gently stroked his long beard with his fingers. "Yes, it takes most of my time these days." He picked up a letter from his desk. "They are all special to me. I read each one carefully and when I get the time, I write back. For the most part though, I read their wishes, check my naughty list and, if the child has been good, I send their letter on to the elves to make or buy their special toy."

An old wooden desk lit by a candle sat in the center of the room with several large books upon it. The top book lay open and on its pages were listed rows of children's names, their ages, and where they lived. Many had a check mark beside their names; others had an X, while others had a question mark.

"I wonder what mark you have beside your name, Taddy Boy?" Holly speculated.

"I've been good; I've been good," he said defensively.

"Why do they call you Nicholas? Isn't it Santa Claus…Santa?" Holly asked as they passed Mrs. Claus in her kitchen, by a festively decorated living room, and into a long dining room with one large chair at each end of the long table and many tiny stools along each side.

"My name is Nicholas. I was born many years ago in a place that was once called Myra in a land you call Turkey."

"So, how did you become Santa Claus?"

"I am known by many names. St. Nicholas, Father Christmas, Sinter Claus…"

"But why?" Holly wanted to know.

"It is a very long story. I was an orphan, raised by the church. The monks always tried to help the poor so to do my part I used to make wooden shoes for those in need and crutches for the lame."

"But why do you come to our house on Christmas Eve?"

"Well, Holly," Nicholas scratched his head recalling the story, "in my town, I knew of three daughters of a widowed man who did not have a dowry for his daughters. That's money to get married."

"Oh."

"I knew he was a proud man and would never accept money directly so, wanting to do things in secret, I sneaked into their house late one Christmas Eve and dropped some coins into each of their stockings drying by the fire. I nearly got caught but I managed to get away. All three young ladies were able to get married. They believed the money had come from heaven."

"That was nice of you."

"I liked that they thought it was from heaven and in honour of the gifts the Christ child received from the magi, I continued giving gifts on Christmas Eve all around the world to the poor, especially the children. I think Jesus would have liked that."

"I think so, too."

"I never wanted any recognition but at some point the church made me a saint. It is an honour indeed to be called Saint Nicholas," he said, as a blush of pink rose in his cheeks. "Santa Claus is just a shortened way to say Saint Nicholas, especially when you say it fast."

"Oh, I get it."

"I was so busy making toys and helping people, I never noticed that so much time had passed. Titles still don't mean much to me; that's what others give you. I am just Nicholas to all my friends here. I guess God liked it too and continues to let me live to continue my work."

"Wow." Holly couldn't contain her admiration.

"I like to think that it shows others that keeping Christmas is good but sharing it with others is even better."

"I guess the elves do, too."

"Yes, indeed. The good elves came to help me in the ever-growing work," he said appreciatively. "There is so much to do to ensure every good little boy and girl around the world at Christmastime gets a present. And let's not forget that many individuals also have the Christmas spirit and help in many ways."

"But how do you do it in one night?"

"It's not really one night, like people think. Christmas Eve starts in Jiji and New Beeland the day before and I end up in Kiwiwi and Ramoa twenty-four hours later."

"Oh, but you go everywhere in one night?"

"Thank goodness some folks celebrate Christmas on different days. There are those who celebrate on December 6th or the 19th, which is Saint Nicholas Day, many on Christmas Eve some on December 25th and others on January 6th. This gives me lots of time, especially when I use the magic fairy dust and, of course, my flying reindeer."

"Well, I'll be," muttered a dumbfounded Taddy Boy.

"You can say that again," Holly gasped, her mouth falling open.

"Ah, here's what you were looking for." They had come to a set of large wooden doors with a sign above it reading *Toyland*.

Holly thrilled with excitement.

Santa opened the doors to reveal a busy, bustling, brightly coloured, and gleaming workshop. In a rhythmic beat, saws and hammers were hard at work, steam engines chugged, conveyer belts both in the air and on the ground moved unfinished toys from one section to another, and the hiss of spray paint all added to the organised confusion.

Holly stared in awe.

Happy elves sang and whistled while busily moving from one location to another, assembling each child's wish, operating machines, hand painting, and polishing each new toy. Holly was amazed at all of the bicycles and skates, skateboards and scooters, trucks and dolls, guitars and trumpets, games and puzzles, and so many other wonderful things slowly moving along the assembly lines.

"This is marvellous!" she cried in glee, gazing in wonderment. "How do you get it all done in time?"

"Ho, ho, ho. Well, I must say, each year it gets a little tougher, especially with all the electronic gizmos such as cell phones, tablets, robots, and flying computer things children ask for but I think we have it all in hand."

Holly passed the lightning bolt hazard sign warning they were entering the *Electronic Thing-a-ma-jigs* section where another production line worked busily with soldering guns smoldering, sparking, and zapping circuit boards. With lights flashing, wires sprang everywhere, and plastic parts and pieces in various stages of construction slowly moved along another conveyer belt.

As they reached the end of the production line, more elves were wrapping gifts while others stacked and piled. Finally, an elderly elf who gave Santa a friendly wink and a smile, ticked off each toy by a child's name after it was carefully labelled and gently placed on a shelf in the large warehouse ready for the ever-nearing Christmas Eve.

"This is *beautiful!*" Holly gasped in wonderment.

Santa chuckled as they passed an already loaded sleigh parked on a runway leading out of the warehouse. "Well, Holly, I hope you have enjoyed Santa's workshop. We should now talk about what brings you here, my dear?"

"We are on a mission to save some dragon eggs."

"Is that so?"

"You see, after the dragon wars centuries ago, Fangor here was the only one left," she said cuddling a purring Fangor. "There was a deal made between King Mo-lar, the human king, King Overbite, and Fangor that if he stayed in the volcano the fairies would go out each night to collect children's baby teeth that had fallen out and leave a coin or two from the rainbow's end Pot-of-Gold. That way, Fangor was fed and forever kept his flame alive and the fairies would have dragon scales to make fairy wings."

Fangor burped a tiny puff of smoke from his nostrils.

"No wonder I have not seen a dragon these many years," Santa said laughing so his belly shook. "They would make me smile when they came to play and frolic around me on my annual journey riding in the sleigh. But I am interrupting you. Go on."

"Well, we heard that recently that a boy in Gumgolia found some eggs after an earthquake. Brushya thinks they are dinosaur eggs but Fangor knows they are long lost dragon eggs. So we are going to Mosjowl to get them."

"Mosjowl? You sure have come by the coldest route to get there."

"King Mo-lar thought it the safest route because the drooling gummies have returned to Bicuspid looking for the last Fairyland. They want..."

"Fairy wings for their nightmare dust," he interrupted, frowning. "I know all about those drooling gummies. They always try to attack us on our journeys, especially when I head to Tonsilvania near their homeland of Plaque. They are bad — really bad."

"I bet they don't get any Christmas presents!" Taddy Boy piped up.

"The roots of all evil are planted deep," interrupted Wizzy.

"That is true little one. Bad boys and girls never get a present," Santa replied.

"We nearly got eaten by a polar bear and her cubs!" Taddy Boy exclaimed. "They shouldn't get presents either!"

"We had some trouble on the way here from some bears who said they knew you. I used some fairy dust to enchant them. It was good for as long as it lasted."

"You mean Agula, Kunwaktok, and Agil? They are my friends but Agula can be in a bad mood every now and then, especially when they are hungry or she's protecting her cubs."

"You can say that again!" Taddy Boy affirmed.

"We give them lots of sugar cookies and they leave us in peace but you are not alone, they also make Dasher and my other reindeer a little nervous as well." Santa opened the doors to the reindeer stable.

In stalls, with their names ornately carved on a wooden plaques above each one, stood Dasher, Dancer, Prancer, Vixen, Comet, Cupid, Donner, and Blitzen, all casually munching fresh hay. When the reindeer realized Santa had come to visit, they became excited and began nodding their heads, snorting, and stomping their hooves.

"Hello, my beauties! How sweet you all are," he said giving the first a gentle rub on his muzzle. The others began calling and nodding for the same attention.

149

"Okay, okay, my precious ones. Settle down, settle down. Nicholas loves you all just the same and you will all get a little scratch and a treat."

"Where's Rudolph?" Holly asked, noticing his empty stall.

"He and the others are playing in the pens outside."

"What about Olive?" Taddy Boy asked.

"Who's Olive?" asked Holly.

"You know the one who used to laugh and call Rudolph names."

"That's not Olive," she giggled. "That's 'All of the other reindeers…'"

"Oh, I always thought that it was Olive. I have always wanted to give her a piece of my mind," Taddy snorted.

"Santa, we also came this way so that those wicked gummies could not find out that Fangor had left Fairyland undefended," Holly said, feeding Prancer some hay.

"Do they not have an enchantment spell to hide the entrances like I do? I never had to use one until humans invented jet aircraft and those pesky satellites."

"Oh yes. So far they have not found Fairyland."

"Good. I will let the elfin world know to keep an eye out for these ugly bats and if necessary, somehow I will help the fairies."

Dasher stamped one hoof nervously when he saw Fangor snort another puff of smoke but soon settled when Nicholas petted his snout. As promised, Santa visited each reindeer handing out treats and dearly loved rubs.

Back at the main house Santa settled into his favourite overstuffed chair and put his feet up on the footstool. "It has been a long day," he said with a yawn.

Just then Mrs. Claus asked entered carrying a tray of steaming hot chocolate, milk, and cookies. "Who would like supper and some hot chocolate?"

"I'll have some milk and cookies, dear," Santa replied, sitting up straighter.

Holly covered her mouth with her free arm and yawned. "It has been a long day, Santa. Would you mind if I had a little sleep now?"

"I would like some cookies," Taddy Boy said but his request fell on deaf ears.

"Why, of course," Santa answered Holly. "Carol has readied a big feather bed for you upstairs."

"We will need to leave early tomorrow and be on our way. Thank-you for all you have done for us."

"I would like hot chocolate, too," Taddy piped up.

"You are more than welcome, little one. Sleep well and to all a good night."

"Good night Santa and Mrs. Claus."

"Oh dear, call me Carol."

"But, but..." was all that could be heard from the backpack.

⸎

In the coastal caves near Bicuspid, Ruthless Toothless Brutus was becoming frustrated at the lack of progress his hunters and prowlers had made. They had found the Rainbow's End Pot of Gold and set up toothpick traps just like his predecessor Pyorrhoea Pete had done centuries before but with less than spectacular results.

"Why can't you get these pesky imps?" screamed the emperor to his cowering hunting patrols.

Apparently, wasps, hornets, and dragonflies escorted each tooth fairy and protected and warned them when gummies were close or when they flew too close to the capture cages the gummies carried. Many of the drooling gummies had returned with welts upon their bodies from multiple stingers, and carrying empty cages.

"We know where they are, my lord," the head hunter protested. "We just can't get close enough or see the encampment."

"Have we heard from any bat patrols around the world as to where our dragon friend might be?"

"No, my lord, but we have, however, stolen many deadly nightshades from the humans," he said, adjusting a pair of white-rimmed sunglasses.

"At least we can attack in the daylight," Queen Hali Tosis said, trying to ease the emperor's mood.

"Not good enough! I want to attack Fairyland *now!* "

"We have captured some fairies and plucked their wings, my lord. They are now children who keep the furnaces burning to make the nightmare dust."

"I want more! I need thousands of fairies wings or the dragon. I need more human slaves to make more nightmare dust and turn this world into one big, bad dream!

"Yes, my lord." The head hunter and the queen bowed low and wisely backed out of the royal chamber.

153

CHAPTER TWELVE

Dragon Eggs

"Yo, yo, let's go.
Thank-you, Santa,
But you can see, can't ya?
Time to blow
Get on the road
Leave this show
Of ice and snow," rapped T-Pick as Hip Hop broke into a dance.

"T-Pick is right. We should be going," Holly donned her cape and slung her backpack over her shoulder. "Thank-you so much for everything, Santa and Carol. We certainly enjoyed our visit."

"You are most welcome, Holly. I have packed lots of goodies for you to eat on your journey," Carol told her.

"And here's a little magic elfin dust I use to get into the houses without a chimney. You can slip through a window or a keyhole. The more you use the smaller you get," Santa said handing over another pouch of magic dust.

"Wow! Thank-you, Santa."

"I have asked Comet to guide you to the Parents' Sea. From there you are on your own and I'll see you next Christmas Eve..." Santa winked, "if you're good, ho ho ho."

"I can't wait to tell all my friends at home all about this place."

"They won't believe you," Taddy Boy said.

"Maybe, maybe not. But *we* know, don't we."

"Yup."

"And maybe we can expect a little less sass if *someone* wants a present left under the tree on Christmas morning, hmmm?"

"You *can't* be talking about me!" Taddy Boy said indignantly more as a show for Santa than from embarrassment.

"Ho, ho, not to worry, little one. Santa never forgets someone who's such a good friend for such a long, long time."

"Ha!" Taddy Boy said smugly into Holly's left ear.

"I can always change my mind though," Santa mentioned.

"Oh, you don't have to do that. Hey, he can hear me."

"Ho, ho, ho, of course, I can. Santa hears everything." Santa winked and laughed again until his belly shook.

"From now on, you'd better be on your best behaviour; Christmas is not that far away," Holly reminded Taddy Boy, knowing full well that was impossible.

**"We must leave little one.
Our task is not yet done.
I need the heat from the sun,
Or become oblivion,"** Fangor huffed.

Holly waved her wand and, poof! Fangor returned to his normal size, and with Holly on his back, he gave a mighty roar and lifted off.

"Good-bye, Santa. Good-bye, Mrs. Claus," she called over her shoulder as they broke through the enchanted curtain and once again burst into the cold arctic weather.

With Comet in the lead, they headed south to the Parents' Sea. Over the vast icecap they flew with the

155

brilliant starry sky above them. Holly cast the No Wind spell and her Fire Spell to keep Fangor warm while the dragon heated the frigid air before him. As it was still late summer, the weather warmed the farther south they flew. Holly was surprised to see massive breaks in the ice appear. It looked like the arctic had shrunk as more and more chunks fell off into the sea, as the air grew warmer.

It did not take long before they reached Denture Land. These islands were the telltale sign they were leaving the Arctic and entering the Parents' Sea. Comet circled to face Holly and pawed the air with his hoof.

"I think Comet is leaving us," Taddy Boy guessed.

"I think so, too."

Comet urged them to continue south with a nod of his head then with a whoosh, headed back north from whence they had come.

"Good-bye, Comet. I'll listen for your hoof beats on Christmas Eve," Holly called hopefully.

"You can never stay awake," Taddy Boy reminded her.

"Well, there's always a first time." Then she turned her attention to the quest. "On to the White Sea, Fangor."

"In the distance I hear a dragon's roar
But not one I've heard before," Fangor rumbled warily.

"I hear it, too." Holly scanned the horizon and saw two white jet contrails coming toward them at a high speed.

"Oh, oh, I don't want to get nuked," Taddy Boy exclaimed.

"The Brushyans must have picked us up on their radar!" Holly hollered pulling Fangor into a steep dive.

156

Holly cast the Spell of Invisibility hoping it would last until the jets disappeared.

"From all the eyes that can see
In shadow or in daylight be
Hide this object perfectly
With a cloak of invisibility."

She then pointed Nova-Cane at Fangor and commanded her magic word, "Jawbreaker!"

As the pair of Brushyan jet fighters roared past, Captain Campbelkov could not believe what he saw. "Ivan, do you see what I see?" said the wide-eyed pilot as Fangor exhaled a fireball at them in defence.

"I, I thinks so but I... don't think so," Ivan replied rubbing his eyes at seeing Holly wave from the back of the dragon.

"Where did it go? It just disappeared."

"I don't think anyone will believe us," Ivan said.

"Neither do I."

"What do we tell the Squadron Commander?"

"This is just between you and me, da?" Campbelkov suggested, remembering Fangor's fierce eyes.

"Da. We'll tell base it was a UFO. They'll believe that before they'll believe we saw a dragon with a little girl on its back. That way they won't think us crazy."

"I would not treasure an extended holiday in Cryberia."

"Da, let's return to base."

The pair of jet aircraft turned away without firing a shot.

A few moments after they had left, the spell evaporated. "Whew, that was close," Holly said, watching the jets disappear. "Any longer and they would have seen us again."

"At least the spell worked. Did you see the missiles under their wings?" Taddy Boy exclaimed.

"Scary, weren't they? I'm sure glad they didn't shoot at us."

"The next time they might!"

"Is this what you tried to warn me about?
Human dragons with no mouth
Fire breath from the...other end
A strange way to attack or defend.
They look rather silly
Or did they eat a bowl of chili?" Fangor questioned.

Holly laughed. "Their weapons are powerful and believe me, they did not eat a bowl of chili."

"I sure don't want to see them again," Taddy Boy said.

"Me neither. We should fly very low to get below the radar. That way, they won't know where we are."

"Yo, yo, no worries
There's no need to hurry.
Back to base they scurry.
Never seen a dragon breathe,
They don't believe
What their eyes see, yo," T-Pick rapped on Holly's shoulder.

"I sure hope you're right, T-Pick."

Fangor dipped low so he was gliding just above the surface of the sea, thrilling Holly but scaring Taddy Boy.

"Really, do we have to fly this close to water?"

"Oh hush, Taddy Boy, this is exciting!"

The tips of Fangor's wings skimmed the heaving waves, frightening off the gulls that were leisurely riding on them. As they made their way, they could see a colony of puffins on some of the rocks then a few whales gliding along in the cold water on their migration. Occasionally, big waves surged and soaked them but Holly thought it better to get a little wet than be hunted by fighter jets.

158

"You know I don't like water," Taddy Boy protested, dripping from the last wave.

"You needed a bath anyway. You were starting to smell musty."

"Musty? Are you saying I'm old?"

"If the shoe fits."

"But, but, I don't wear shoes."

"Oh, never mind. Let's just carry on."

At last, they saw the coastline of Brushya approaching. More seagulls flew out to investigate only to scatter when they saw what was coming. Then Holly saw the first buildings in the distance. From the seaport of Murmurski, ships could be seen moving in and out of the harbour and being more loaded and unloaded at the docks.

"Yahoo! Dry land!" cried a relieved and soaking wet Taddy Boy.

Holly commanded Fangor to hide in whatever cloud cover he could find as they passed over the city. While admiring some of the beautiful old buildings, Holly noticed dark images coming out of a church spire and rising in their direction.

"Look below us. What is that dark smudge climbing toward us?" Holly asked.

"Looks like thousands of birds," Taddy Boy replied.

"At least it's not jets, but I don't think they are birds..."

Before they could react, they were swarmed by thousands of small dark-winged bats wearing Flossack hats. Fangor veered and swerved to evade the horde. Holly covered her eyes with her hands to avoid being attacked by the frantic swarm.

"What did we do wrong?" Taddy Boy asked, tucking his head into the top of the backpack.

"I'm not sure. They are not the drooling gummies."

"Are you going to do something or should we get scratched to death?'

Just as Holly reached for her wand Fangor swooped into a steep dive. The bats followed close behind. The sudden jerk caused Holly to hold on tight and she was unable to use her magic.

"Whoooooooa!" Holly yelled, barely keeping her grip. But rather than losing the bats they were being met by thousands more coming out of empty buildings.

"Go up! Go up, Fangor. They cannot fly as high as you," she shouted. "We will have to risk the radar."

Fangor belched a fireball, clearing a path through the bats, and spiralled upward. The sudden swing caused Holly to slip off the saddle and nearly lose her grip on Fangor's reins. Fangor flipped back over and now Holly hung upside down. The next moment, Taddy Boy slipped out of the backpack.

"Heeeeeeelp!" Taddy Boy yelled as he fell.

With one hand wrapped around the reins, Holly flung her arm out and backward and grabbed Taddy Boy's foot, just in time.

"Be careful, Fangor," she said, panting. "Remember, we're on your back."

Fangor straightened out when he was well above the winged menace and safe from the marauders. Holly climbed back into her saddle. "Whew, that was too close," she huffed, out of breath, as she stuffed Taddy Boy into the backpack.

"Thanks for saving me, Holly," Taddy Boy said in a tiny voice. "You never know what the Brushyans might do to a bear trying to steal dragon eggs."

"No problem, but I think all spies go to droolags in Cryberia,"

"That doesn't sound very nice."

"I don't think it's supposed to be," she said and then quietly added, "I wonder why they attacked us?"

"Maybe they were just curious?"

"Somehow I don't think so. I think they were waiting for us."

Indeed, the Flossack bats had been watching for them. Their sonar senses had received the alert that had been sent out by the gummies to all bats around the world. Now, messengers had already been sent back to inform their gummy relative, Emperor Ruthless Toothless Brutus.

Once clear of Murmurski and the bats, Holly resumed their course south to Mosjowl. To avoid detection, they kept to the rural country away from towns and cities by flying over lakes and forests and soaring low above the trees. If anyone did see them, Holly thought no one would believe what they saw anyway, as many centuries had passed since a dragon had been seen flying in the Brushyan sky.

Just as the leaf from the Tree of Knowledge described, they had flown over Lake Omegski, Lake Belogski, the Rybinski Reservoir and followed along the Yoga River. Finally, they turned south along the Mosjowl Canal and it wasn't long before they saw the glowing lights of Mosjowl.

"Well, I think we're here."

"At last," Taddy Boy said. "Dragon scales can rub a stuffed teddy bear raw."

"This is a big city!" Holly observed. "Way bigger than Bicuspid. I hope we can find the place where they keep the dragon eggs."

"How are you going to find the place without getting noticed?" asked Taddy Boy.

"We," Holly corrected.

"What do you mean 'we'?"

"*We* are going to find the eggs."

"Oh sure, I've heard this one before. Don't you know they have soldiers in there...with guns? *Big guns!*"

"Remember, you are your own doctor when it comes to curing cold feet," Wizzy intoned.

"Who's gonna put a filling in that enamelled smart aleck?"

"Oh hush, Taddy. Who's going to shoot a girl with her pet dragon anyway?" Holly said optimistically.

"Ah...the soldiers, with their guns?"

Looking around for a place to hide, Holly spied a dense forest on the outskirts of the city and directed Fangor to land in a small clearing.

"We'll wait here until after midnight then we'll find the eggs. That way, fewer people will be around to see what we're up to."

"What about the Mosjowl bats?"

"We'll just have to take that risk."

They settled down for a well-deserved rest. Fangor was fed another sack of teeth while Holly ate a pie that Mrs. Claus had packed for her. As they had some time, Holly decided to learn a new spell while she waited.

"Now let's see..." she said as she thumbed through her *Beginners Magic* book. "Walking Spell," she read. "I don't think so...he would get into too much mischief..."

"I heard that," Taddy Boy said, not amused.

"Rain Maker Spell — no. Can't Speak Spell — now that I could use..."

"I heard that, too!"

"Oh hush, Taddy Boy. I was only kidding. Hmmm, Common Tongue Spell. I like that. Seeing that we are in Brushya, that might help." She read further. "To make a person, beast, or thing speak your tongue or release one from a Gibberish Spell, an apprentice may use a magic potion of Universal Tongue, a Translation Scroll, or point the wand at the person, beast, or thing and read

162

the following incantation followed by their secret magic word."

Holly looked around and saw sitting on a branch, a sparrow happily singing. "Now let's see..." She read the new spell:

> "You who speak the tongue of your land
> To you I make this command
> Turn them into words I can understand
> And to all of those from Fairyland."

She pointed her wand, concentrated hard and yelled "Jawbreaker!"

From the tip of Nova Cane, a bolt of blue energy shot out and surrounded the bird. The friendly chirps turned into, "tra la la, tra la la, sol le meo, sol le meo Tra la la."

"Hello, little sparrow."

"Hello, tra la la, tra la la, " the bird answered.

"Nice to meet you."

"Hello, tra la la, tra la la, " the bird said again.

"Hello again. I wonder if you or your friends could help us? We need to find dragon eggs. We think they are somewhere in this city."

"Hello, tra la la, tra la la " the bird repeated.

"Yes hello, but I wonder..."

"Forget it, Holly. He's not going to talk to you," Taddy Boy interrupted.

"What do you mean? He can understand me, can't he?"

"I don't think so. I think he's a bit of a bird brain," Taddy Boy said with a snicker.

Holly giggled.

> "I can smell them with my nose
> And I can tell that they are close
> So do not despair
> I will sense them from the air." Fangor roared.

"But you are so big, I know the guards will see us."

163

"Unless they can't," Taddy Boy said.

"Oh, I don't know if my invisibility spell is strong enough..."

"A closed mind is the most difficult thing to open," Wizzy mumbled from the backpack.

"Or last long enough to get there," Holly continued, frowning.

"It isn't gonna happen unless we try," Taddy Boy said. "Good grief, now I sound like Toothy Peg in there."

"But you're right. We have to try. Come on let's go," she said climbing on Fangor's back.

> "From all the eyes that can see
> be it in shadow or daylight be
> Hide this object perfectly
> with a cloak of invisibility."

She then pointed Nova-Cane at Fangor and commanded with the word, "Jawbreaker!"

Now invisible, they soared above the great city of Mosjowl. As Fangor circled to get a sense of where the eggs were, Holly could see all the cars and bus headlights moving along the streets below. The hustle and bustle of the night and the noise of city life filled her with excitement but also fear of being caught. She recognised the Dread Square and the Brushyan parliament building called the Tremblin from pictures she had seen at school, along with lots of churches with roofs that reminded her of tulip bulbs.

It didn't take long before Holly noticed her spell was wearing off when she started seeing Fangor's scales begin appear. "Oh oh, we had better find the eggs fast. The spell isn't lasting."

Just as she said that, several bats flew out of an abandoned building and flapped toward them.

"They sensed Fangor," Taddy Boy whispered urgently.

"Come on Fangor, we have to land quickly," Holly cried.

"I know we are close
I can smell them with my nose."

"He'd better sniff them out quick cause the bats are coming, the bats are coming!" Taddy Boy shouted.

Just before he totally rematerialized, Fangor glided down to touchdown on the flat gravel roof of a large, red brick building called the Mosjowl Museum of Palaeontology.

To Holly's great relief, the swarm of bats passed overhead and disappeared into the night, "Whew, that was close," Holly whispered.

"Well, we're here so how do we get in?" Taddy Boy asked. "I bet you there's a security guard."

"I am sure you are right," Holly replied, checking for entrances.

"With a gun."

"Probably."

"And he's not going to let you just walk out with the dragon eggs."

"Probably not."

"Sooooo?"

"We have to sneak in, just like Santa does."

"Okay then." Taddy Boy shrugged.

"Yo, Yo
Sneaking in like a gangster
Or a prankster
A midnight hamster
A thief in the night
Through the skylight..."

"That's a good idea," Holly said, interrupting T-Pick's rap and Hip Hop's dance. "We'll go through the skylight!"

"Shall we leave Big Boy here?" Taddy Boy asked.

"This is a big place. We'll need Fangor to sniff out the eggs. I'll use some of Santa's magic dust to shrink him then I can carry him."

"Yo, yo
Dig fast in the sack,
The bat's are coming back,
From the sky of black
They're coming to attack," sang T-Pick.

Fangor looked up in the sky and belched a fireball in the direction of the black mass coming down, scattering them for the moment. Holly hurriedly sprinkled the magic dust on Fangor and in an instant he shrank to the size of a cat. Scooping him up in her arms, she yanked open the skylight and climbed in, closing the hatch just in time. The bats thudded clumsily on to the Plexiglas window now stunned, they slid off the skylight, one flattened and squirrely-eyed bat after another.

"Ooooh, that's gotta hurt," Taddy Boy said, watching them and wincing.

"They're going to need a dentist for sure," Holly giggled as she climbed down the access ladder.

"I hope he pulls the tooth, the whole tooth, and nothing but the tooth," Wizzy said from the backpack.

"Hey, that's the first time Tooth Ache in there said something funny!"

Holly crept along the hallways of the museum cradling Fangor in her arms. In the quiet of the night, the displays of dinosaurs' bones in frozen poses stood eerily, as if they were still alive. A complete Tyrannosaurus Rex stood in the centre of the big hall with his mouth open as though in mid-roar. A Velociraptor in the mid-attack of a horned Triceratops dangled in an alcove, and even a Pterodactyl hung suspended from the high ceiling in silent scream. All stood in an ominous silent guard of a time long passed.

"It's creepy in here," Holly whispered, staring around, wide-eyed.

Fangor could sense the death as well and shot a defensive little roar and a puff of smoke toward the fearsome figures.

"I got goose bumps on top of my goose bumps," Taddy Boy muttered with a shudder.

"Hush, Taddy Boy, we don't want to be discovered," Holly whispered, hiding behind a pillar as the security guard passed nearby.

"Who would want to steal a pile of bones?" Taddy Boy asked.

"We're here, aren't we?"

"Yeah, but..."

"But what?"

"They didn't know we were coming?"

Holly rolled her eyes then slid behind the gigantic leg of the largest of dinosaurs, a Titanosaur, when another guard passed by.

"Which way, Fangor?"

Fangor snorted toward to a set of stairs leading down into the basement and she scooted to the door undetected and quietly sneaked in. Creeping down the stairs, they entered a lower hallway. Overhead, security cameras silently observed her every move.

Fangor began to squirm with anticipation as they tiptoed along the passageway and he almost wriggled right out of her arms when they came to a laboratory door at the end of the corridor.

"This must be it."

Holly slipped through the door and there, displayed on the table before her, were five beautiful eggs, their shells rippling with vibrant colours.

Fangor yelped, jumped up on the table, and entwined himself around each enormous egg, nudging

167

and cuddling each one like a mother finding her lost children.

"They are so beautiful," Holly exclaimed looking at one more closely.

"Yeah, but there's no time to hang about," Taddy warned. "Don't ya think we should get going?"

Holly heard footsteps coming down the hall. "You're so right. We gotta go." She scooped the eggs up, stuffed them into her backpack, then grabbed Fangor under her arm and ran to a second door and peered out. As the security guards came in at one end of the room, she silently left through the door at the other. Looking back to make sure she had not been followed, she dashed up the stairs to the main floor and through the door…straight into two armed security guards waiting for her.

"Excuse me sir, I am looking for a place to re-charge my phone," she said feebly, gazing up at the moustachioed guard glaring down at her.

Before she had time to snatch out her wand or fairy dust, they seized her by the scruff of her neck, lifted her off the ground, and marched down the hall with her dangling between them. In a windowless security room at the back of the main building she was plunked her down in a hard chair.

She could not understand the Brushyans as they spoke to each other. All she knew was that after searching her backpack and finding the eggs, became both began shouting furiously at her.

Fangor spat tiny fireballs at them when they touched the eggs but they swept him aside, tumbling him into a corner of the room.

"Oh, oh. Fangor ain't gonna like that," Taddy Boy said.

Fangor roared, spat out a fireball, roared again, and started to shake.

"Oh, oh," Holly warned.

The startled guards backed up in fear as Santa's magic dust on Fangor began to wear off. The more he grew and filled the interview room, the louder his fierce roar became. When he shot out a huge fireball at them, the guards ran for their lives down the main hall.

In the commotion, Holly quickly stuffed the eggs back into her backpack as Fangor outgrew the space and burst out through the ceiling. The guards seemed as petrified as the bones in the displays and hid behind anything they could find that gave them cover. Fangor roared once more in fury, split open the roof of the building and, as Holly jumped up on his back, he took flight into the night sky.

CHAPTER THIRTEEN

Dark Skies Looming

"I don't think we can hold them back much longer. The bats seem to be getting much stronger," said King Mungmouth at the Kings' Counsel in Fairyland.

"They guard all the fairy doors and our secret ways in
Day and night they wait like gargoyles and goblins
Ready to attack
When our tooth fairies come back
To make them human children, I trust
And slaves to their nightmare dust," said King Toothhurty.

King Mungmouth continued the discussion:

"We have knocked down the Gummies who have broken through the curtain
None have escaped to tell, that is for certain
We hold them in cages in the mountain deep
With a sprinkle of fairy dust to make them sleep."

King Wisdom also spoke:

"We must hope that Fangor and Holly get back soon
Before the time of the waning Dragon Moon
Our friends with their talons and stingers are truly bold
But before long it will be too cold."

Then it was King Jeb's turn.

171

"More and more humans scream in the night
With nightmares that give them terrible fright
We must send more magic fairy dust
To fight the evil nightmare dust."

King Mo-lar drew himself up and commanded:

"Of course, my friends, you are all correct
Your counsel I do respect,
Their attacks are truly relentless
We must strengthen our defences.
Arm the ballistas and catapults
And oil to burn in our moats
Make sure the ways into the hive are narrow
And all are armed with bows and flaming arrows.

Kind Mungmouth looked worried.

"Of course, we will do as you ask
One and all of these tasks
But will all these plans be enough?
I think we will need some luck."

King Mo-lar paced back and forth in the center of the Kings' Counsel circle.

The dragon and the wizard are what we need
Before these drooling gummies succeed.
We must trust in our magician's apprentice, Holly
To make it back in time, by golly."

All fairies worked hard to shore up all the defences of the hive. The old general ordered fairies to pile sandbags against the toadstool homes, walls, and battlements. Frenzied fairies made arrows from donated porcupine quills; others sharpened large sticks tipped with melted silver acquired by the crows that are attracted to shiny things humans make. Others used eagle feathers to make the flights for the ballista arrows.

172

Thousands of fairies buzzed with work on the defence of the last fairyland hive.

Forest friends once again showed up to help as they had many centuries before. The swifts and swallows made mud nests in the trees for fairy archers' outposts. Beavers dammed up the nearby stream to create moats around the villages for the burning oil, and honeybees used their precious honey to cover the spiked horse chestnuts so that they would stick to their targets when fired by the catapults. Dragonflies with fairy riders patrolled the perimeters, always on watch for any drooling gummy that happened to get too close.

"The SPCA is overcrowded with captured bats wearing stolen sunglasses and the government states it is overwhelmed with the problem." Mr. Johnson heard the newscaster report on the television.

"Bats with sunglasses?" he said out loud to no one in particular. "What on earth are they doing with sunglasses?"

The newscaster continued: "Blaming the bats for the disappearance of their pets, some of our citizens have formed posses to hunt them down. Not knowing if these animals have any diseases, City Counsel of Bicuspid warns all citizens that these animals are to be considered unsafe and hunting them is not recommended. The mayor also reminds us that the uses of firearms is not permitted within the city limits of Bicuspid." Visuals appeared of citizens wearing camouflage hunting outfits and carrying crossbows, bows and arrows, and slingshots while patrolling the streets.

The concerned mayor of Bicuspid appeared on the television screen. "My fellow citizens of Bicuspid, I ask that you don't take the law into your own hands. Let the police do their jobs. These bats are extremely dangerous and we ask that our citizens stay clear of them at all costs by remaining indoors whenever possible. Researchers still have no idea why the new species of bats is here but our best guess is that it is a rare migratory event and that they will be gone soon."

"The citizens are becoming frustrated with the loss of pets. Mayor, are children in danger?" the news reporter asked.

"Our children are our most important concern and we ask all parents and teachers to ensure children are never left alone outside without adult supervision. To ensure the safety of our citizens, Council is taking every measure to investigate and rid us of these bats one way or another. Extra police and security patrols are in place twenty-four hours a day and we have put the army reserves on full alert. Helicopter patrols and tactical teams are searching the area to find out where they are nesting."

"Did you hear that, Connor? Make sure you are with Mommy or Daddy when you go outside," Mrs. Johnson ordered.

"Yeah, Mom." Connor wrapped his hands around his throat and staggered around before flopping onto the floor, faking his own death.

"That's not funny!" Mrs. Johnson said firmly. "I just hope our little Holly is okay and not bothered by these beasts!"

"I wish she was home," Connor said, getting up.

"Me too," said Mrs. Johnson.

"Me too," said Mr. Johnson sadly.

The newscaster interrupted their thoughts. "Hospitals and clinics are being swamped with people seeking relief from bad headaches, migraines, and nightmares. To make matters worse, pharmacies and drug stores report that their shelves are completely bare of all forms of pain medications."

"I wonder if these bats have anything to do with that," Mr. Johnson said, turning to his wife.

"In international news from Brushya," the newscaster continued, "the Mosjowl Museum of Palaeontology suffered a building collapse and other widespread damage. The official reports say that a natural gas explosion occurred but several bystanders report seeing a dragon. Yes, that's right folks, a dragon."

"Have you heard of anything more ridiculous?" asked the co-anchor.

"Butterflies, fairies, and now dragons! What is this world coming to?" Mrs. Johnson voiced, staring in disbelief at the television.

"Somehow I think our daughter has something to do with it," Mr Johnson suggested.

"Really? No, not my little girl."

Deep within the caves northeast of Bicuspid an ear splitting shriek echoed. "Brushya! Why would the dragon be in Brushya?" screamed Ruthless Toothless Brutus looking for answers from a bat in a Flossack hat.

"We do not know, master. They came from the north, flying low as if they were looking for something."

"Looking for what?" Brutus screeched. "I know they're up to something, but what?"

"The Mosjowl bats report that they saw them sneak into a building that keeps old bones."

"A cemetery?" asked Queen Hali Tosis.

"No, the humans call it a museum," replied the Brushyan bat.

"Humans! I will never understand humans. What do they want with house of old bones?" Ruthless Toothless Brutus asked.

"Bone soup?" offered the head hunter.

"Don't be silly. Even we wouldn't eat bones that taste like stone!"

"How old?" Queen Hali Tosis asked.

"Ancient. They are of beasts from long ago that no longer roam the earth."

"Do you think they are as old as dragons?"

"Yes. Some are even older."

"Why would a dragon want old dragon bones?" asked Ruthless Toothless Brutus.

"Spare parts?" replied the Brushyan bat with a shrug.

"No..." the Emperor muttered in disbelief. "Surely not spare parts?"

"Do they keep eggs there?" Queen Hali Tosis asked shrewdly.

"Yes, many old eggs but they are hard and look like stones, my queen."

"He's after dragon eggs," she said quietly. "I'm sure of it."

"What do they think they will do with them, once they have them?

"Hatch them," she said with a nod.

"Hatch them! But if they're stones, how will he hatch them?" Brutus asked.

"There must be a way," replied the Queen, "and if he does, that means more dragons; and more dragons mean more dragon scales for us!"

"Aye!' the Emperor hissed. "The more scales, the more fairies..."

"The more nightmare dust!" finished the queen.

"But more dragons also mean more dragon fire," cautioned the head hunter. "Our ancestors did not fare well with dragon fire."

"True," answered the Queen. "But we need the scales at all costs!"

"Yesssss, at all costs," stressed the emperor. "Continue following them and report back to me as soon as you hear anything."

"Yes, my lord. Your will is my command." The Brushyan bat bowed and left to return on his long flight back to Brushya.

Turning his attention toward the head hunter, the emperor asked, "What about production?"

"Unfortunately, my lord, production of the warlock shale has been slower than expected. We are running out of dragon scales as well as rattles from rattle snake tails but we do have fillings from silver jackal's nails and pools of midnight hail."

"And our raids on the fairies?" the queen inquired.

"The fairy king enchantments on Fairyland have been impossible to break but we continue to try."

"Is there any good news?"

"Yes, my lord. At great risk and with the help of the dark shades, we have captured with our traps many tooth fairies in the early evenings when they leave to collect teeth and at dawn when they return from the rainbow's pot of gold near the forest fairy doors."

"Good! Anything else?"

"We have changed them into human children and they now work the furnaces."

"And?" asked the queen.

"Many humans are *enjoying* our dreams, mistress," the head hunter replied with an evil grin.

"Good. We'll show those pesky pixies who are the bringer of *sweet* dreams! Heh, heh, heh," she cackled.

"Aye, keep up the good work!" Ruthless Toothless Brutus ordered then asked, "But what about our invasion of Fairyland?"

"We have made several attacks on an open glen in the mountains but it's heavily defended. Our warriors have taken many casualties."

"Can we not make a full-on assault?" demanded the Emperor.

"We cannot attack what we cannot see, my lord. Fairyland still eludes us but we know it's there. It seems that all forest creatures are helping these fairies. Each time we attack we lose several hunter patrols."

"And even if we did find it, we cannot commit all our forces in case we need them to protect us from the dragon," Queen Hali Tosis cautioned.

"Or *dragons*," the head hunter added.

CHAPTER FOURTEEN

The Captured Princess

In the abandoned ruins of a medieval castle in a wooded area somewhere several miles east of Mosjowl, Holly glided Fangor down to land unseen in the open space that was once the stronghold's courtyard.

"Whew! That was a close call!" Holly gasped brushing off building dust. "They are gonna be really mad we wrecked the place."

"Someone will have a lot of explaining to do. I wouldn't want to be in their shoes," Taddy Boy said.

"They will probably send out the whole Brushyan army after us," Holly guessed as she gathered wood to light a fire. "We'll have to scram as soon as we can."

"Yo, yo,
Get scrammin'
Before guns go blammin'
Cell doors slammin'
Too much bangin'
And homey don't want no hangin,'" rapped T-Pick as Hip Hop gyrated.

"I know, I know, but we need some rest and..." Holly sighed, "we don't know where we're going."

"Before we get too comfy, we should check out this dive in case there's any of those critters' watching us," Taddy Boy suggested.

"You're right!" she agreed, gazing up at the ramparts. "We certainly don't want to be attacked by

180

the gummies or their friends while we sleep." Holly got up to start searching the ruins and the overgrowth that had taken hold of the abandoned fortress.

"What do you mean sleep? Who's gonna be able to sleep now?" Taddy Boy squeaked.

"You don't sleep. You're a stuffed teddy bear."

"I rest my eyes to keep them moist."

Holly rolled her eyes and started searching.

Fangor sniffed the air then looked toward to what was left of the remaining tower.

"I sense something strange over there
Not a beast but it still stares
Always sighing
Always crying
In sadness grieves
And wants to leave," Fangor rasped.

"*Oooooohhhhhhh*," moaned whatever was inside the tower.

"What on earth could that be?" Holly asked, making her way over to the castle keep from whence the noise came.

"Hold on there, Baba Louie!" Taddy Boy protested. "Shouldn't we think about this? It could be some crazy Brushyan Monk or some crushin' Brushyan bear!"

"Well, if it is a bear then you should be able to talk to him, being a cousin and all," Holly joked.

"I, I, I'm a stuffed bear, not a real one and, and, and he couldn't hear me even if I tried to talk to him! I think I should just stay here by the fire and keep warm."

"Sounds like I hear a scaredy bear again."

"There's nothing wrong with being cautious now and then," Taddy Boy reasoned.

"It's okay to use caution but even a turtle never gets anywhere without sticking its neck out," Wizzy advised from the backpack.

"You're becoming a big tooth ache," Taddy Boy snapped back.

"Caution is what we call cowardice in others," Holly added.

"Now you sound like toothy peg over there!"

"Oh, come on. Let's check it out."

Holly entered the dark door of the tower and pulled out her wand. She thought this was a good time to try the new spell, the one she had learned the first night.

> "Element of fire with your flame and sparks
> Bring your light to take away the dark
> Where you go is of no concern
> My wand will point the place to burn."

"Be careful where you point that thing. I've been its victim and never want to get scorched again!" Taddy Boy warned.

Holly pointed her wand up dark the empty tower, concentrated hard, and yelled, "Jawbreaker!"

A bolt of flame shot out of her wand and flew up the entire length of the tower hitting the wooden joists of the roof. Instantly the wood beams burst into flame lighting up the entire inside of the tower. The glow lit up the circular stairway leading aloft revealing several wooden doorways at each level.

"Well, I don't see anything, not even bats," Taddy Boy observed.

"True, but I don't see what Fangor was talking about either."

"Maybe that's a good thing."

"Maybe, but I had better put the fire out before it becomes a beacon for all to see, if you know what I mean."

"Oh yeah, if they haven't seen it already."

Holly dug out her *Beginners Magic* book and looked up the Water Spell.

"To make a splash, rain, water spout, or river, to cool or put a fire out or release a person or thing from a Fire Spell, the apprentice may use a magic potion of a Sea Wave, a magic scroll of Drench or Douse, or point their wand at what they wish to soak and read the following incantation followed by their secret word..."

Concentrating as hard as she could, Holly pointed Nova Cane at the burning flames and read the incantation.

> "The fire that burns so bold and bright
> Be cooled by a Storm of Might
> Do not resist
> Do not fight
> On your way out, shut off the light."

"Jawbreaker!"

Nova Cane rumbled like thunder, shuddered, and then gushed out a huge torrent of water out from the tip as if it were a fire hose. The surge of water soaked down the entire roof turning the fire into steam with the rest coming down in a deluge, drenching Holly and Taddy Boy. Holly held desperately onto Nova Cane with both hands, as water spewed from the thrashing wand until it poured out of doorway like a river.

"I don't know how to turn this thing off!" she hollered, grappling Nova Cane as it spun her out of control.

"I think *"storm of might'* had something to do with it," Taddy Boy yelled over the noise of gushing water.

The water continued spraying, spinning Holly around and around. "Whoa," she screamed as she rode the wand like a bucking bronco.

"I'm getting dizzy!" hollered Taddy Boy.

Fangor came over and stuck his nose into the archway and was saturated with a straight stream each time Holly made a circle. After being splashed several times, he backed out spluttering and vigorously shaking water off his head.

Finally, Holly couldn't hold on any longer and let go of Nova Cane causing them to both to drop to the ground. Separated, the flowing water suddenly stopped.

"A fine mess you have got us into, Holly!" Taddy Boy hollered. "It will take days for my fur to dry out!"

"I'm sorry, Taddy Boy. I didn't know my own strength and I guess I have a lot to learn. Please don't make a fuss. I know how much you hate water but at least I learned to drop Nova Cane when a spell goes out of control."

"You'd think they would have said that in that nothin'-but-trouble book of yours."

"Oh look, it does say that right after the spell," she said reading the next passage.

"Oh goody, at least we've got that straight," he groused.

"Hey look, the water washed the floor," Holly exclaimed.

"Uh, that's nice, one less thing for the maid to do."

"No really, look what it uncovered." Holly found a set of keys, a pewter mug, some plates, and a knife, evidently left behind centuries ago.

"I could use a sharp knife, a plate, and the mug."

"Eeeew! You don't know who's used them."

"I'll make sure I wash them really well," she said stuffing them into her backpack.

Having seen nothing else and still completely sopping wet and shivering, they went back to the campfire to dry off and eat some of the rations provided by Mrs. Claus.

T-Pick used his long tongue and Hip Hop grabbed with his praying arms a few slow mosquitoes that still hung around now that the season was changing. Fangor crunched on another bag of teeth. Just when they all started to relax, they heard another groan come from the tower.

"*Ooooooooohhhhhhh*" the mysterious eerie cry moaned.

"What was that?" Holly exclaimed.

"Not again," Taddy Boy sighed.

"It must be that 'thing' Fangor sensed earlier."

"What joy. I guess you're going back over there to check it out," Taddy Boy surmised aloud as she got up. "Yep, that's what you're gonna do. I knew it."

This time, Holly took a burning log from the fire to light her way. She wasn't going to make the mistake of needing the Water Spell again.

Holly stuck her head in the entrance and tentatively looked around with the torchlight held high but again, could not see anything. Then coming from up above her, she heard the groan once more echoing through the inside of the tower.

"*Ooooooooohhhhhhh...*"

"It sounds like it's coming from one of those rooms up the stairs," she said looking up and moving toward the stairs.

"I know, let's go and check it out...not!" Taddy Boy warned but Holly had already started climbing the stairs.

She stuck her torch through the bars that were in the first door and looked. She could see a small cobweb-filled room that was empty except for a stone bed in the corner and a bucket beside it. Some chains with manacles hung on the wall and across the room was a barred window.

"This is a prison cell!" said Holly, shocked.

"Ah yes, a medieval necessity," Taddy kidded. "Parents would lock their kids in there if they didn't brush their teeth twice a day."

185

"Really? Mean parents in those days," she said with a shrug. "I guess kids don't realize how lucky they are today."

"Just kidding…" Taddy said. "I think."

"In any case, I can't wait to give my Mom and Dad a big hug when I get home. I miss them."

"Me too."

They carried on up the stairs and at the next door Holly heard a moan but this time gentler and very sad. Holly looked through the bars and there, in the middle of the cell was a ghostly apparition suspended in the air with her hands covering her face.

"That, that looks like Princess Pearly White!" Taddy Boy exclaimed.

"Princess Pearly White? You mean King Overbite's queen?"

"Yes, yes. She's a lot older but that's her!"

"Free me," the ghost moaned. "Let me out."

Holly tried the door but it was locked. She dug out her Beginners Magic book and started looking for an Unlock Spell.

"You have used your spell today, Holly," Taddy Boy reminded her.

"Oh, darn it! That's right," she said slamming the book shut. "Now what do I do?"

"You could always try the keys."

"What ke…? Hey, wait a minute. I remember," she raced down the stairs and grabbed the old keys that were revealed by the water. She raced back up the stairs and tried the key and it started to turn.

Holly flicked her eyes toward Taddy Boy and said, "Maybe the Water Spell was a good thing after all."

"Luck, just pure luck."

"Luck is a wonderful thing. The harder you work, the more it seems to happen," Wizzy's barely audible voice said from the backpack.

The door creaked open and a gush of air rushed by her. The apparition now floated in the air beside her.

"Thank-you, thank-you so much. I am free! Now I can return to my beloved one," Queen Pearly White gushed with excitement.

"You are welcome, my queen."

"Don't be so formal, sweet one. I was once a magician's apprentice just like you. Please, call me Pearly White."

"My name is Holly."

"Nice to meet you, Holly."

"Princess, I mean Pearly White, don't you recognise me? I'm Taddy Boy," he said knowing that Princess Pearly White was a tenth level magician and could hear him.

"It cannot be. Is this Garth's companion from so long ago?"

"Yup. That's me," Taddy Boy said proudly.

"Time has not been good to you, I see."

"I, I *am* 800 years old and, and…"

"Has had a lot of hugs," Holly said giving Taddy Boy another.

"That is true. You look like you have been very loved. I apologise, Taddy Boy. I have become insensitive during my time in that cell. Eight hundred years! Wow, I never realised how time flies by."

"Are you able to move from here?" Holly asked.

"I have waited so long for this moment. Of course, I can, now that my curse has been lifted." Pearly White shouted with glee as her ghostly body swooped and spun around inside the tower.

Another sound came down the stairs and Holly quickly looked up.

"Who dared to release you? You are mine, mine!" the ghost of Admiral Igor wailed.

"A mere magician's apprentice, Admiral. So much for your great Brushyan wizard! Had he not taken my

187

wand from me you would have never have kept me!" Princess Pearly White shouted. "Holly, give me your wand and be quick."

Holly tossed Nova Cane to her and Princess Pearly White grabbed it in mid air with her wispy fingers. She pointed the wand at the spectre and spoke the incantation.

"Wind of howl
Wind of night
Blow away this ghost of white
Scatter him to the four winds
As payment for his sinful sins."

Then she shouted her magic word, "Amalgazam!"

A blue bolt of energy flew out of Nova Cane and circled the room, spinning faster and faster until a whirlwind formed. The twister moved and enveloped the Admiral's ghost and carried him out through the window and up into the sky.

"We won't be seeing him again," said Pearly White as she handed the wand back to Holly who stood gaping in awe of the power she had just seen.

"Now you are free to return to King Overbite!" Taddy Boy said eagerly.

"After eight hundred years, my darling king would be long passed as he was human, not a demigod, pixie, fairy, or even Elvin."

"But he does exist! We saw him," Holly said excitedly. "He waits for you in the ruins of the castle in Bicuspid!"

"Really? I thought he would have banished me and married someone else after I left without any word."

"No. He anxiously waits for your return. He's a ghost just like you, wandering the halls of the Bicuspid castle. I guess true love never dies."

"I can't wait to get out of here," said the queen, sighing at the thought of King Overbite.

Fangor bellowed in fright when he first saw the ghost appear out from the tower but Holly calmed him down. They had all settled around the fire when Holly asked the queen the obvious question. "How did you get in there in the first place?"

"It is a long, dreary story."

"Please tell us."

"Well, as you know, I am the daughter of King Neptune and I am also the Princess of the Sea. My duties come with a lot of responsibilities. After King Overbite and I were married, we had our son, Poseidon. I knew my king wanted him to rule Bicuspid but Poseidon was the grandson of a sea god and had to take over the ocean realm. If I was to stay with my darling king, Poseidon had to rule the sea, so one night we left without telling the king so I could train our son in the underwater realm. We planned that I would return later to give the king an earthly heir to Bicuspid."

"Wow, what happened for you to wind up here?"

"Unfortunately, when we were helping the whales migrate in the Frantic Sea, we were caught in the nets of Igor the Dreadful, a cruel Brushyan Sea Admiral. You met him on the stairs. Anyway, I was able to cut the net to free Poseidon but Igor captured me before I could use my wand."

"Why would he do that?"

"He wanted me for himself but when I refused, he locked me away in this tower. His magician, Ivan, put a spell on the door so that only another magician other than me could unlock it. Thanks to you, young lady, I am now free. Freeeeeeeee," she sang out in merriment as she rose in the air, spinning and twirling in obvious joy.

Holly saw that Fangor was staring curiously at the phantom floating around in front of him as if she were a mere fly bothering him. "Don't you try to catch her,"

Holly warned. He closed his jaws and dropped his great head.

Princess, or Queen, Pearly White, returned to the glow of the fire. "I will need to leave shortly to find my way back to Bicuspid and find my beloved but before I do, is there anything I can do for you?"

Opening her overstuffed backpack, Holly replied, "You could tell my great, great, great grandfather Garth that we have found the dragon eggs and will be returning with them as soon as we can. He will have King Dentin the Monarch of the Butterflies let King Molar know."

"Dragon eggs? I am afraid they won't be much good to you like that."

Fangor snapped his head toward the princess and said,

"Dragon eggs need to come alive
They must for my kind to survive
And of course
For Fairyland's hives to thrive."

"In my studies at the yearly gathering of the Wizards of the Plantagenet Order in the Stone Circle, I read an ancient scroll telling of the first Chin Emperor, Chinny Chin Chin, bringing a dragon back to life using one of its egg over two thousand years ago."

"How did he do that?" Holly asked.

"Here it comes. Something dangerous, I can tell," Taddy Boy groaned.

"He used a Moon Pearl. The largest one ever found. Dragons and pearls are often shown together in the many drawings of ancient Chin and other Grin dynasties. It has mystical powers."

"Well, that didn't sound *too* bad," said Taddy hopefully. "We just need to get it. You can do that, right Holly?"

"Where do we find a Moon Pearl?" Holly asked.

"As far as I know there is only one," Pearly White explained.

"This doesn't sound good. *And...?*"

"And it is buried with the emperor deep in his earthen pyramid tomb in central Chin in a place called Doublechin. It was Chin's capital for over a thousand years and the emperor's name Chinny Chin Chin is where Chin got its name."

"Great! First the Brushyans and now the Chins!" Taddy Boy cried. "Is there anyone else we may want to start an international incident with?"

"Oh hush, Taddy Boy. We got through didn't we?"

"We're not through *yet.*"

"Go on, my queen, ignore him. Tell me more about this tomb pyramid. I thought they were only in E-chipped."

"This tomb is not a stone pyramid but an earthen one found in Doublechin. It's near the city of Lip, nestled in a dragon's mouth. There are many burial pyramids in Chin but this one is very special. It was made for the first emperor. Ancient writings say the emperor Chin created an entire underground kingdom and palace, complete with a ceiling mimicking the night sky, set with pearls as stars. The underground caverns contain everything the emperor would need in his afterlife. Nobody has been in it out of respect for the emperor but they say his tomb is guarded by an underground moat of liquid silver and outside, over eight thousand enamel soldiers stand guard."

"Enamel soldiers?"

"Yes, they are supposed come back to life if they are ever needed to defend against the enemies of the emperor or anyone else trying to rob the tomb."

"I knew it! We're all gonna get killed!" groaned Taddy Boy.

"I agree it's not going to be easy," Holly said, "but killed, *really*?"

"Let me see...eight thousand soldiers against a girl, a stuffed teddy bear, a rapping lizard and a dancing bug. Sounds like an even match to me."

"You forgot about Fangor."

"Even he has his match. Remember all the other dragons were killed by knights in the Great Dragon Wars," Taddy Boy recalled.

"Once we get the pearl..."

"*If* we get the pearl," Taddy Boy cautioned.

"*When* we get it," Holly insisted, "then what?"

"I am not sure but I do know it can only be used only once a year when the Dragon Moon occurs," Pearly White went on. "That's when the stars align to form the dragon in the sky. In fact, that is only a few days away so you need to get to Chin as soon as you can. The emperors of Chin considered themselves the guardians of dragons and even today, dragons are highly regarded in Chin culture. How the Moon Pearl is used is a secret that the Chin emperors must have kept to themselves."

"Well, one step at a time, I guess." Holly said with a nod.

"Never stop trying through trying times," Wizzy said from the backpack.

"Thanks for the support, Wizzy."

"Yo, yo Keep on flying,

No backsliding,

Always striving,

No room for crying

Gotta keep on trying," T-pick rapped as Hip Hop instantly broke into another dance.

"There was something else I recall from the ancient writings," Pearly White said. "The dragons nest."

"What about the dragons nest?"

"It is essential to bring an egg back to life along with the Moon Pearl. Where did you get the eggs?"

"At the Mosjowl Museum of Palaeontology."

"There's no way we're going back there!" Taddy Boy insisted.

"I agree. We did not leave on good terms."

"You can say that again!"

"We didn't see anything there that looked like a nest anyway," Holly explained.

"You must find the nest where the eggs came from. It probably won't look like a bird's nest but a hollow in the ground lined with what might look like petrified dirt or grass. Dragons are loners so look in areas that are remote," Queen Pearly White suggested.

"We need to go to Gumgolia," Holly blurted out. "I remember the little boy on the news and the newsman saying they found the eggs in Gumgolia."

"Gumgolia is a big place," Pearly White said, frowning. "To find the nest will be a challenge."

Fangor roared,

**"A dragon knows night or day
Where their dragon eggs may lay.
I am no magician
But I see them with my heat vision."**

"Thank-you, Fangor. We will need your help for sure."

"Well, my friends, my time here is almost done." Queen Pearly White grasped Holly's hand in hers. "It has been too long since I have seen my beloved. I thank-you once again for your help and wish you well in your quest, Holly Johnson. But before I go, I give you this gift." She pinned a brooch with a living silver seahorse onto Holly's cloak.

"Thank-you, Queen Pearly White," Holly received the gift and watched as it changed into solid form before her eyes.

"If you ever need help, return the seahorse to the sea and my son will come to help you."

"Poseidon? Wow! Thank-you."

"I will pass on your message to your great grandfather."

"Oh, thank..." she began, but it was too late. In a wispy swirl Queen Pearly White was gone.

"Well," said Holly, touching the seahorse pin, "my friends in school won't believe this one."

"Tell me, what part of this journey do you think they *will* believe?" Taddy Boy asked, raising a shaggy brow.

Holly yawned. "I'm so tired. I have to remember the Water Spell tonight, and tomorrow will be a big day, so for now, we rest."

High in the attic of the tower, several ears had listened to the plan and when the coast was clear, bat scouts were sent on their long journey to Bicuspid and the awaiting gummy emperor.

CHAPTER FIFTEEN

Black Skies

It was nearly daybreak when Holly awoke and climbed out from under Fangor's protective wing. As she stretched and yawned trying to shake away drowsiness she saw Fangor's large eye pop open.

Good morning Fangor" she said.

> "Good morning, little one
> A new day has begun.
> Time to find the dragon's nest
> Head east, not west."

"Not so fast. I'm starving."

"Yo, yo time to eat
Faster than a heart beat
A little bug meat
Better than pig's feet
But ain't no chick, chick chicken feed, see?" T-Pick chimed in. Hip Hop promptly got up and started dancing.

"I agree, T-Pick. Before we go we have to have something to eat. But I'm not having bug meat."

"What do you expect from the rainbow reptile and a creeping stick?" Taddy Boy grumbled.

"Don't be so grouchy, Taddy Boy."

"The longest days are those you start with a grouch," Wizzy observed.

"Somebody's looking to get his tooth knocked out," Taddy grumbled.

"Now, now, Taddy Boy, we just don't talk like that."

"Ya, but..."

"*Taddy...*" Holly warned.

"Hmph!"

The fire had become just a wisp of smoke and Holly shivered in the damp air and morning dew. She cast a small Fire Spell to relight the fire and noticed that dawn had been getting later by a little more each day now that summer edged into fall. She rummaged through her backpack and pulled out a meat pie to eat for breakfast. When she saw Fangor eyeing her pie she gave him another sack of teeth while Hip Hop and T-Pick picked off a few gnats that buzzed around the campfire heat.

"Well, what do we do now? Queen Pearly White said we need to find the dragon's nest," said Taddy Boy.

"I am sure that it is in Gumgolia...but where in Gumgolia?" Holly mused.

"And how do we get there without being seen?"

"Time to ask the leaves from the Tree of Knowledge, I guess."

Holly pulled the branch out of her bag and plucked another leaf.

Only three left, she noticed then started to chew. She was still not used to the bitter taste and she gagged again. Her eyes rolled up and once again she went into a stupor. As before, a wise and older woman's voice softly spoke.

"To keep from being detected, go northeast away from the cities and into the mountains. Fly into the clouds if you think you are being followed. Fly past Tonsilvania and Decayville but avoid the land of Plaque at all costs as it is the home of bats known as the Drooling Gummies. Turn southeast to find

the Hanging Mountains then south to the Allrain Mountains. What you seek are in the foothills. You will know if you've gone too far if you see the Goblin Desert below you."

"Are you kidding me? We fly past the *home* of the drooling gummies!" said a shocked Taddy Boy.

"It looks that way," Holly said coming out from her trance.

"You know they'll rip us to shreds!"

"I don't think they eat stuffed bear."

"You never know what those things will want for dessert!"

"True. There's nothing like a soft bear paw or fluffy ear to help dragon meat go down," she giggled.

"You're just kidding me, *right?*"

"Yo,yo, don't forget Tonsilvania
Vampire mania
Howlin' nights
And werewolf bites
Evil bats and black cats
In the land of Demonomania," rapped T-Pick.

"Huh? Vampires? Werewolf bites?" Taddy Boy's voice quavered.

"I have heard about vampires but I don't think they are real. I just hope I don't get tonsillitis," Holly said.

"Don't *think*? Before this adventure I'd never heard of a rapping reptile and a break-dancing bug. There are some that don't believe in Santa but they're all real."

"The fact that nobody wants to believe something doesn't keep it from being true," Wizzy said.

"You have a point there. My brother doesn't think you can talk," Holly agreed.

"My point exactly!" Taddy's ears stood straight up.

"Well, I guess we just have to go and see."

"Of course we do." Taddy Boy said, resigning himself to his fate. "Of course we do."

"Gumgolia!" the scream of Ruthless Toothless Brutus echoed through the sea caves on the coast of Bicuspid, "Are you sure they are going to Gumgolia? Why Gumgolia? They are plotting something; I know it! What else did they talk about?"

"My lord," the head hunter replied, "the ghost of Queen Pearly White said they also have to get the Moon Pearl from the Emperor Chinny Chin Chin of Chin to bring the dragons' eggs back to life."

"Aha! I knew it!"

"I believe that was me," said Queen Hali Tosis, examining her nails.

"Yes, yes, my dear. Any other bright ideas?" he inquired.

"Actually, yes, I have. If they are in eastern Brushya and they are going to Gumgolia, *and* our reports are correct, I believe they will fly right through Tonsilvania and our homeland, the Land of Plaque! *Dear*," she replied with a sneer.

"Of course! They fly right through our own back yard. We shall attack them with every last blood sucking hunter bat there."

"But our army is here. All we have there is the old and the very young and none of them have teeth."

"Wait a minute. Maybe their plot *is* to attack us while we are here?"

"Interesting and very clever if..."

"Maybe they knew they were being watched all along and all this stuff about Gumgolia and Emperor Chinny Chin Chin is just to put us off the real plan to wipe us out in my own empire!"

"Perhaps, my lord, but I hardly think that one dragon and a girl with butter-coloured hair would be able...."

"Will the vampire bats help us, my queen?" asked the head hunter.

"You can never tell with them. They are possessed by the moonlight and I don't like the idea of having a vampire dragon hunting for our blood," replied Queen Hali Tosis.

"We must defend our land at all costs!" claimed the agitated emperor. "We fly now!"

"But, my lord, what about our ongoing attacks?" asked the head hunter.

"Or the furnaces, the production of our nightmare dust, or our hunters out on patrol?" added the queen.

"Stop the presses, recall the hunters, prowlers, and scouts, and cage the children. We will come back for them once we have this dragon," he cackled. "Then we'll deal with the fairies."

"Do you think we need to send all of our..."

"We fly! *NOW*!"

"From all the eyes that can see
be it in shadow or daylight be
Hide this object perfectly
with a cloak of invisibility."

"Jawbreaker!" Holly pointed the wand at Fangor.

"Just in case we were being watched." Holly senses tingled. "I just hope the spell lasts longer this time."

"I get the feeling..."

"Me too," Holly replied.

Fangor took off, concealed from the ever-watching attic bats and headed northeast looking for the forests of eastern Brushya.

It was too late. The Brushyan bats had long since reported their position. Rain started to fall when they approached the outer edges of Tonsilvania and Holly pulled her hood over her head. She could tell that

Fangor was becoming excited at the thought of getting closer to bringing his kind back from extinction because his pace had more energy and he flew harder and faster than before.

Holly thought that by travelling during the daylight hours, they would avoid most, if not all, vampire bats even if her Spell of Invisibility wore off. "Let's keep our fingers crossed," she hoped out loud.

"Garlic or holy water and a few stakes might be better," Taddy added.

Unfortunately, the bats on the bat line had been pre-warned and were indeed ready for them. She saw the fluttering dark figures rise from below and because of their exceptional hearing, they could easily detect the flap of Fangor's wings. Their honing senses could also detect the body heat of such a large dragon.

"Here they come," Holly warned.

Swooping and diving, the bats searched frantically for their warm blooded victims and came so close that Holly had to duck to avoid being bitten. Sliding from one side of the saddle to the other and back, she dodged each attack. One beast latched on to Fangor's invisible neck and was about to clamp down its fangs when Holly swooped under Fangor's neck like a circus rider, knocked the startled bat off, and came up the other side swinging back into her saddle.

"Woooooaaaaa,'" Taddy Boy screamed from almost falling out of the backpack. "That's some trick riding."

"Yeah, I'm getting the hang of this."

Another bat latched on to Taddy Boy and sank two fangs down in his neck.

"Yeow! That one bit me!"

Holly pointed her wand and quickly recited the Fire Spell.

"Element of fire with your flame and sparks
Bring your light to take away the dark
Where you go is of no concern
My wand will point the place to burn,"

Then, "Jawbreaker!"

A fireball flashed, knocking the bat off Taddy Boy neck but the bolt singed his fur once more. "I'm so sorry, Taddy. I didn't mean to burn you."

"I'm getting used to it," he said. "At least I won't turn into a werebear seeking blood on the full moon. Or will I?"

"We'll know if your fur grows shaggy, your teeth turn into fangs, and you get the hankering to howl at the moon," Holly answered taking a swing at another passing bat.

"Really?"

"No, I'm kidding," she assured him. "You have no blood so you won't turn into a vampire. You'll be fine."

"Except for the two holes in my neck and my singed fur."

"Right."

She could see the black of the bats' eyes, wild with rage, and their sharp fangs dripping with saliva as they flew all around her. But with nothing to see and their sonar having nothing to bounce back on, they eventually lost interest. After what to Holly was far too long, they returned to their dark damp caves to wait for easier prey during their midnight prowls.

"That was close. I wouldn't want you to get bitten by one of those ugly critters," Taddy Boy said once the throng had gone. They all felt giddy with relief.

"Supper would get very boring always sucking blood from someone's neck in the moonlight."

"Yeah, can you imagine your mom when you ask, 'What's for supper tonight?'" Taddy Boy said with a muffled snicker.

"She'd say, 'I got a two-for-one special of old man pints down at the Blood Bank,'" Holly replied, imitating her mother's voice.

"I know what you would say. 'Aw, Mom, couldn't we have nice sweet organic young people blood for a change?'" he mocked.

"'It's too expensive. Blood doesn't grow on trees. If you want organic, go hunt your own but right now young lady, drink your supper.'" She giggled along with Taddy Boy.

Below them, the beautiful spires and castles perched on the steep cliffs of the Spittle River passed by.

"Now for the latest news," said the newscaster on Mr. Johnson's television. "The bats have vanished, apparently moving out over night. There have been no sightings since yesterday and the day-to-day activities of the city of Bicuspid are finally returning to normal."

"Maybe the mayor was right," he commented. "Maybe they were just migrating and have gone to where bats go."

"To the Bat cave, Robin!" Conner yelled from the den.

"Thank goodness," Mrs. Johnson said, ignoring her son.

"Even the bats that were being kept in the SPCA broke out of their cages. That indicated the strong internal urge of these creatures to migrate."

"Wow, a break out at the SPCA!" Connor hollered.

"I wonder if they'll ever find my sunglasses?" Mrs. Johnson said as she folded another towel.

"Is it true, is it affirmed
All our Tooth Fairies have returned?
The first time in many nights

None were captured by the Gummy blight," said King Mungmouth.

"Yes, I believe it's true.
All gone right out of the blue,
Unless they hide, out of view.
So beware—it could be a ruse," replied King Jeb.

"Let us send out the eagles,
Seagulls, and beagles.
Search the caves where the sea rages,
And release our kin from the toothpick cages.
Let's make sure the bats are all gone
So the collection of teeth can carry on," said King Mo-lar.

Fairy scouts, along with the other prowlers, were sent out to search for and release any captured fairies at the hive's fairy door entrances and also at the favourite spot for the drooling gummy hunters, the end of the rainbow Pot of Gold where the fairies pick up the money to pay for the children's teeth.

They searched for any evidence of the drooling gummy army still lurking in the area. The forests, abandoned mines, and cabins were all investigated, with no sign of the horde.

The sea caves on the coast were the last and scariest of all for the fairies to patrol. Hesitantly, they entered the dark grotto. They were immediately met with the foul stench that told them it had not been long since the bats had been there. The skeletal remains of the unlucky gulls and rodents lay scattered everywhere. To their relief, and with great excitement, many of the captured fairies were found, released, and sent back to join their families back at the Fairyland hive.

But not even one eerie bat was found. It was like they had just disappeared, right off the face of the earth.

The fires had been extinguished and the molten pots of nightmare brews lay tipped over. The children held in cages, unaware they were once tooth fairies, were released and shown the way to the Bicuspid orphanage.

"Your Majesty, everything tells us the gummies are no longer here.

We have searched and searched and all is clear," said the scout.

"I believe this has something to do with Fangor and Holly.

I just hope and pray they will get through, by golly," King Mo-lar mumbled under his breath.

As they flew into reeking, grey, gritty smog, Fangor jerked and snorted as the pungent smell, like rotten eggs, hit his nostrils.

"Yuck! What is that stink!" Holly gasped, covering her nose with the sleeve of her coat.

"Sorry, Holly. I can't smell anything." Taddy Boy's nose twitched as he sniffed the air.

"Lucky you! This stench is disgusting," she said, gagging. "We must be near Decayville."

"For once!" Taddy shouted with glee. "I don't get the bad stuff!"

"They should have rules about pollution, and clean up their city streets and rivers," Holly declared.

"Just like your Mom, who says you have to brush your teeth twice a day if you want to prevent bad breath and tooth decay," Taddy said.

"I guess so."

It was like flying through nothingness. The brown grey cloud hid everything from view, even the blue sky. When they could get a glimpse below, all they saw was dirty brown rivers, dry grass, and dingy trees. Holly could not see one bird flying, no animals in the fields, nor people in the streets.

"How does anything live down there?" Taddy Boy asked.

"At least there are no bats hounding us."

"I hope we don't catch anything," Taddy Boy said.

"My throat's already sore and I'm getting stuffed up."

"I will fly higher
Before I lose my fire.
Before you get an infection
And I lose my direction," Fangor growled.

"Be careful, Fangor. I cannot tell which way we are going. We have to avoid the land of Plaque at all costs. There is no way we could hold off a whole nation of gummies."

No sooner had they broken into the sunlight and cleared the black skies of Decayville, than they saw, lined up in huge army formations, another ominous black sky.

The entire massive army of drooling gummies, wearing sunglasses and bandana masks, were waiting for them. Emperor Ruthless Toothless Brutus was in the lead with Queen Hali Tosis next to him.

CHAPTER SIXTEEN

Dragon's Nest

"Pull up, pull up, Fangor," Holly screamed as they just about slammed into the hoard. Fangor lurched and spat a huge fireball at the nearest company of drooling dummies, scattering them in all directions. Several bats screamed as they plummeted to the ground, burning as they fell, while others careened into the ranks of their brothers smouldering with singed wings and fur. For a moment, the confusion allowed Holly and Fangor to swoop and twist, narrowly escaping the trap.

"Get them!" ordered Ruthless Toothless Brutus as he and his elite guard followed the dragon.

Fangor flew as high as he could go, followed closely by the dark cloud of yellow-eyed bats. Holly could hear the slurping and gnashing of teeth behind her as she reached in her backpack for Nova Cane.

> "Element of water turn into crystals of ice
> Make my aim true and precise
> Make them solid if you please
> My wand will point the place to freeze."

"Jawbreaker!"

A massive bolt of ice crystals streamed from Nova Cane and exploded amongst the chasing throng behind her. Instantly, the nearby gummies froze solidly in mid-flight and dropped from the sky. Again and again she fired like a cowboy riding his horse and shooting his six guns, scattering the evil surge.

"Jawbreaker!"

"Jawbreaker!"

Each time, more and more bats fell from the sky. But the mass kept coming. Fangor swerved and veered as he manoeuvred in the sky like a jet fighter. He used his fire and Holly used her ice.

"We are not winning this," shouted Taddy Boy as the bats surrounded the dragon.

"Not now, Taddy Boy," Holly yelled, zapping several of the closer gnashing vermin. "I'm a little busy."

Several bats had avoided the ice and now attacked Fangor, forcing him to whip them off with a thrash of his tail that also caused him to rapidly lose altitude. Those able to hang on tried to bite and slash at his hide but found his shielding scales too tough to pierce.

"Catch him!" screamed Queen Hali Tosis.

To force a dragon to submit, they needed to have several hundred gummies attack at the same time and, by using their sheer weight, hold him down so that others could find the vulnerable neck and while biting at his throat, try to suffocate him.

Fangor fought for his life, twisting and turning and belching fire. At each turn, more and more bats attacked but with Holly's ice bolts, they shook the bats off, freeing them to attempt an escape.

Unnoticed by Holly, the head hunter attempted one last try and closed in from behind from the direction of the sun. He was just about to grab Holly by the scruff of her collar when T-Pick shot out his long tongue and smacked him in the eye, knocking off his sunglasses. The head hunter reeled off, his eye quickly swelling from the piecing light and sending him screaming as he tried to cover his stinging nocturnal eyes.

"Well done, T-Pick!" Holly cried.

T-Pick fist pumped Hip Hop along with a finger blast and explosive noises.

Holly pulled out the bag of magic dust Santa Claus had given her and sprinkled the sparkling crystals into the air. Any bat that flew into the cloud immediately shrank to the size of a tiny bee.

"What is happening?" Ruthless Toothless Brutus voice squeaked as he too shrank and started to fall. "This is not forever sleep dust!"

"Withdraw!" yelled the Queen, instantly recognising the dire situation. "Avoid the fairy dust at all costs!" She scooped the emperor in her claws and swerved away to retreat back to their dark caves.

It was too late. Hundreds of salivating bats caught in the frenzy of the hunt did not hear their Queen in time and flew right through the cloud of sparkling sand.

"Dive, Fangor! Dive!" Holly shouted, seizing their only opportunity in all of the confusion. "Back into the smog."

Fangor folded his wings back and bolted straight down, streaking through the confused black mass. With fire belching as he went, he cleared a path while Holly continued to cast ice spells. As soon as they entered the stinking black cloud, Holly pulled on Fangor's reins, yanking him into a hard right and they watched the chasing bats pass by them as they dove further into the putrid black void.

"I never thought I would prefer being in this rotten abyss than in fresh air but..."

"It's better than us being a furry bloodsucker's dinner," Taddy Boy finished.

"Exactly."

"I wonder where they got sunglasses," said Taddy Boy. "They never had them the last time."

"I don't think they were invented back then but now it looks like they can attack during daylight."

"Oh great. Now they can eat us twenty-four/seven."

"Can't worry about that; we have to get a move on."

Holly guided Fangor north as fast as she could urge him to fly. She wanted so desperately to get away from the homeland of the drooling gummies that her hands shook and sweat poured down her forehead. She realized the smog had bewildered them and they had flown farther south than they had planned. She vowed not to make that mistake again. It was time to put Decayville and this dreadful Land of Plaque behind them and carry on to Gumgolia. They were lucky to be alive.

Back in their bat caves, squatting on his throne, Ruthless Toothless Brutus felt the magic dust wear off. Hundreds of bats were being bandaged up; some were on crutches while others lay on stretchers.

"I told you they were going to attack our homeland," he said, shaking and jerking up to full size.

"Yes, my lord," the head hunter said, one eye swollen shut.

"I'm not so sure they were attacking us or just flew into us," the queen mused.

"Of course, they did," Brutus snapped. "Look around you. See the damage one dragon can do?"

"And one magician's apprentice," added the queen.

"I can see now how my ancestor Pyorrhoea Pete could not succeed."

"*And* his Queen Ginger Vitis," she emphasized.

"Yes, yes, of course, my dear," he said, dismissing her comment with a wave of his creepy wing.

"We should follow them."

"No! For now we must defend our homeland in case they attack again. Send out patrols, guard our borders, and fill the skies with our hunters. Remind them they must save their Emperor at all costs."

"Yes, my bravest one, but perhaps we can spare just one? *Just* in case they are indeed headed for Gumgolia."

"My lord, I am willing to follow them," offered the head hunter.

"Oh, all right. Take a messenger with you so that you can report back."

"As you wish, my lord, my lady," he replied as he hobbled back out, bowing in respect.

Their clothes still reeked but Holly was relieved when they finally cleared the stench and darkness of the Decayville cloud. Below, the leaves in the forests became green, the waterfalls flowed clear, and the rivers were blue once again. It was such a pleasure to breathe in the fresh air, ridding lungs of the putrid smog. Even Fangor perked up and flew with more vigour.

"That was soooooo close," Taddy Boy said, breaking the silence.

"It sure was. Thank goodness for Fangor's fire," Holly agreed, patting him on the neck.

"You were blasting them, too."

"When the going gets tough, the tough get going," uttered Wizzy's low voice from the backpack.

Holly shrugged off the compliment. "They were waiting for us and we flew straight into them. I wonder how they knew we were there?"

"Bats have got big ears?"

"They must have. From here on in we must be careful when we speak and we are going to have eyes in the back of our heads."

"Carrots are definitely good for the eyes. Have you ever seen a rabbit with glasses?" Wizzy said.

"If the gummies are here then they are not in Bicuspid. If they are not in Bicuspid then the fairies are safe," Holly observed feeling somewhat relieved.

"Great. Now they are *all* here. Brushyan bats, Vampire bats and Drooling Gummies with odds at a million to two." Taddy Boy pointed out.

"That's not so bad, is it? Remember, I have my secret weapon," she said cheekily.

"And what is that?"

"You."

"Humph!" was all she heard.

"We must hurry on before the bats realize we have dodged them and try to follow us again."

The Fangai Mountains rose in the distance, all beautifully dressed in whitecaps and purple frocks. The sun was warm but Holly knew it would get cooler as the sun moved into the late afternoon. She wanted to find the nest as soon as possible but she had to be cautious. She continued to survey the sky behind her but saw nothing following so for now she felt safe and carried on.

"This is where we turn south for the Allrain Mountains."

'What you seek is in the foothills' she recalled Queen Pearly White saying. She looked back one last time and this time, she thought she could see two small black dots following in the far distance.

"Are we being followed or are those just birds?"

"I can't see behind me," Taddy replied.

She couldn't be sure. Not wanting to give away her destination she decided to fly straight rather than turning south and head for the cover of the Hanging Mountains. She thought that *if* someone was following her, they could lose whoever it was in all the cracks and crannies, dead end canyons, and mountain exits.

213

She selected a deep ravine with many twists and turns and instructed Fangor to fly low so his green scales would disguise them in the foliage of the trees. When she saw a large crevice with a waterfall, she steered Fangor sharply into it and directed him to cling on the chasm wall and hide behind the wall of falling water.

"Be as quiet as you can, especially you, Taddy Boy."

"Me? Why me? What about the singing lizard?"

"Let me guess," she mused.

"But, but..."

"Now shhhhh."

It didn't take long before she heard the slow, loping flap of wings coming up the ravine. Wearing sunglasses, the large drooling gummy in charge was alert and in hunt mode.

Over the roar of the water Holly could hear them talking.

"I am sure I saw them come into this ravine," he hissed.

"Yes, master," said the messenger.

"Keep your eyes peeled; they could be anywhere."

"Yes, master."

"Are you sure they didn't see us?"

"Yes, master."

When the bats had passed by and she was sure the coast was clear, Fangor took off, flying through the cascading falls, and retraced their route back down the ravine. Once out they turned south to continue their journey to the Allrain Mountains.

"Couldn't go around the waterfall, we had to go straight through it! Yup, let's not think about your best friend. Eh?"

"Oh hush, Taddy, in case they hear you!"

Holly knew she had bought some time but was not sure how much. She kept looking backward but saw no one and for now, breathed a sigh of relief.

"Do you think we lost 'em?"

"I sure hope so, Taddy." The last thing she wanted was to face the giant hoard of drooling gummies again. She might not be so lucky to escape a second time.

"I'm drowning in here," Taddy Boy complained, breaking the silence, "We're soaked and the backpack is full of water."

"We're all wet..." She giggled, realizing what she just said. "I mean...you know what I mean."

Taddy Boy giggled as well, breaking the tension they had all felt.

While still in flight, Holly un-slung her backpack and poured out the water making sure to keep Taddy Boy, Wizzy, T-Pick, Hip Hop, and the provisions from tumbling out.

"I hope you didn't ruin Mrs. Claus' sugar cookies!" Taddy said.

"All is good. Even the pies and magic dust."

"Whew! What a relief. But you could have lost the tooth."

"Wizzy's fine."

"Rats! What about the lizard and the bug?"

"Hip Hop and T-Pick are fine, too."

"Rats!"

They carried on with Holly checking nervously behind them every few minutes. All seemed clear but she couldn't be sure. The terrain became grassy and windswept as they flew out of the mountains and into the foothills.

The first sign that they were nearing their destination was Fangor tugging on his reins and making a deafening shrill noise Holly had never heard him make before.

"What's the matter boy? Are you okay?"

"Fangor smells a mother's nest
My heart beats fast in my chest
Sweet sensation of great cheer
Now that we are finally here."

Fangor suddenly dove down, back flapping his wings to slow down, and landed. He sniffed and scratched at the very site where the boy from Gumgolia had found the eggs just days before, raised his head, flapped his wings, and roared in triumph.

CHAPTER SEVENTEEN

Gumgolian Nomads

"It doesn't look like much." Taddy Boy said as Holly inspected the hole where the eggs had lain.

"They were buried here a long time," she said, figuring the earth had covered the eggs over for thousands of years but the original nest material that had been under the missing eggs would have survived. Sure enough, petrified grass and twigs could be seen tangled in the soil. Using her pewter mug as a ladle, she dumped the scraped samples into her backpack beside the colourful vibrant eggs.

"So much for keeping your mug washed," Taddy Boy commented.

With all attention focused on the ancient nest, no one had noticed the movement behind them.

"Hello?" said a young curious voice.

"Whoa!" a startled Holly shouted, spinning around to face the sound. Even Fangor snapped his head toward the voice roared and snorted a puff of black smoke from his nostrils.

Standing in front of them was a young Gumgolia goat herder holding the reins of a jittery reindeer. He stood open-mouthed, staring in awe at the giant dragon that, now nose-to-nose, stared back at him suspiciously.

"Hey, I know you. You're the boy on the news," Holly said, breaking the tension. "Hello, my name's Holly," pointing to herself in universal sign language, "and yours?"

Looking back down the hill, the boy started rambling excitedly in Gumgolian all the while pointing at Fangor.

Holly looked down the hill to see a nomadic Gumgolian village below and a number of men on horseback riding up the steep bank toward them with several other villagers following on foot.

Holly quickly pulled out Nova Cane and pointed at the boy.

> "You who speak the tongue of your land
> To you I make this command
> Turn them into words I can understand
> And to all of those from Fairyland."

She pointed her wand and commanded, "Jawbreaker!"

All the words the boy was shouting she could now understand.

"Come see, come see the dragon!"

"Hello, my name's Holly," she said again.

The boy spun around surprised he could understand her. "Huh?"

"My name is Holly. What is yours?"

"Er, my name is Bataar and this is my best friend Koshi," he answered pointing to the reindeer.

"Hello Bataar, hello Koshi," she said giving Koshi a friendly scratch behind the ear.

"You can judge a man by his enemies as well as by the friends he keeps," Wizzy offered.

"And what does that say about you Holly, with a bug, a lizard, and a dragon as yours?" Taddy Boy asked.

"And a talking stuffed teddy bear."

219

"Yeah, well, everyone has a pet teddy bear."

Holly turned her attention back to the boy. "You are the boy who found the eggs. I saw you on television."

"I am. I found them after the earthquake that destroyed my village."

"I hope everybody is okay."

"Yes, thank-you for your concern," said Bataar, now starting to relax.

At the first sight of the dragon, the frightened horses reared up as soon as they reached the crest of the hill causing several of the men to fall off. Feeling threatened, Fangor reacted by making himself look larger. Standing on his back legs, he stretched out his wings, which scared the horses even more.

"Stop, Fangor, stop! You are scaring them," Holly said raising her arms to calm him as the horses bolted back toward the safety of the village.

"Watch out behind you," Taddy Boy warned.

The men got up, grabbed their rifles, aimed, and surrounded the odd band of travellers.

"Stop, Father," Bataar pleaded jumping between the mean and Holly. "I believe these are friends."

"Yes, we are friends on a mission," Holly pleaded as Fangor settled back down.

"What kind of Mission?" Chuluun, Bataar's father asked, still keeping an eye on the dragon.

"To save the dragons," Holly replied petting Fangor on the snout.

"Dragons? Those eggs..."

"Yes, the eggs that Bataar found were those of ancient dragons. We have a plan to bring them back to life just like in ancient times."

"Dragons are sacred to us, Father."

Holly opened her backpack and showed Chuluun the eggs. "We got them back."

"We would be honoured if you would come to our village and share buuz and milk tea and tell us your story."

"Booze! You can't have any booze, Holly. You're too young." Taddy Boy knew the Gumgolians could not hear him.

"Thank-you for your offer but I do not drink alcohol, sir," Holly replied.

"Buuz is a traditional Gumgolian food of steamed dough pockets stuffed with onions, minced beef and vegetables and milk tea is just... milk tea," informed Bataar.

"Oh," she said sheepishly. "In that case, we would be honoured, sir. Thank-you."

"My name is Chuluun," Bataar's father said as they went back down the hill to the rebuilt yurts, or nomad tents.

Seeing Holly's stunned face at the devastation left by the earthquake, Bataar calmed her. "No one died and we will be moving the village before the winter sets in."

"Thank goodness," was all she managed to say.

"…and are now on our way to Chin to bring them back to life." Holly finished her story while and sipping milk tea given to her by Yula, Bataar's mother.

"It seems to me to be an honourable quest by an honourable person. Not like the strange men from Brushya who came to take the eggs. They showed no respect of our customs. But Chin? Why Chin?" Bataar's father wanted to know.

"Ancient scrolls said that Chinny Chin Chin, the first emperor of Chin, was the guardian of the secret and his tomb holds the Moon Pearl," Holly explained while Bataar patted Fangor's head that poked through the front door.

"He held only one part of the answer," Chuluun told her.

"What do you mean? We thought that if we can put the eggs, the nest, and the Moon Pearl together, the eggs would come alive and we would have dragons once again."

"There's much more to it."

"Oh, no," Taddy Boy muttered.

"Many years ago the Gumgolian Empire ruled most of the eastern lands and also held the dragon as sacred. Mandible the Cannibal, a powerful warlord, ruled the horde and fought the Grins and the Chins. He was merciless and vindictive toward anyone who opposed him. For many years they all fought, causing many deaths. Peace only came between then when they agreed to share the Secret of the Eternal Dragon."

"How do they share this secret?"

"Emperor Chinny Chin Chin has the Moon Pearl and Mandible the Cannibal has the Ring of Myth."

"Ring of Myth? What does the Ring of Myth do?"

"I am but a humble herdsman of goats," Chuulun spoke softly. "The answers you seek are above me."

"What do we need to do?"

"You must find the warlord Mandible the Cannibal."

"Mandible the Cannibal! Merciless and vindictive, really? *Really?*" Taddy Boy yelped. "Will this nightmare *never* end?"

"Did he not die many years ago?" Holly asked, ignoring Taddy Boy.

"If you mean like you and I are in this world, then yes. But as one of the sacred guardians, he and Chinny Chin Chin live on in the afterlife to keep their sacred promise to the dragons."

"Wow. How do we find this Mandible the Cannibal?"

"There are many rumours and legends. Some say he is buried on the plains of the Goblin Desert; some say in a hidden cave in the Hanging Mountains, while others say in a temple on a mystical island."

"Oh great. Are there any bats there?" Taddy Boy asked.

"We could be searching forever. What should we do?"

"Go on to Chin. Find the tomb of the emperor. Do what you know you must do and let the answers reveal themselves to you, little one."

"And his eight thousand enamel soldiers," Taddy Boy added.

"My thanks to you and your family," Holly said, getting up, "but we should get going now."

"We are on our second candle since the sun has set. Tonight, you sleep here; tomorrow you travel on your journey."

Holly looked around at the crowded tent. She was, after all, a little girl amongst strangers.

"Don't be concerned, Holly. We are used to this," Bataar said, calming her anxiety. In no time, curtains were hung and she had her own private partition.

That night, lying on her bedroll, she decided to try to learn a new spell. Using a candle to read, she opened her *Beginners Magic* book. As the others slept, she quietly flipped through the worn pages by the light of a single candle, stopping on the Super Shove Spell. *This could be handy*, she thought.

It read: To push or repel a person, persons, or thing back, reverse or strike with a Power Push spell, an apprentice may use a magic potion of Push Off, Scroll of Ramming magic scroll, or point his or her wand or staff at the one or ones they wish to ram and read the following incantation followed by their secret command word.

> "You who come too near
> Go away get out of here
> So far back you disappear
> Never again to reappear."

223

"Don't say it..." Taddy Boy warned.

"Of course, I wouldn't say 'Jawbreaker'."

"You just..."

The wand glowed, shook, and then sent a pulse of energy flying through the tent, ripping the yurt off of its foundation and sending it flying into the night air.

"...did."

"Oops."

Chuluun, Bataar, his mother and sister were all suddenly awake. They sat up and stared at Holly in stunned amazement and alarm.

"Look at all the stars," Holly said innocently pointing upward. "Aren't they beautiful?" For the first time she noticed several stars shining a little brighter in the outline of a dragon. She knew that it would not be long before the Dragon Moon occurred.

"Impressive. A *great* way to make friends, Holly," Taddy Boy remarked, unable to resist mocking his friend.

Fangor chased the yurt like a puppy chasing a ball and caught it just before it fell into the ravine the earthquake had created. Unfortunately, when he returned it, his teeth had punctured it in several places.

Holly worked hard helping put the yurt back up and also helped sew the torn fabric. By the next morning, it was awkwardly standing again, complete with a patchwork of reinforcements.

"I am so sorry, sir. If there is anything I can do..." Holly said, packing food Bataar's mother had given her into Fangor's saddle.

"Don't be concerned, little one. We have lost yurts before and I am sure we will lose more," Chuluun said.

"Just save the dragons and perhaps I will see a tooth fairy before I lose all my baby teeth," Bataar added.

"I will do my best."

"Remember that the best of glues cannot fix a broken promise," Wizzy said from the backpack.

When Chuluun and Bataar had left to tend their animals, Yula stayed behind and gave Holly something wrapped in a silk cloth.

"A gift," she said, smiling. "This may help you solve the mystery of where the tomb of Emperor Mandible lives."

"But why give this to me and in secret?"

"I believe your quest to be true and I did not wish to embarrass my husband."

"Excuse me?"

"This treasure has been handed down in my family for many centuries. A great ancestor of mine was a handmaiden of Emperor Mandible. Our family was once very favoured by the warlord of the Gumgolian Empire. My beloved husband, whom I loved since I was a little girl, is a humble goat herder and knows not of these things."

"Thank-you, Yula. Can you tell me what it is?"

"It is one of three jade flutes given to the Gumgolian generals after the death of Mandible. Each has secret inscriptions in a language so ancient that only they could read them. For a thousand years, only they and their descendants knew of where he was buried so grave robbers and enemies wishing revenge could not find him. He was called Mandible the Cannibal for a reason."

"I see," Holly said as she began to unfold the silk cloth.

"No, no, not here," she said, placing her hands on Holly's and looking around. "I do not wish my husband to see."

"But what about the ancient writings?"

"I do not understand them; my ancestor was a humble handmaiden, not a Gumgolian general."

"Of course. Thank-you, Yula." Holly packed the wrapped object and turned to stow it in the backpack.

"You could always give them a parting gift," suggested Taddy Boy.

"What do you mean?" Holly whispered.

"She gave you a flute. You could give her a smarty pants molar or the lizard and the bug."

"I'm not sure that would be a gift or a burden."

"My point exactly!"

"Maybe I should give them a stuffed teddy bear instead? I'm sure Bataar's sister would love a cuddly and very *quiet* teddy bear."

"Oh no, please don't leave me out here in the wilderness! I'd miss TV; I'd freeze in winter, reek of goats, or reindeer or, or..." he gasped. "Maybe I was a little hasty. Forget I even mentioned it."

"Okay. I thought that might be the case. I will give her a leaf from the Tree of Knowledge." Holly plucked the third leaf and gave it to Yula, explaining that she could only use it once to answer one question.

Yula accepted the gift graciously, storing it in the pocket of her coat.

Then Holly hopped on Fangor's back, waved at the family of Gumgolian nomads, and flew south toward the Goblin desert.

The heat hit her like a tsunami wave as they passed from grasslands and into sandy dunes. Something was bothering her but she couldn't put her finger on it. She looked back but saw nothing. Was she imagining things? Was she being followed? She thought about what to do. Should she carry on to Chin or look for Mandible the Cannibal?

"What's the matter Holly?" Taddy inquired.

"I am not sure what to do. Do we go to Chin or find Mandible's tomb?"

"That's a tough one."

"Always take plenty of time to make a snap decision," Wizzy advised.

Something told her she should check out the flute so she asked Fangor to circle and land in a hollow of one of the dunes.

The head hunter and the messenger, thankful they had sunglasses, hid on their bellies behind the crest of a nearby sand dune. They had indeed been following but this time had been undetected.

"How beautiful!" Holly gushed when she pulled the flute out of its silk wrapping.

The flute had truly strange markings etched along its entire length. Its shape reminded her of the recorder she had practiced on in school with a mouthpiece at one end and holes down its length. She couldn't resist trying to play it.

"I don't hear anything," Taddy Boy said.

"Neither do I. Maybe it's broken."

Off in the distance and out of site, she heard a scream of pure agony and then the flap of wings rushing away.

"I wonder what that was?" Holly looked around then shrugged and went back to checking out the flute. The inscriptions were extremely peculiar to her. She had only just started to learn French and Spanish but never ancient Gumgolian.

"I don't know, Taddy Boy. I cannot make any sense out of it."

"So what are we going to do, Holly? Fly to Chin?" Taddy Boy asked.

"I guess we have no choice. I was just hoping to get a clue on which way to go from the flute."

"Well, we can't stay here. Look, even Fangor is panting in this heat so we won't last long in this desert if we don't get moving."

"I agree. We should be on our way." As she got up to go she picked up the silk cloth that had wrapped the flute and noticed that it appeared to have an unusual pattern sewn into it. Puzzled, she looked at it more closely and noticed that in the centre a ring of sparkling blue thread surrounding a symbol sewn on top of an oddly shaped circle in gold thread. The outer edges were wiggly and lined green thread.

"I wonder what this means," she said aloud.

"You got me. I can't read."

"Wait a minute, this could be a map."

"Cool! A treasure map."

"I guess, kinda. But where is it?" she said turning it around several times.

"Yo, yo, where's the beef?
This Goblin heat
Gives me grief
I gotta leave
It ain't sweet but
Eat a leaf, chief," rapped T-Pick. Hip Hop was too hot to dance.

"That's a good idea, T-Pick. Maybe the Tree of Knowledge can help us." She rummaged in her backpack and found the branch now with only two leaves left. She plucked one more and chewed it. The harsh taste was not getting any better but her eyes rolled up as before and she began to speak.

"The ancient writings on the flute read; 'Play the tune for the dead at the tomb of the warlord Mandible the Cannibal lying in the Goldcrown temple to be found on the Island of Lockjaw, in the Sea of Cavity.'"

"But how do we get there?" Taddy Boy asked.

"What you seek is on a path of grave peril. One that many have attempted but never succeeded. If you choose to go further, you go with this warning: Enter at your own risk. To reach the Sea of Cavity, you must leave this desert and travel

southwest to the jungles, cross the Land of Plaque and pass through the Canker Mountains."

"The Land of Plaque!" Taddy Boy screeched.

CHAPTER EIGHTEEN

Capture

"Oh no, we have to go through the Land of Plaque," Holly said as she came out of her dreamlike state.

"No, we don't. We could just go home."

"For the first time I get a bad feeling about this as well, Taddy Boy," Holly said, suddenly overwhelmed by the enormity of the quest still ahead.

"Finally, you're coming to your senses. Let's go back to Santa's house. I really liked Santa's house."

"I do miss those sugar cookies but we can't let down Fangor and all those depending on us in Fairyland." She sighed, looking at the vibrant coloured dragon eggs.

> "I understand your reluctance to go.
> The bats are indeed a worthy foe.
> But my kind and I have faced them many times before
> And have sent many to knock on death's heavy door.
> I will get you through this evil horde
> And make the Lockjaw Island shore,"

Fangor said.

"Don't listen to him! I want to sit on your comfy bed again not on a bat's supper plate. Let's go home."

"Don't let fear frighten you. Face it a little at a time," Wizzy said.

"Thank-you, Fangor. Thank-you, Wizzy. I needed that. We have to go on, Taddy Boy," Holly said, re-energized.

"Rats!"

"What? They are in the Goblin Desert?" Emperor Ruthless Toothless Brutus screeched. "Why are they in the Goblin Desert?"

"The head hunter sent me back but he's staying with them to watch their every move," said the messenger, his ears still ringing.

"It looks as though they are going to Chin after all," the Queen commented, knowing she had been right all along.

"We couldn't take any chances. We had to defend my empire," Brutus sniffed. Turning back to the messenger he asked, "What else did you see?"

"I'm sorry, my lord. What did you say?" the messenger asked. "My ears are still buzzing and I don't hear so well."

"What else did you see?" Brutus shouted.

"They had flute that screeched in my ear."

"A flute? Why would they have a flute?"

"It was a gift from the human nomads."

"Judging by our messenger, perhaps it is a secret weapon," the queen suggested.

"Nonsense! What kind of flute would be a weapon?" The Emperor mocked the queen by pretending to play a flute. "It's probably nothing but a stupid gift."

"Perhaps, my lord. Shall we send out the elite forces?" asked the queen.

"Yes, let my beauties fly. I cannot wait to feast on dragon tonight!"

With a flick of the queen's head, two hunters left the room to send the elite guard to the Goblin Desert.

> "From all the eyes that can see
> Be it in shadow or daylight be
> Hide this object perfectly
> With a cloak of invisibility."

"Jawbreaker!"

Suspicious of the noise she had heard earlier, Holly rightfully thought that it would be better leaving in stealth mode just in case there was someone watching. Or perhaps the pair of gummies that shadowed her earlier had found them.

Flapping his wings, Fangor lurched into the air, circled to find his bearing, and headed southeast toward the Canker Mountains.

The gritty sand from the flurry of wind caused the head hunter to cover his face but he knew where they were headed even if he couldn't see them. Unable to follow an invisible Fangor and wanting to get out of the hostile desert, he decided to return to the Land of Plaque to report to his emperor. He took off west flying as fast as he could, knowing he had to inform his Emperor that their prey was heading to the Gold Crown temple on the Island of Lockjaw, in the Sea of Cavity, and not as originally thought, to Chin.

As he approached the empire borders, he saw the entire elite army of drooling gummies heading the other way toward the Goblin Desert.

"Hey, where are you going?" he hissed at the first mate of the pirate horde.

"We head to the Goblin Desert and on to Chin in pursuit of the Dragon," the hunter said after his salute.

"But they went this way."

"We saw no dragons, Head Hunter."

"You cannot see him but you must turn around, *now!*"

"With respect, Head Hunter, we are on orders from the Emperor and it would be my head if I disobeyed."

With that, the horde carried on eastward and slowly disappeared out of sight while the frustrated head hunter flew west.

To avoid the populated areas of the Land of Plaque, Holly, as planned, had flown southwest toward the Canker mountain area. The ground below them had changed from desert to jungle foliage.

As she approached the Land of Plaque, she sensed the evil that loomed over the land. Gloomy sentry posts of trees stripped of leaves and looking like masts from sailing ships with rows of horizontal spars poked threateningly up above the jungle canopy. Piles of animal bones and skulls dotted the border warning all who neared to beware that no one was welcome.

Normally, these sentinel posts would be lined shoulder-to-shoulder with drooling gummy pirates hanging upside down with their yellow eyes watching and waiting for any trespasser. But today, Holly was surprised when she saw very few gummies sentries after the experience they had mistakenly flown into earlier.

"Where are all the gummies?"

"At lunch?" Taddy Boy offered.

"I hope they haven't returned to Fairyland."

"Don't worry. With our luck, I'm sure they're around here somewhere."

"The best way to make someone worry is to tell them not to," Wizzy said from the backpack.

"Shhhh, someone's coming," Holly warned.

"They can't hear me," Taddy Boy whispered back.

"Oh yeah, I forgot."

Upon hearing the flap of wings, one old grey-bearded gummy pirate flew out of his perch in the jungle canopy to investigate but after seeing nothing, promptly went back and settled on his roost for an afternoon nap.

Smoke rose above the jungle from the boiling cauldrons of nightmare dust at each deserted camp they passed. Holly was proud that her Spell of Invisibility had lasted much longer than ever before. Even old gummies could spell trouble.

"Whaaaaaaat! They are on their way back here?" screamed Ruthless Toothless Brutus, "I knew it. They wanted to attack us here all along."

"My Lord, they head for Lockjaw Island in the Sea of Cavity."

"But why? There's nothing on it except an overgrown temple."

"To seek a treasure from the tomb of the ancient Gumgolian Emperor, Mandible the Cannibal."

"Mandible Shmandible. What scallywag would want some trinket from a long dead, crazy Gumgolian? They're here to attack us. I know it!"

"My lord, the Goldcrown temple has always been rumoured to hold great secrets. Some say it has great powers, others say treasures beyond one's wildest dreams," Queen Hali Tosis reminded him.

"Avast ye! Sounds to me like you have a bad case of rumourtism!"

"Shall I recall the army, my lord?" asked the head hunter.

"Of course, you lazy dog. Bring my mates back and find these rapscallions. I want these scoundrels in chains."

"Yes, my lord. To get to the Isle of Lockjaw they will need to go around the Canker Mountains."

"Or over them," added the queen.

"We know they are too cold and too high for anyone to travel over," slobbered the emperor. "They will need to go around and we will be ready for them. We will block the valleys and patrol the coastline."

"They did cross the North Pole, my lord," the head hunter reminded him.

"Why would they, if they don't have to?"

"Of course, my lord."

The looming Canker Mountains approached fast. Holly could see that these peaks were high indeed with snow already deep on their summits.

"Well, what do you think, Taddy Boy? Go around or go over?"

"I don't like the cold so I..."

"Ain't no mountain high enough,

Ain't no valley low enough..." T-Pick began singing.

"Excuse me!" Taddy Boy snapped.

"He can't hear you."

"Oh, yeah."

"It will take us too long to go around so button up. It's gonna get cold," Holly said as her Spell of Invisibility faded.

"We'd better climb fast before they see us," Taddy boy cautioned.

No sooner had he spoke, than a dark cloud rose from the jungles below. Holly could see they were coming fast.

"Faster, Fangor! Fly with all your might!"

As they reached the base of the mountain and started to climb its steep walls, a huge steel net suddenly flew out of nowhere entangling Fangor's wings and bringing him heavily to the ground and knocking out the band of heroes.

"We have them!" shouted an old, sparsely-toothed gummy sporting a blue beard and who had blasted the large slingshot.

"The Emperor will be pleased," shouted the blue fang leader.

The putrid smell from the boiling cauldrons woke Holly. She shook her head to clear the cobwebs and it took a second or two before she realised she must have been knocked unconscious in the fall. She tugged at the chains now securing both her arms and feet to a post placed in the centre of a Blue Gum colony.

Getting her bearings, she looked around and saw layers of caves in a cliff wall surrounding an open square strewn with banners featuring blue claw marks and topped with several skulls. Large elephant rib bones created ominous looking fences, and their tusks forming a gateway at one end. Numerous cauldrons bubbling over smoky fires continued to make the dreaded nightmare dust. With horror, Holly realised she was now the captive of the Blue Fang Tribe of the drooling gummy empire.

"Oh no," she gasped in fear. Her next thought was of her companions and scanning the area, she saw T-Pick and Hip Hop hiding with their heads poking out from under an overturned bowl near one of the cauldrons. Taddy Boy was motionless in the backpack. Not far away, she could see Fangor still wrapped under the steel net, continuing to struggle to free himself all the while belching fire to keep the surrounding gummies at bay. The more he struggled, the more ensnared he became.

"Don't struggle, Fangor. I'll get you out somehow," she yelled, trying to calm him.

"And how do you think you will do that, young missy?" a glaring Ruthless Toothless Brutus hissed.

Holly spun her head around to the sound of the voice to see the emperor's entourage in all its gory glory. The emperor and queen in full pirate regalia sat on bejewelled thrones carried by a dozen hulking gummies as several others cooled the royal pair with ornate feather fans on long poles.

"We will soon have all the dragon scales we'll ever need, won't we, my dear?"

"Yes, my lord," the queen replied. "As soon as we can get close enough to harvest them."

"You won't get away with this!" Holly snarled, bravely tugging hard on her chains.

"You tell those dummies, I mean gummies," Taddy Boy encouraged bravely from the backpack sitting near the stake.

"I don't think you can do much about it, little girl, but I admire your resolve and determination," Brutus said, with a sinister giggle. "I have always wondered how sweet the meat of a young human girl might taste. A tender thigh or one of your skinny arms perhaps?"

Holly gulped as her heart went up into her throat. She didn't feel quite so brave anymore. For the first time on this journey she actually felt scared.

"Break out the rum, boys. It's time to celebrate after all these years," the emperor said to the roar of the multitude of slobbering gummies.

"Don't you think we should deal with these vermin now while we have them chained, my lord?" the queen suggested. "She would make a great appetizer and her small bones the best toothpicks for when we eat the dragon."

"Where are they going to go? The dragon is tiring and will soon run out of flame so why risk our troops? After all this time, we can wait a few more hours, so my hearties, it's time to party!" Brutus uncorked a bottle of rum to a renewed roar from the crowd. The celebrations and dancing lasted well into the night with many a drunken pirate's song sung to the music of the fife and drums.

Holly could smell the putrid rum-soaked breath of the gummies who came up to sniff her and lick their lips in anticipation of devouring her. In the firelight, she could see that Fangor was resisting less and less as time passed and she could tell he needed another bag of teeth soon or his fire would go out forever. She kicked herself for not giving him one prior to leaving the desert.

Eventually, as in all gummy celebrations, the sound of song was soon replaced by the heavy snores of sleeping and drooling gummies drunk on too much rum. The sound of hundreds of gummies snoring along with other rude noises was almost deafening.

Holly knew it was her chance to escape, but how? With both her arms and legs tied behind her she knew she needed help. Suddenly, an idea came to her.

"T-Pick, Hip Hop come to me," she whispered as loudly as she dared.

T-Pick, with Hip Hop riding on his back, scooted out from under the cover of the pot and raced over to Holly, barely avoiding a stumbling gummy that fell face first and out cold right in front of them.

"Yo, yo, Holly
I heard you call me
They nearly caught me
Time we got free
Here to help, see?
By golly, yo."

"T-Pick, can you grab Nova Cane out of my belt and put it into my hand?" Holly asked hoping he had the strength.

T-Pick climbed up to his favourite perch on her shoulder and shot his long tongue out, grabbing Nova Cane from her waistband. With one giant tug the wand sprang out of her belt, swung in an arc over her shoulder and landed gently in her hand behind her.

"Thank-you, T-Pick. That was awesome. Okay now, Quill, are you there?"

Quill leapt out from the band of her magician's apprentice cap, somersaulted as he always did, and stood in mid-air in front of her nodding eagerly.

"Can you write an Unlock Spell in the sand in front of me? Rat Rat."

Quill nodded, spun, and quickly wrote in the sand.

"Ropes, chains, or things that bind,
Or doors and padlocks locked in kind,
Release your grip or knots unfold,
Free the prisoner that it holds."

Once finished, Quill spun, flipped with flourish, and returned to her cap.

After reading the words Holly pointed her wand at the padlock fastening her chains and fervently whispered, "Jawbreaker!"

Instantly the chains dropped to the ground and she was free.

"Yeeeeeesssss!" she whispered a shout of victory. She quickly grabbed her backpack and ran over to Fangor. She pointed her wand again and commanded, "Jawbreaker!"

Fangor stretched his wings as the chains broke loose from the strain and he rose, grateful for his freedom. Holly threw a bag of teeth into Fangor's jaws and his flame returned with a vengeance.

The noise of them leaving woke the queen in time only to see the dragon taking off with Holly on his back. "Get them!" she shrieked. "They're escaping!" She poked Ruthless Toothless Brutus in the ribs so hard he leapt up from the bed as if he were stung by a bee.

"Yeow!" he hollered, "What was that for?"

"They're escaping, you idiot!"

The emperor whirled around and saw the dragon in flight belching fire down on the camp and setting it aflame. "Get after them!" he ordered the stirring and groggy horde. He staggered around, kicking and pushing passed out bats that slowly woke and took reeling chase. Several, too drunk to fly, crashed into the cliffs and fell to the ground.

The queen and emperor stared up, stunned by the events. "I told you we should have eaten them," the queen shrieked, "but no, you had to have a party. Maybe this will teach you to get the job done before you make merry."

"You should watch your tongue, my queen, as even a queen can push too far," the emperor snapped back.

The queen flew out of their bedchamber to join the head hunter and the drunken, ragtag gang of pursuers.

Fangor climbed as fast as he could up mountain's steep crevasses, swooping and twisting to lose the bats that followed close behind. Holly knew if she could climb high enough they could escape as the air would become too thin and too cold for the bats to chase them. Having seen him in the arctic, she just hoped Fangor, being a reptile and cold blooded, could also make it.

"Up Fangor, up as fast as you can."

Up ahead, Holly saw another crew getting ready to propel another steel net at them but this time she was ready.

"You who come too near
Go away get out of here
So far back you disappear
And never again to reappear."

"Jawbreaker!"

The shock wave left the tip of Nova Cane and hurtled toward the catapult striking it just as they fired. The gummies manning the weapon never knew what hit them when the pulse of air punched with an unseen thump, flinging them in all directions. Some were splattered on the mountain while others were sent hurtling over its edge.

Fangor spiralled to just barely steer clear of the deployed net that now rocketed down toward the pursuing gummies. Holly grinned with glee when she saw the gummy faces below change to shock at the sight of the mesh hurtling toward them. With no time to react they were quickly ensnarled by the net, sending them spiralling out of control to the ground.

CHAPTER NINETEEN

Upper Palate Temple

"That was close!" Taddy Boy couldn't help but overstate the obvious as they soared higher.

"You can say that again! That net almost got us a second time!" Holly agreed, glancing back over her shoulder.

"They would have eaten Fangor for sure if they caught him again."

"Don't forget those slobbering things wanted to eat me as well!"

"Yeah, that too."

"I can't believe such evil exists in this world," Holly sighed as they reached the snow line, now far out of reach of the drooling gummies.

They flew up until they found a pass between the snow-covered mountains. As soon as they entered a deep ravine, the wind picked up, whirling the deep snow that covered the rugged terrain below and causing a blustery white out condition. The cold desolate peaks loomed above them and the frozen lakes and waterfalls dotted the landscape below as they made their way through the rugged canyon. No life could be seen as the sun peeked through on the horizon to the east behind them.

Suddenly, Holly heard a loud crack followed by a rumble.

"What was *that*?" she Holly as the thundering noise echoed off the canyon walls.

Gigantic slabs of ice had broken loose from the steep mountain slope and the thunderous avalanche forced Fangor to dip and wheel to evade the hunks of tumbling ice. Bouncing boulders struck his wings and he roar in pain. With an injured wing he struggled to stay aloft through the falling debris but managed to swoop up just in time before being caught in the deathly grip of plummeting snow and ice.

"That was close, too!" Taddy Boy shouted.

Holly shivered and tugged on her hood. The extreme cold made her eyes water and she could barely feel her toes. She knew Fangor was being affected as the temperature dropped and he had expended a lot of energy trying to save them. Both had slept little during their ordeal with the slobbering, foul-smelling meat eaters of the Blue Gum Colony and exhaustion was taking its toll. They would soon need rest.

> **"To land you must ponder**
> **The pain is much stronger**
> **I cannot last much longer**
> **A spell you must conger,"** Fangor cried in distress.

To help ease the bite of the blizzard, Holly decided to cast a Stop Wind spell to give some temporary relief.

> **"Winds, winds, please die down,**
> **Go up down or all around**
> **Give us rest from your biting chill**
> **Leave this space calm and still."**

Then she shouted, "Jawbreaker!"

Instantly, an invisible bubble formed around them just like the one in the arctic, and the wind stopped right away, but Fangor was labouring. He would have to land soon or he would die. She wiped her eyes and when they became adjusted to the dawn glow she looked around for a sheltered perch.

Holly's teeth chattered. "I'm freezing." She wrapped her arms around herself to keep in any heat that remained but it was no good. Her lips and fingers were turning blue, she couldn't feel her hands, and she was becoming drowsy from fatigue and hypothermia.

With the deep glacial snow, nothing seemed suitable and, if there was a cave it had to be deeply buried. Then, as they came around one the shoulder of a mountain she saw what looked like the twinkle of light in the distance.

"Look! Do you see that?" Barely peeking out from her frost encrusted eyelids she was unsure of what she had seen.

"No, what did you see?" stammered Taddy Boy.

"A light, over there." she said weakly, pointing. "See?"

"I, I, I think you're right."

Holly rubbed her eyes in disbelief. "There's another, and another," she said with a spurt of new energy but then slumped feebly in her saddle.

"Yes, yes!" Taddy Boy said in jubilation now seeing what looked like the walls of a temple.

Fangor unsteadily glided down, his talons clipped the tiles on the wall as he just made it over, landing and finally collapsing in the temple courtyard. Holly had passed out in the saddle on Fangor's back. He just slumped in the corner, out cold.

When Holly awoke, refreshed and in strange surroundings, she was delighted to see that this time there were no chains. Instead, she lay nestled in a warm, soft bed with clean sheets and a pillow.

"Oh dear, how long have I been out?" She slowly stretched out her arms, yawned then looked around the strange room.

"One whole day," Taddy Boy said from his perch on a chair next to her.

"A whole day!" she said, shocked. "We need to get going right away." When her bare feet hit the floor she suddenly realized she was wearing a nightgown and leapt back into bed and quickly covered herself up.

"Whoa, what happened here?" she said peeking out from under the covers.

"While you slept the monks brought you here, washed you and your clothes, and put you to bed."

"Monks? What monks?" Her clothes lay neatly folded at the end of the bed.

"The ones that live here. You did crash their home."

"Oh yes, I almost forgot." She got back up and this she time got dressed. "What about Fangor?"

"He's as snug as a bug; to keep him warm they lit fires around him and covered him in blankets."

A gentle knock came at the door. "Hello, young traveller. Are you awake?" called a voice with an unknown accent.

"Come in." Holly backed up against the bed.

The ancient wooden door creaked as it opened and in the entranceway stood a kindly, oriental-looking, old man, stooped by age and with a long white beard. He wore a bright orange robe. "I am sorry to intrude but we thought you might like some breakfast." In his hands was a tray with a steaming bowl, tea, bread, and a spoon.

"That would be very nice, thank-you. I am rather hungry."

The monk placed the tray on a small table beside the bed.

247

"You are most welcome, dragon rider." He bowed gently then folded his arms, tucking his hand up each sleeve. "You have slept for a day and need nourishment."

"My name is Holly Johnson and I am very thankful of you for saving our lives."

"You are most welcome Holly. My name is Floss Sing. "

"Hello Mr. Sing."

"You may call me Floss."

"You speak my language, Mr. Sing, er, I mean, Floss."

"We are the monks of the Upper Palate. We live in this remote place to meditate and find enlightenment. We seek all paths to this end including the languages of the world. I heard you talking in your sleep and I knew your words."

"I hope you didn't say anything embarrassing," Taddy Boy whispered.

"I hope I said nothing that might offend?" Holly replied, eagerly scooping the porridge in the bowl.

"No, you talked mostly of dragon eggs and the infestation from the lower valley."

"The drooling gummies!" she said, her mouth full.

"We call them a different name but yours works. We know they are very evil but as in all life they seem to have their place in this world."

"In the molten lava at the bottom of a volcano would be a good place," Taddy Boy suggested.

"I may not share your belief about their usefulness," Holly said, shaking her head. "Those things almost killed us and they like to spread nightmares to all they touch."

"We monks believe kindness to all creatures is on the path to being enlightened. I will leave you now.

Please join us in the temple when you are ready." He gracefully bowed and closed the door behind him.

"Well, he seemed nice," said Taddy Boy.

After finishing her breakfast and gathering her things, Holly, following the sound of deep-voiced chants and went down a set of stairs that opened up into a large hall. Sitting in rows were at least a hundred orange-draped monks nodding as they chanted in prayer. The leader noticed the stranger standing at the bottom of the stairs.

"What brings you here, child?" The chanting stopped and all eyes turned toward Holly.

"I, I...Mr. Floss said for me to come..." Holly stuttered not knowing what else to say.

"No child, we know why you are here, but why did you come to the Temple of the Upper Palate?"

"We seek the tomb of Mandible the Cannibal on the Isle of Lockjaw."

"You seek the Ring of Myth."

"How did you know?"

"You have dragon eggs of stone."

"Yes, but..."

"Long ago, we knew that to stop the bloody wars and keep peace in the land, each of the warring emperors had to have an equal purpose. One they could both share. As dragons were the protector of both peoples it seemed wise to make them their guardians."

"So, how did you know we are after the Ring of Myth?"

"We are the ones that forged the Ring of Myth and gave it to Mandible the Cannibal. We also harvested the Moon Pearl and gave it to Emperor Chinny Chin Chin. This way they both were responsible to ensure the dragon's eternal place in this world."

"Oh. So that's how you know."

249

"We wish you well and are pleased a new champion will bring back the eternal dragons and help the fairies."

"Well, we will try," she said not feeling as confident as he sounded. "You know about the fairies?"

"We are one with nature as they are. King Toothhurty and the eastern fairies are our friends and we have missed them in this part of the world, as we have the dragons."

"Wow! Cool. I can't wait to tell them back in Bicuspid."

"We must see that you are safely on your way but you must hurry as this is the eve of the Dragon Moon."

"Yes, we must hurry if we are to have any chance. Thank-you very much for saving me. If you would show us the way we will be moving on."

"You cannot leave through the mountain pass. It is too cold and the beasts will be waiting for you at the other end."

"Which way should we go? We can't go back."

"The shaft," said Floss.

"They're trying to give us the shaft!" Taddy Boy shouted.

"Shaft?" Holly asked.

"We are a long way up here. You don't think we bring up all our supplies through the bitter snow do you?"

"I guess not. What supplies?"

"Gracious gifts from the people are brought to the base of the mountain and we bring them up by the shaft."

"Oh, I see. What about Fangor? Will he be able to go through the shaft?"

"I am afraid your dragon is far too large for the lift. He is welcome to stay here until the spring melt if you wish. He will be well looked after."

"No worries," Holly agreed. "I can help with that. On our travels we met Santa at the North Pole."

"Ah, our old friend Nicholas. What did he give you?"

"Some of his magic dust that shrinks him so he can get into houses on Christmas Eve."

"Oh yes, his yearly trip to give presents to all good children."

"That's right."

"Very well then, we'll be on our way."

"Once again they escape our grasp," hissed Ruthless Toothless Brutus. "Why am I surrounded by such idiots?"

"My lord, the girl with butter hair has become a powerful wizard." The leader of the Blue Colony grovelled in front of the emperor and the queen.

"You still failed, oaf. We had them in our clutches and your men let them escape," Brutus said, glaring at the snivelling bat before him.

"But, my lord..."

"Get out of here! I do not want to see your face in my presence."

"Our greatest fears are being realized, my lord husband. A dragon and a wizard defeated the great Emperor Pyorrhoea Pete the Pirate when they attacked Fairyland, did they not?" Queen Hali Tosis recollected.

"They won't defeat me," the emperor snarled, slamming his fist on the arm of his throne. "We know where they are going and we'll be waiting for them on the other side of the Canker Mountain pass."

"Yes, my lord. I will send the army around to greet them," said the head hunter.

"I will lead the attack. It seems that if you want something done right, one has to do it himself!" the emperor snarled.

"Are you quite sure you are up to it, husband?"

"Of course, I am!" He rose to his feet. "I am Ruthless Toothless Brutus, Emperor and Supreme Leader of the Gummy Empire and the Land of Plaque," he boasted.

The queen rolled her eyes and shook her head.

The shaft turned out to be a long-dormant lava tunnel that had boiled up from the center of the mountain many eons ago. Now it was a dimly lit vertical cavern with a downward spiralling, rickety bamboo staircase on the outside walls and a wooden lift similar to a freight elevator in the center core.

"This looks creepy. Not much light down there," Holly said as she surveyed the tunnel with Fangor tucked away in her coat.

"Oh, not to worry Holly. We have little friends for that," Floss assured her.

"Friends?"

"Yes, fireflies. Beacon, my little friend, where are you?" Floss called.

A glow appeared across the cavern and came toward them then the firefly hovered in front of Floss.

"There you are, my friend. May I ask a favour of you?"

Beacon nodded and spun excitedly in the air. His tail grew brighter as he flew up, somersaulted, and returned.

"Do you think your friends would help us light the passage so our travellers can see as they descend the shaft?"

Beacon nodded eagerly and zipped off. The next moment, thousands of lights appeared, lighting up the gloom like stars on a clear night.

"Wow, so cool!" Holly exclaimed, a smile instantly lighting her face. "They are so beautiful."

"Now that's some kind of flashlight!" Taddy Boy gasped as the fireflies floated all around them.

"Well, I guess we'll be on our way. How can we thank-you, Floss? You and the monks have been so kind."

"Our pleasure, little one. We will pray for your success. Safe journeys to you, and to you, Fangor," he said giving a friendly ear scratch to a purring Fangor. "You must go quickly now as the Dragon Moon is upon us."

Holly was not convinced the series of frayed ropes and pulleys could hold their weight as they climbed into the elevator. She pulled the lever that released the brake and the rickety elevator started to descend. When the wobbly lift jerked, Holly grabbed the sides to steady herself and let out a little scream. Even Fangor burped a puff of smoke and squirmed uneasily inside her coat.

"Yo, yo, no fuss
No worry
No muss
No hurry
No crashin'
No bashin'
Ain't gonna hit it
Ridin' with it
No mistakin' it
We're not breakin' it
We're makin' it, yo," rapped T-Pick as Hip Hop did a wobbly dance.

"Thanks boys, I'm okay now," Holly said, still maintaining a firm grip.

Holly looked up at the fading sight of Floss Sing's smiling face and it calmed and reassured her. She gave an uneasy smile and waved back one last time until his face disappeared into the darkness.

The creaking and moaning of the cage lashed together with twine around bamboo poles, jerked and shook as it continued its slow unsteady plunge into the darkness. Beacon and the fireflies stayed with her to light the way, helping to ease her nerves.

"Hey, at least you don't have to climb down all those stairs," said Taddy Boy looking amazed as they passed by the thousands of ancient wooden stairs on their spiral downward.

"Can you imagine someone having to climb *up* all those steps?" Holly asked.

"No way. Heart attack city right there."

Wizzy's voice perked up from the backpack, "If at first you don't succeed, try, try again."

"Then quit. There's no point in making a fool of yourself," added Taddy.

Down they went on their seemingly endless journey until Holly heard the distant flow of water.

"We must be coming to the bottom." Just as the words left her mouth, the shaft opened up into an enormous cavern. She could feel a refreshing breeze hit her face. A waterfall off to one side supplied a large pool of water with a dock that had several small boats tied up to it.

"Those must be used to bring in the supplies to the Upper Palate Temple."

"I don't see anyone here." Taddy observed.

"You're right, Taddy. I wonder how we're supposed to get out of here."

"You could always use your last leaf from the Tree of Knowledge."

"That would be a waste. I think I'll save it in case we need it later."

The elevator landed gently on the ground and they got out. Holly looked around and saw some grain bags, boxes, cases of jars, and urns stacked on the dock. There were no passageways or doors that she could see, just a dimly lit dock.

"Beacon," she called.

The firefly came immediately and hovered in front of her.

"How do we get out of here?"

Beacon and several other fireflies flew away, following the current of the water to the cave wall. Their light exposed a dark tunnel where the waterway made its mysterious journey out.

"It looks as though we have to borrow a boat," Holly said reluctantly.

CHAPTER TWENTY

Mandible the Cannibal

"Where are these stomach-churning vermin?" screamed Ruthless Toothless Brutus. "We have been lying in wait for more than a day."

"My lord, the mountain passage is treacherous. Even in the summer we have lost patrols in those valleys," the head hunter advised.

"The winds can quickly rise and steer them into dead end valleys. And don't forget about falling rocks," Queen Hali Tosis reminded him.

"They made it over the north pole, didn't they?" the emperor snapped.

"Yes, my lord," they both answered.

"Are you sure we have both ends covered?" the Emperor asked for the fourteenth time.

"Yes, my lord. Our *divided* army is amassed at the snowline at both ends. There is no way to escape without us seeing them," the queen said, tired of answering the same question again.

"Thank-you, Beacon, and to the rest of your friends showing us the way," Holly said. "May I ask one more favour before you leave?"

Beacon readily nodded and flipped once more in mid-air.

"You are so kind, my friend. I need to read my *Beginners Book of Magic* to find a light spell."

Beacons tail lit up but with only one firefly's light it was hard to read. "Beacon, can you shine a little brighter? I have difficulty reading the passages."

Beacons tail burst into such a bright light it lit up the entire cavern. Holly covered her squinting eyes.

"Too bright, too bright,' she shouted.

Beacon instantly lowered the intensity.

"Now that's a dimmer switch!" Taddy Boy commented.

Once her eyes had adjusted, Holly flipped the pages of her book until she found the Light Spell.

> "Element of light with your beams and rays
> Make the dark turn into day
> Light my wand and make it glow
> Light the way to show the way to go."

"Jawbreaker!"

Pointing in the air, Nova Cane shuddered then sparked in her hand forming a white light that lit up the dock.

"That's better. Now we'll be able to see. Thank-you, Beacon, for all of your help." After one last wave goodbye, Beacon and the rest of the fireflies returned up the shaft to the temple.

"I guess we're on our own from here, Taddy Boy."

With Fangor still small and cuddled inside her coat, Holly boarded one of the boats. Being too small to operate the oars, she pushed away from the dock. With one hand she held the wand up and with the other grabbed the tiller to steer the rudder and let the current carry the boat downstream.

Slowly they made their way bumping the sides of the channel several times along the way. Using all her

258

strength, she tried to steer clear of white water rapids that seemed to have sprung up out of nowhere. The boat jostled and jounced, almost tipping them overboard. Holly pulled on the tiller as hard as she could to avoid the torrents but down they went.

"Whoooooooooa!" both Taddy Boy and Holly screamed as they spun and dipped going ever faster as they rode the churning waves.

"I don't like getting wet!" screamed Taddy Boy as wave after wave splashed into the boat.

"I don't like to drown," Holly yelled back as another surged in.

Fangor slipped out of Holly's coat and hastily flapped his wings, but his wings couldn't lift him. He was too small. Instead he jumped and clung to the prow of boat digging his talons deep into the wood and puffed fireballs in defiance at the water — to no avail.

T-Pick and Hip Hop scurried into the safety of the backpack with Wizzy.

"I don't want to *die!*" screamed Taddy as they spun again.

"Nor do I," Holly yelled back, yanking hard on the rudder.

As the boat was about to tip completely, they banged against a large rock that steered them into a sideslip of calmer water allowing them bypass the rest of the rapids.

"Whew, that was close!" Taddy Boy gasped in relief as the boat settled back into the easy glide downstream.

"You say that a lot."

"I do?"

"And by the way, stuffed bears can't drown."

"They can't? That's a relief."

Keeping to the calmer waters, Holly avoided the remaining run offs and small waterfalls until she saw an opening of daylight approaching.

"That must be the way out," she said proudly after having navigated the stream.

"Nicely done, Holly," praised Taddy Boy

"Why, thank-you, kind sir," she said as they broke into the daylight.

Getting her bearings, Holly looked around at the jungle shores as they continued to drift. She looked up and saw a huge black cloud way up in the distance surrounding the snowy mountain pass.

"It looks as though they were waiting for us, Taddy."

"What if they see us?"

"You're right," Holly tucked Nova Cane away then grabbed a tarp from the bottom of the boat and covered herself along with Fangor. They slowly eased their way along the stream trying to look like a regular boat returning from bringing supplies for the temple. The deception seemed to work until the magic dust started to wear off Fangor.

Within seconds the dragon grew back to his normal size easily capsizing the small boat. Holly, not wanting to go down with the ship, leapt up and grabbed onto the saddle horn just as he took flight. With a roar and a mighty flap of his wings they were once again airborne and, like a bareback trick rider in the circus, Holly swung a leg up and over and regained her seat in the saddle. She looked up, hoping they hadn't been seen but the black swarm had indeed noticed them. They swirled and turned in a mass dive and streaked toward them. Holly could even hear Ruthless Toothless Brutus scream, "Aaaaattttaaaaaaaack!"

"Oh no! We've been seen."

"They just don't give up do they?" Taddy Boy said.

"Evil never does," she answered.

"The best way to escape evil is to pursue good," Wizzy said from the backpack.

"Fly, Fangor, as hard as you can. We must reach the coast and beyond to the Isle of Lockjaw."

Fangor flew like the wind as they travelled over the stunned onlookers in the jungle villages of Plaque with the dreaded bats in hot pursuit. They were nearing the coast when Holly felt the sudden sharp pang of pain in her shoulders as a gummy gripped her with his claws and tried to lift her from her saddle. His slobber drooled down her face as she tried unsuccessfully to swat him off.

"They're on us!" she cried.

Several other gummies attacked Fangor, trying to use their combined weight to bring him down. T-Pick lashed out his long tongue and smacked the gummy attacking Holly in the eye while Hip Hop boxed him in the other eye, forcing him to let go his grip and peel off with an ear-splitting scream of pain.

"Thanks, T-Pick; thanks Hip Hop," she said, now free to pull out Nova Cane and start the incantation of the Power Push spell.

> "You who come too near
> Go away get out of here
> So far back you disappear
> And never again to reappear."

"Jawbreaker!"

Several gummies blasted off Fangor's wing after being hit with the sonic wave.

"Jawbreaker!"

More gummies skyrocketed off the other wing.

"Jawbreaker!"

Finally the rest of the gummies jetted off the tail allowing Fangor to regain his speed and agility. But they kept following close behind, nipping at them repeatedly.

Holly tried but couldn't keep up with the demand of her spells.

"I can't get them off our backs."

Finally, Fangor rolled on his back, curled his head back and blasted the chasers with a huge fireball sending many singed gummies into the Sea of Cavity. With the break they needed, Fangor surged ahead putting a short distance between them.

"Land ho!" shouted Taddy Boy.

"There, up ahead, Fangor. An island."

In the mist ahead, a sliver of green appeared on the horizon with a golden glint glowing brightly like a lighthouse.

"That must be the temple. Fly toward it before these things catch up."

The gleaming top of the Gold Crown Temple poked out of the almost completely vine-covered stone ruins below. Fangor found the remains of a stone terrace at the top of the stairs rising from the jungle and landed quickly while firing a ball of fire toward the pursuing horde. Holly hopped off and ran toward the temple and pulled aside the vines clinging to its walls. Stone carvings marked the entrance and she bravely plunged through it.

"Fangor, guard the entrance while I find the tomb!"

Fangor backed up to block the doorway and discharged fireball after fireball toward the black throng that had now reached the island. Each furnace blast scattered them and kept them at bay for moments. With Fangor in position, the gummies landed in the surrounding jungle trees and vines, reluctant to get burned and unsure how to attack and avoid the dragon's breath.

"You can't keep this up, dragon," hissed Ruthless Toothless Brutus.

Fangor hunkered down, swinging his long neck and glaring furiously at the thousands of bats. The stone ruins protected his back but he remained alert, making sure the enemy couldn't sneak up on him. But the gummies did try. They climbed the vines, tried to come up from below; they attacked from above and straight on but each time Fangor stopped them with another blast of scorching fire.

Holly ran down the dark hallway while invoking the Light Spell.

"Element of light with your beams and rays
Make the dark turn into day
Light my wand and make it glow
Light the path and show the way to go."

Then she shouted, "Jawbreaker!"

Nova Cane lit the way as she descended the stairs looking this way and that for Mandible the Cannibal's tomb. Just before she entered the inner chamber of the temple, Holly thought she saw something move in the darkness ahead. She crept forward and as soon as she stepped on the stone floor she felt something slither over her foot. She screamed. The floor of the temple appeared to be moving, wriggling, and slithering. She looked down and saw snakes writhing everywhere.

"Snakes!" Shocked, Holly jumped back to the safety of the stairs, starring in horror at the sight before her.

"Don't like snakes. They're creepy," Taddy Boy muttered.

"You can say that again."

"Don't like snakes. They're creepy," he repeated.

"It's just a saying, Taddy. You don't have to really say it again," she sighed.

The snakes had made their home on every ledge and crevice of the stone walls and hung from the vine roots that draped the ceiling and walls. To investigate the newcomer, a large boa constrictor dropped in front of her, sensing the air with his long forked tongue while still clinging with his tail to the root above her. Holly screamed again and raced back up the stairs to the entrance.

"Whew, *that* was close!" she gasped still trying to catch her breath.

"Let's get outta here!" Taddy Boy demanded.

"Yo, yo no, no
You know
You can't go.
Gotta get the bling
Spring the magic ring, yo."

"T-Pick's right. We can't go. We need the Ring of Myth."

"Okay, let's look at the situation we're in," Taddy Boy reasoned. "If we go back downstairs we die a slow death by poison or if we're lucky, we get eaten whole by the big squeeze. If we go outside, we get ripped to shreds by bats."

"I am so sorry, Taddy Boy. It's a real nice mess I got us into."

"Even Garth never got us into this much trouble."

"I know, but we still have to think of a way to get the ring."

"I think we should take our chances with the winged rats…with Fangor's help, of course."

"I think we have to scare the snakes away somehow," she said ignoring Taddy.

"Fear can be a great motivator," Wizzy's voice said.

"That's it! I can shrink Fangor and he can scare them."

"What about the bats?" Taddy Boy reminded her.

"Oh yeah, maybe that's not such a good idea."

"Yo, come on baby light my fire,
Try and set the night on fire, yo."

"That's it! Thank-you, T-Pick. We can light torches. All animals are afraid of fire."

Holly gathered a dozen sticks and broken roots lying around and stuffed them into her belt like ammo. She lit the first one using the Fire Spell and went back to the stairs leading down.

"I could keep Fangor company..."

"Scaredy bear."

"At least I admit it."

When she got to the bottom of the stairs, the boa backed off, hissing in protest away from her torch. She pointed Nova Cane, lit and threw one of the torches onto the chamber floor. The snakes hissed and slithered away from the fire forming a clear place to step. She lit another and stepped again trying carefully not to put out the torch. She made her way to the centre of the chamber placing several lit torches around her keeping the snakes in the far corners then raised her torch to see.

"Where is this tomb?" she wondered aloud, seeing no coffin. Peering into the gloom, she saw several stone carvings of different jungle animals lining the walls. A tiger, gorilla, snake, and elephant were just a few but one on its own caught her eye. It was a dragon.

"Dragon's on walls? Here we go again," Taddy boy said.

"I hope it's not a trap as well. We were lucky the last time."

Holly stepped toward the dragon to get a closer look stumbled, and came face to face with a hooded cobra that had coiled, ready to strike at any sudden movement. Holly's torch was the only thing between her and the snake and for one frozen moment, they stared at each other until the snake turned and backed away from the flame. Holly got up very slowly to avoid startling any of the other slithering belly crawlers and stepped back.

"The torches are getting low, Holly," Taddy Boy observed, glancing nervously around.

Holly lit a couple more but as she did, she noticed what she had tripped over. "Look, on the floor. It's the same dragon and pearl symbol as my amulet, etched in deep grooves."

"There's a hole in the dragon's eye."

"Looks like some kind of fluid goes into the groves then goes down the eye."

"Maybe it's supposed to be blood from some sacrifice ceremony!"

"I'm not sacrificing my blood! I'm too little," said Holly.

"Me either."

"You don't have any."

"Whew."

Holly looked up at the stone dragon and saw that its mouth was open and realized the fluid, whatever it was, came from its mouth. "There must be a lever or secret button somewhere."

"Yo, yo, little sleuth,
Find the truth,
Check the flute,
With a sound that's mute.
Leafy said
Through your head
Play the tune for the dead, yo."

"That's right! Play the tune for the dead." Holly quickly got out the jade flute given to her by Yula and started to play. Again, she heard no sound but all the snakes rapidly slithered away into hidden crevices. A thousand frantic screams could be heard echoing from up the stairs and then followed silence.

A groaning, bubbling noise echoed in the chamber sounding like it was coming from under her feet.

"Is that your tummy again, Taddy?"

"I'm hungry but not that hungry."

The clamour and hissing got louder and the stones started to shudder.

"Do you smell something burning?" Taddy Boy asked. "Check your pants."

"Yes, its smells like sulphur but it's not me."

The eyes of the dragon started to glow, smoke came spewing from the mouth followed by eruptions of spitting fire and lava oozing as it fell to the floor.

"Wow, we must be on a volcano," Holly said.

"Exit stage left, and back up the stairs!"

"Let's see what happens, Taddy."

"Awesome, first bats, then snakes and now…I can smell my fur singeing!"

"Oh, hush, scaredy bear," Holly said as she watched the flow of molten lava snake its way into the grooves of the dragon symbol. The fiery contour outlined the symbol of the dragon and pearl then flowed into the dragon's eye.

"Cool!" Holly said, eyes wide with amazement.

The lava dripped from the dragon's eye into a dark room below the floor and dropped onto a lavishly carved jade sarcophagus. The magma seeped into a hole in the top of Mandible the Cannibal's tomb lighting up the inside with a green radiance. Through the jade carvings the silhouette of a human formed and started pushing the coffin lid from the inside.

Holly continued to play the flute until the molten lava stopped spewing and crusted over in dark grey pumice.

"Well, that's that," Taddy Boy said. "Looks like we're done here. Here I come, you lucky pillow!"

"Just hold on to your horses there, my furry friend. Let's see what happens next."

"I don't like horses. One kicked me in the…um castle stable back in Garth's day."

267

"You probably deserved it."

Holly smiled at the, "Harrumph!" that followed from the backpack.

The floor shuddered, rumbled then started to separate and retract like an elevator door, forcing Holly to jump back once more. She peered down into the cavern below and saw Mandible the Cannibal's tomb begin to rise. Once the tomb reached the surface, the split floor reversed, closing off the chamber below.

"Wow, that was cool. Now what?" Holly watched in awe.

A few moments passed. The coffin continued to glow when, SMASH!, like broken glass, the lid of the jade coffin shattered outward into grains of sand that spiralled like a whirlwind and formed a funnel rising upwards.

When the powder settled, from beyond the veil appeared the regal and fierce form of Mandible the Cannibal in his full Gumgolian battle armour. His feet stood apart, one hand grasped the hilt of his sword while the other rested on his hip. His head was held high. The glow from the fires of lava slowly faded from him leaving the figure completely regenerated with only steam rising off his human form.

269

CHAPTER TWENTY-ONE

Ring of Myth

"I think the sulphur has just left me," Taddy Boy said dramatically. "I gotta go, gotta go."

"Oh-oh. Maybe we *should* run?"

"Many are those so filled with fear that they go through life running from something that is not after them," Wizzy said.

"At least they're still alive!" Taddy Boy said. "Holly, get your feet doing what they are made for...run!" But it was too late.

"Who dares enter my sacred tomb?"

Not knowing what else to do, Holly bowed deeply in respect. "Lord Mandible, my name is Holly Johnson," she said with humility and grace, and a quavering voice. In the awful moments that passed with her head bowed, she heard chuckling. It was not from Taddy Boy. She raised her eyes to see a giddy and dancing emperor.

"I'm free, I'm free," he giggled in excitement.

"My lord?" she inquired, standing back up.

"I have been dead for centuries, lying cold in my fancy tomb that was supposed to entertain me in my afterlife. As my world faded and my riches left me, only the promise of the monks kept me with the slim glimmer of hope of ever returning to the living world. I have waited to hear the Tune of the Dead for centuries so that I might rise and keep my promise as a Dragon Guardian."

"That is why I am here, my lord."

"You are?"

"My lord, I am here with the last dragon and these eggs."

"Eggs! Got any bacon? It has been centuries since I have tasted real food," he said, laughing heartily.

"These are dragon eggs, the last of the species. I am here on a quest to bring them back to life."

"How wonderful!" he said clapping his hands. "They are *so* cute when they are babies."

"Isn't he supposed to be mean and cruel and terrible?" Taddy Boy whispered into Holly's left ear.

"My lord, you seem so…happy. Unlike the stories I have heard."

"I had a good public relations department. If they ever saw me like this they would have tarred and feathered me and run me out of town. Rumours and fear kept the people in line and with a face like mine, they believed it." He struck the formidable pose once more. "All I had to do was to look fierce and they cowered like wimps and showered me with gifts."

"But, but…"

"Now that I am free, I am as scatter-brained as a kid at recess," he chuckled as he moonwalked across the floor.

"My lord, I am here on a serious mission."

"Wheeeeee," he sang as he spun on the spot, then he stopped. "I know, I know but I can't help myself. I don't deserve to be this happy." And he giggled once more.

"Sir?"

"Yes, yes, you are here for the Ring of Myth placed in my care by the monks from the Upper Palate."

"I am, my lord."

"You have dragon eggs?"

"Yes sir," Holly opened her backpack and showed him the colourful eggs.

"You said that you have brought the last dragon? Too many centuries have passed since I have seen a dragon. May I meet your friend?"

"Of course. He is upstairs guarding the entrance," she said and turned to start climbing the stairs.

"How come there is only one dragon? In my day there were plenty," Mandible asked, scratching his chin.

"An ancestor of mine by the name of Garth woke Fangor from his sleep, something one must never do. Fangor got angry and started the dragon wars with the human knights. When the war was done, a deal was made between the King of the Fairies and the human king to have Fangor remain alive and feed him children's teeth for gold from the pot-of-gold at the end of the rainbow in return."

"I see. That makes Fangor a very special dragon indeed."

At the top of the stairs they could see Fangor's rear blocking the entrance and his tail swishing back and forth.

"Fangor, are we safe?"

Fangor moved to let Holly and Mandible out onto the terrace. He continued his guard but was no longer being attacked. Not one drooling gummy was anywhere close but in the distance they hung like black blobs in the jungle trees keeping a very sharp eye on the temple.

"Why do they not attack?" Mandible the Cannibal asked.

**"They dropped to the ground
When they heard a sound
Howling like hounds
They all left town,"** Fangor roared.

"Did the sound from the magic flute drive them away?" Holly asked.

"It did," Mandible answered. "It was meant to drive all evil away to protect me when the tomb opened."

"I see, but we could not hear any sounds?"

"Only beasts and evil can hear the tones and to them it's like a banshee howl screaming in their ears and driving them insane."

Mandible gave Fangor a scratch behind the ear as though they were old friends. A low guttural growl like a cat purr came from Fangor and he turned his head for Mandible to get just the right spot.

"He likes you," Holly said.

"There's an ancient Gumgolian saying, 'The best recipe for making friends is to be one yourself,'" Mandible said.

"Hey, he's starting to sound like the big tooth ache in your pack," Taddy Boy said.

Mandible the Cannibal drew a ring from his finger and handed it to Holly. It was the Ring of Myth.

"Thank-you, my lord," she said, slipping the ring on her thumb as it was the only finger large enough for it to fit. "Now, we will seek the tomb of Chinny Chin Chin and with his Moon Pearl, bring the dragons back to life."

"A very good plan. The monks of the Upper Palate will be very pleased," agreed Mandible with a grin. "But you must move fast as the Dragon Moon is upon us."

"Yes, I know. We must hurry."

All of a sudden a black blur with outstretched claws whistled by just missing the head of the emperor.

"How dare these beasts attack their emperor?" Mandible shouted.

Holly played the flute once more and more screams arose from all around them. Without being seen, the gummies had been creeping up the temple walls and down the vines to try another sneak attack but one blast

273

from the flute flushed them out and sent them madly writhing in pain back to the safety of the jungle.

"My lord, I do not think they know you. It has been a long time since you have walked this earth."

"I don't think Ruthless Toothless Brutus would care anyway," Taddy Boy added.

"They must obey me. I am Mandible the Cannibal, Emperor of the Gumgolian Empire. They are dishonouring the Gold Crown Temple and my tomb," he snarled. "They must have a lesson in humility."

"The only thing they listen to is that flute," Taddy Boy observed.

"You are much larger than I, sir," Holly said. "You could play the flute much louder."

"You make good reason," he said taking the flute from her. "I am no musician and will play many sour notes for them."

"We must leave this place for Doublechin but we are surrounded."

"Oh, don't you worry. I will play such a screeching tune that it will make their ears bleed. That will keep them at bay while you make your escape."

"Yo, yo, which way to go?
Back through the land of ice and snow?
Can't go up,
Can't go down,
How do we leave,
This Golden Crown? yo," T-Pick rapped.

"The rainbow lizard has a good point. How do we get out of here?" Taddy Boy asked.

"Well, we can't go back to the jungle or we'll be caught for sure. We can't go through the mountains again or we'll freeze. The only way out is over the ocean," Holly surmised.

"Every time we have to do anything, we have to go over, under or through water and you *know* I hate water. I really hate water and you know I CAN'T SWIM!" complained Taddy Boy. "You know what wet fur and stuffing smells like?"

"I know very well what you smell like. Get over it."

'What? I smell?" Emperor Mandible said. "You know I haven't had a chance to have a bath in centuries."

"Oh, I *am* sorry, Emperor. I was not speaking about you. I was talking about my best friend, Taddy Boy."

"Oh, I see you have an imaginary friend."

"No, he's my real best friend."

Taddy Boy sighed, feeling loved once again.

**"We can always use the favour,
Promised by Queen Pearly White.
Right now we need a saviour
Poseidon with all his might,"** Fangor suggested.

"Yes! Poseidon could help. Thanks, Fangor!" Holly ran down the stone steps of the ruined temple with Mandible playing the flute, Fangor spitting fire, and the black horde following as close as they dared behind them. Once they reached the shore, Holly grabbed the Seahorse brooch from her cape and threw it into the water.

They all waited. Seconds went by as they anticipated something happening but — nothing.

"Well, that was exciting. I was expecting bubbling water, steam, flashes of light, anything! But we got nothing!" Taddy Boy complained.

Holly was first to notice a movement far off on the horizon. Initially, it appeared to be a cloud but as it approached, she saw that it was not a cloud but an enormous wave rolling in. It was not just any wave either, but the mother of all waves forming a wall five stories high. Riding a surfboard in his dogger baggy surfer shorts and hanging ten at its crest was a tanned surfer with a bushy blond hairdo, wearing a crown ringed in live seahorses. Around his waist hung a hefty conch shell and strings of puka shells circled his neck and wrists. When the wave curled forming a barrel, the rider hot-dogged it, did a double spinner, shot the tube then flipped back up onto of the crest with perfect precision.

"Holy...Holly!" Taddy Boy screamed in Holly's ears.

"RUN!" yelled Holly as the big surf approached and scampered as fast as she could up the temple steps.

With every breath Mandible gasped, blowing the flute while running but the bats were no longer trying to fight. They too had seen the oncoming wave and were fleeing to save their greasy black skins.

Fangor leapt into the air and with one mighty flap of his wings landed safely on the upper terrace of the temple.

Holly reached the top step just as the wave hit and crashed into the shore.

"Cowabunga!" yelled the stranger riding the wave in, clearly enjoying himself immensely. When the wave broke, his board slammed unto shore and stuck into the wall of the temple with a mighty THWANG!

"Wow, dude! That was slammin' and you're my witness, dude," said the stranger. "I spent a ton o' time in the green room and I never took a Neptune cocktail or sand facial. What a cruncher!"

"Excuse me?" Holly said.

"He said dude just like you do," Taddy Boy remarked. "Do you know what muscle beach boy's saying?"

"Did you see my toes on the nose?" the surfer cried, running both hands through his shaggy hair. "This boy doesn't cheater five on my big gun."

"Excuse me?" Holly said again.

The stranger looked at his board stuck into the wall. "Bummer, dude," he said and dislodged it with a mighty yank. He carefully inspected his board for damage. "Cowabunga! That was gnarly."

"This beach bum's going to rescue us? He's such a dweeb!" Taddy Boy exclaimed.

"Hush, Taddy Boy," Holly whispered.

The surfer then spied Fangor. "Whoa! Gnarlatious, dude! Where did you come from, big boy?"

Fangor stretched his long neck down to get a closer look at the stranger, snorted, and decided he was in no danger. He would keep an eye on this stranger while still keeping watch for any gummies still bold enough to attack.

"Well, I know what dude means," Taddy Boy muttered.

"Did you see the heavy honker? It was mondo gnarly man."

"Do you speak English?" Holly asked, shaking her head.

"Sure Hodad, I mean girly without a board. You called?" The surfer handed the silver seahorse brooch to Holly.

"Are you Queen Pearly White's son, Poseidon?"

"Yo sis, I was so stoked to get your call. I was havin' lunch with the big Kahuna and he said 'better go save your damsel in distress' so here I am. Dude in servitude."

"Yo? Yo? I hope he doesn't rap," Taddy Boy said, rolling his bead eyes.

"We need your help," Holly told him. "We are surrounded by the drooling gummies. We have to get off this island and we cannot go back to shore."

"Oh, fer sure. Mama told me about them black stains long ago. They're really hairy."

"You can say that again," Taddy Boy agreed.

"We are heading for Chin and the tomb of Chinny Chin Chin," Holly explained.

"All you need to do is cross the Sea of Cavity, pass my favourite place to party, Tie-wan-on, then on to my happy place they call Grin, The Land of Smiles. Then shoot over to Chin."

"I told ya! Grin, the Land of Smiles." Taddy Boy looked around smugly.

"Okay, but if you can delay the bats somehow we would really appreciate it."

"No problem, little dudette. I'll just call a few friends of mine." He reached for his conch shell and gave it three short blasts and one long one. Within minutes, huge blue and gray whales and hundreds of dolphins approached out of the depths and formed a row just off shore. "These guys can handle them fer sure."

"I thought you were going to call for your giant clam Chariot of the Sea pulled by Seamore and five other white sea lions," Holly said recalling Taddy Boy's story of long ago.

"That old thing? It's covered in seaweed back at the Sea Palace. That's Mama's ride. It's an out-dated mode of transportation, dude. Not environmentally friendly, as it were, sis. Giant clams are on the extinction list so using sea life to pull us royals around is a no-no. We're amped about green power these days. That's why I ride the waves and it's sooooooo ex-cel-lent!"

"Oh, I see," Holly replied.

"Your scaly buddy wouldn't fit in it anyway," Poseidon said, looking up at Fangor. "If the emperor dude will play the flute while you take off south across the Sea of Cavity, my beauties will stop them. When you are out of site of the shore, turn east toward Tai-wan -on."

"Thank-you, sir," she said.

"Dude is good."

278

"Okay, thank-you, Dude."

Poseidon laughed. "We'll make a grommet out of you in no time."

"A grommet?"

"A young surfer girl."

"Oh," she replied, shaking her head again.

"I wish you safe journeys," said Mandible.

"Aloha, Hodad," shouted Poseidon as they flew away.

CHAPTER TWENTY-TWO

Emperor Chinny Chin Chin

While Mandible played the flute, Holly, riding Fangor once more, headed south across the Sea of Cavity. Ruthless Toothless Brutus immediately called his army to follow, scattering to avoid the ear-demolishing sounds. Waiting for Holly off shore was the wall of whales and dolphins led by Poseidon on his board.

As soon as the pursuing horde was over the ocean, Poseidon blew his conch once more and the whales and dolphins went into action. First, the whales formed a wall of water by spraying streams high into the air from their blowholes. The blasts knocked the first wave of gummies out of the sky, sending them splashing into the sea.

Bats cannot swim so the downed gummies floundered in the water until rescued by the clawed feet of a comrade who lugged them back to shore to dry out. Other whales flicked their tales creating waves of water; hitting the pursuing bats and leaving them gasping for air through mouthfuls of seawater. The wet bats, now unable to fly well, had to turn around.

The dolphins cheekily sprayed jets of water from their mouths with great accuracy, knocking down the few hunters that had escaped the water wall. They too returned to the safety of the jungle jeered by the dolphins' infectious laugh.

It wasn't long before Ruthless Toothless Brutus saw the senselessness of the attack and called for a retreat. "We'll have to go the long way around, my hearties. We know where they are going."

"We will have to cross the Goblin Desert and away from this wretched sea," Queen Hali Tosis interjected.

"My boys can put up with a little heat..."

"And the freezing cold at night?" she inquired.

"Anything's better than those big squirts and laughing fish."

Holly made great time crossing the Sea of Cavity and caught the party noises long before they came upon the shores of Tai-wan-on.

"Somebody's having a good time down there," she said, hearing the loud music and voices.

"Looks like the whole island's there," observed Taddy Boy.

"Nothing makes you more tolerant of a neighbour's party than being invited to it," intoned Wizzy.

"Yo, yo, gotta love the music
Cause I lose it
When they groove it
Just can't quit it
When they hit it
You gotta love the music, yo," T-Pick rapped excitedly as Hip Hop break-danced on Holly's shoulder.

"Okay, okay, I get it, you two. I love the music too, but we can't stop. We have to find the tomb of Emperor Chinny Chin Chin before the Dragon Moon passes."

None of those whooping it up on the island paid any attention to the skies as the large dragon flew overhead and carried on toward the land of Chin.

"Okay, don't get a lip on...By the way, where is Lip?" Taddy Boy asked.

"Good question, Taddy. We don't know exactly where the Emperor Chinny's tomb is to be found. It could be in a jungle or buried in a desert, for all we know. All we know is that it is near Lip on the Lip-on River."

"Knowledge becomes wisdom only after it has been put to use," Wizzy's muffled advice mumbled from the backpack.

"Is he trying to lip us off?" Taddy quipped.

"That's it! Thanks Wizzy. We have one more leaf from the Tree of Knowledge! It's our only hope."

"Are you sure? It's our last leaf and you may need it once we get there. You know, like how we get past the eight thousand enamel warriors guarding the temple!"

"I know, Taddy, but there's no point unless we find Lip."

When they had reached the coast, Holly steered Fangor down to land unseen on a sandy beach in a secluded cove.

"Why are we landing, Holly?" Fangor asked.

"I don't want to be flying when I go into the trance from chewing the last leaf from the Tree of Knowledge."

"Good idea. You wouldn't want to get an impaired driving charge from the dragon police would you?" Taddy commented, smirking at his own cleverness.

"Very funny."

As the waves rolled in, Holly chewed her last leaf and asked her question. "How do I find the entrance to Emperor Chinny Chin Chin's tomb?" Holly went into her trance. Her eyes drifted closed and her voice changed once again.

"Fly north east over the Land of Smiles called Grin. Follow the Gingiva River until you pass the Bite Wing Falls. You are now entering the Land of Chin. Avoid the terraces where the people of Chin grow crops by following the ridge of

the Dragon Spine Mountains. To the south you will see the River Lip-on and the great city of Lip. Carry on until you find the Dragon's Head in a place called Doublechin. Nestled in the jaws of the dragon's mouth, you will find the pyramid tomb of Chinny Chin Chin covered by an earthen jungle. Seek the side of the rising sun and wait for the Dragon Moon to rise between the dragon's teeth and its mystic glow will reveal the hidden entrance."

"Why does it always sound so eerie and dangerous?" muttered Taddy Boy.

"It does sound mysterious doesn't it?" Holly replied, coming out of her trance and sitting upright.

"How do you get mysterious from 'eerie or dangerous'?" Taddy said. "Holly, the day is getting on so if we plan to be there by the time the Dragon Moon rises, we had better get a move on."

"You're right but I think we will fly low so any bat spies cannot tell the gummies where we are."

"Good idea. Let's go, honcho." Taddy Boy tucked himself lower into the backpack as Fangor lifted off once more.

Ruthless Toothless Brutus, Queen Hali Tosis, and the black horde had made their way across the Land of Plaque. They were flying into Gumgolia, on their way to the Goblin Desert, and onward to Doublechin and the emperor's tomb.

With sweat dripping off his hairy brows, Brutus hollered, "Fly faster, faster, me mateys. We have to get to the tomb."

"If you push them any harder, they will fall out of the sky with exhaustion," cautioned the queen feeling faint from the long, hard flight.

"Without water we won't be able to fight," panted the head hunter, clearly not used to such heat.

"Don't worry about my mateys. They can do it. Believe me, there will be plenty to drink at the celebrations after. But now, we go faster, faster!"

Fangor flew low over the jungles of the Land of Grin. Holly could have used a Spell of Invisibility but knew she would need her power later and decided to save her magic. They crossed the Gingiva River and reached the cliffs of the Dragon Spine Mountains. They stopped briefly to drink and fill water canteens at the Bite Wing Falls but soon carried on to the ridge. She could see the great city of Lip in the distance and the brown haze covering the skyline.

"Wow, I can smell the pollution from here," Holly said.

"Air pollution is something for which we all have to pay for through the nose," Wizzy droned from the interior of the backpack.

"I think we already are!" Taddy Boy said, coughing.

Higher and higher they flew, hugging the craggy ridge called the Dragon's Spine and into the cleaner air.

"Yo, yo, big city,
Ain't it a pity?
Streets are dirty and gritty,
And it sure ain't pretty,
In the big city yo," rapped T-Pick.

Finally, Holly saw the mountain ridge split, forming the shape of a head. In the open jaws she saw the pyramid she had been searching for.

"There!" Holly shouted.

"There!" echoed Taddy Boy.

"That's what I said, Taddy,"

"No, I mean, THERE!"

Holly looked and saw in the distance an ominous black cloud approaching from the north.

"Oh dear, we won't have much time. The drooling gummies are coming. We have to get into the pyramid and fast!"

Fangor circled and landed in the mountainous jaws of the dragon with crevasses and rocks forming its teeth. On the west side, Holly saw where many archaeologists' excavations had taken place. They had obviously been trying to find the tomb entrance but without success. *False entrance,* she thought.

Remembering what the Tree of Knowledge had said, Holly looked eastward in the twilight sky and saw that the large Dragon Moon had half-risen. She looked toward the pyramid but saw nothing unusual. The glow from the moon was lighting the base of the pyramid. Worried, she looked north and saw that the moving blackness was getting closer as each second passed. She could almost hear the flap of their wings.

"Come on," she whispered desperately, as if to will the impossible of making the moon rise faster.

She looked eastward again. The moon had risen only slightly but its creeping glow now lit the bottom third of the pyramid.

"This is taking too long."

"Patience is a quality that is most needed when it is exhausted," Wizzy said.

"I can see the dragon!" Ruthless Toothless Brutus shouted. "It won't be long now, boys. We'll have all the dragon scales we'll ever need!"

"We will trap them in the jaws of those mountains; there will be no escape," added Queen Hali Tosis excitedly, now feeling a rush of new energy after the long journey across the Goblin Desert.

"Shall I order the army to split and encircle them, my lord?" enquired the head hunter.

"Yes, yes! Blue Gums left; Red Gums right and surround them. Make sure they can't escape! I will keep my elite Green Gums under General Puss in reserve with me!"

"Yes, my lord," the head hunter acceded.

Holly saw the ever-closer black swarm split into two arms and knew they were going to encircle them. She knew they had to act fast or it would be too late. To come this far only to fail now was unthinkable.

"I hate to be an alarmist but the rats with wings and gnashing teeth are almost upon us," Taddy said.

"I know, I know, Taddy Boy," Holly said, obviously worried. "We will hold them off as long as I can."

As the sun set in the west, she looked once again to the east. Finally, the Dragon Moon had risen and was now perfectly framed by the rocky dragon's teeth. Quickly she turned to see the moon glow shimmer on a spot in the middle of the eastern side of the pyramid.

"There!" she shouted, pointing. "That's where the entrance will be."

Fangor leapt and clung to the steep side of the pyramid over the exact spot she had pointed out the glimmer. With his fiery breath and a swish of his tail, he turned back the first wave of gummies making their attack.

Holly snatched Nova Cane out of her waistband and repeated the incantation of the Power Push spell.

"You who come too near
Go away get out of here
So far back you disappear
And never again to reappear."

"Jawbreaker!"

At once, thirty or forty gummies were hurled back and slammed onto the rough ridges of the dragon teeth. Knocked for a loop, they slumped down, dazed, confused, and slow to get up.

Fangor fired his flaming breath again and again and swished his huge tail knocking off all intruders that came near. Battered and befuddled, the first wave of gummies retreated to the safety of the jungle covering the hills. It would not be long before they regrouped and attacked again.

"Why are they attacking in small groups?" Taddy asked.

"I think they are testing us."

"Why?"

"Checking for any weaknesses."

Holly could see Ruthless Toothless Brutus directing his armies to move and amass to the south while the queen moved troops to the north.

"I think they want to attack from two sides at once," Holly perceived.

"We'd better get a move on."

"We have them now, my queen," the emperor chuckled. "There is no escape! General Puss, prepare to attack!"

"Yes, my lord."

Making use of the pause in action and under the cover of Fangor's wing, Holly pointed her thumb wearing the Ring of Myth toward the shimmer. It was the only thing she could think of to do and prayed it would have a result.

"Maybe we should have brought the broken pipe?" Taddy suggested.

"You mean the jade flute? Oh, I hope not. Mandible still has it."

Undaunted, she continued to point the ring. The glow from the Dragon Moon appeared to throb then shot a narrow pulsing beam of light through the opal stone in the ring. Then, magnified a thousand times it hurtled like a bolt of lightning, hitting the gleaming spot on the pyramid.

"Wow! Maybe you spoke too soon."

The earth rumbled and shook and fell away from the pyramid exposing a giant engraved stone. The stone reverberated then slid back exposing the entrance. Holly was about to enter when a wispy shape appeared and formed into the ancient Chin emperor, Chinny Chin Chin.

CHAPTER TWENTY-THREE

Dragons

Wearing striped pajamas, slippers, and a housecoat, a short, yawning, and unshaven emperor stood scratching the nape of his neck. "Who dares disturb my sleep?"

"That's the emperor?" a stunned Taddy Boy asked.

The drooling gummies attacked once more with a frenzied Ruthless Toothless Brutus screaming and commanding his troops onward. Fangor roared and shot several fireballs but it was clear, there were too many bats to hold them off for long. Holly quickly turned and fired her Power Push spell several times. Each time she fired, clusters of bats flew backward like a bowling pins hit by the ball.

Fangor was able to snatch General Puss out of the air and with one gnashing bite he lanced him like a boil.

"Wha...what's going on?" The sleepy Emperor Chin looked up and in sudden amazement realized a giant dragon stood over him defending the tomb entrance. Seeing the battle before him, he immediately pushed Holly aside, stepped forward, and raised his out stretched arms. In a low chant the emperor mumbled words Holly couldn't understand.

The swarm of bats almost blotted out the moonlight but Holly was still able to see the plains below in the dim light. The ground started to shake and shudder and, as if frozen, all involved turned and paused to see what was happening.

Suddenly, a fist broke through the earth, next a head, and then the body of a legendary enamel soldier surfaced. Covered in dust, he stood motionless at attention and appeared to wait. A second later another appeared, then a third emerged, and soon many soldiers had materialised, standing in rigid formation. Each warrior looked like a real person, in ancient armour and armed with shields, spears, swords, bows, and arrows. Enamel horses and war wagons also rose until the plain looked like a sea of thousands. In no time, battalions of the famed enamel soldiers stood in regimented order ready for battle.

Stunned, Ruthless Toothless Brutus was not sure what to do. Queen Hali Tosis saw that the situation against them was becoming worse by the second and ordered an immediate attack. The noise from the remaining gummies taking flight at once from the surrounding jungle trees was deafening. With such a mass, there was no way Holly or Fangor could ever hope to stop them. She braced herself for the worse.

With a wave of the emperor's arm the entire army saluted their leader then raised their weapons and cheered. At a second wave the army swiftly moved into regiments establishing positions of attack.

Once in place, the archers fired thousands of arrows, forming a dark cloud of deadly quills hurtling toward the attacking bats. When they struck their targets, hundreds of bats fell from the sky at once. Next, waves of javelins from the spear throwers struck down even more of the black horde while the remaining foot soldiers climbed up each side of the slope to form rings around the pyramid, ready to defend their emperor's tomb.

With the gummies' attentions distracted, the emperor raised his hand toward Fangor and in an instant Fangor shrank to the size of a lap dog and fell into his arms. He quickly ushered Holly into the pyramid and the stone door slammed shut behind them.

Once inside, Holly saw the magnificent interior of the pyramid as the emperor led them into the throne chamber. Soft, soothing music played as they crossed ornate arched bridges straddling the rivers, ponds, and streams of liquid silver that flowed past peaceful islands. Lavish pagodas and tranquil gardens of all kinds adorned each of the islands.

Even more majestic than Queen Pearly White's description, the ceiling mimicked the night sky, set with glowing pearls as stars. The entire underground glittered in gold and gems like a mystical palace. Silk curtains draped the walls and covered the furniture. Smooth white marble lined the floors supporting columns imbedded with jade. Room upon room really did contain everything the emperor would need in his afterlife.

"What are those things attacking my dragon?" Emperor Chinny Chin Chin asked while slipping on his imperial yellow robes adorned with white cranes.

"Those are the drooling gummies, makers of nightmare dust, and Fangor is *my* dragon...my lord"

"You tell him, Holly," Taddy Boy whispered.

"Perhaps so but I am the guardian of *all* dragons," Chinny said, now sitting on his throne and stroking the purring Fangor under the chin, "and who are you?"

"Oh, my apologies, my lord." Holly bowed. "My name is Holly Johnson from Bicuspid on the Root Canal."

"You may call me Imperial Highness. I have eaten mere lords for breakfast!"

"My apologies again, Your Imperial Highness," she said, bowing low. "How did you shrink Fangor? I have to use Santa's magic dust."

"As I said, I am the Guardian of Dragons and it has been a long, long time since I've had a baby dragon on my lap." He affectionately picked up Fangor and rubbed noses with the adoring dragon, then rubbed Fangor's belly saying, "Kitchy kitchy coo."

Taddy Boy rolled his eyes. "Are you kidding me? That's a fire breathing tinderbox and a bone crushing dragon!"

Outside Holly could hear the clamour of battle still raging. "Are you sure we are safe in here?"

"Do not worry dragon rider, my imperial army will keep them at bay," Chin Chin said, unconcerned. "Now go on."

"Those parasites have been chasing us since we started on our quest. They want Fangor's scales to make their hideous dust that disturbs people's dreams."

"Tell him they were going to eat us and, and pluck fairy wings, too!" Taddy Boy said excitedly.

"They have come very close to capturing us but we have been lucky, Your Imperial Highness."

"Lucky! Floooky, you mean! We have made it only by the skin of our teeth!" Taddy Boy retorted.

"There's no such thing as luck but just in case, it's good to have it on your side," Wizzy's muffled voice said from the backpack.

"Excuse me?" questioned the emperor hearing Wizzy.

"Pay no attention to Wizzy, Your Imperial Highness. He says things like that all the time. To answer your question, we have had some help from friends along the way."

"I assume you mean Mandible, my former arch-rival?" Chinny frowned.

"Yes, and others. The Monks from the Upper Palate monastery, Queen Pearly White, Santa..."

"Yes, yes, it takes all kinds to help our friends," he said impatiently still cuddling Fangor on his lap and nestled on his throne. "Now tell me, what is your quest?"

Holly opened her backpack and showed the emperor the eggs. "Fangor is the last dragon and we have brought the old eggs found in Gumgolia."

"Ahhh, wonderful. You want to bring back the eternal dragons."

"Yes, Your Imperial Highness."

"Did Mandible give you anything?"

"Yes, Your Highness, the Ring of Myth," she said showing the ring on her thumb. "We traded it for a jade flute. Now, as legend has it, we need the Moon Pearl."

"Very good. What do you bring me in exchange?"

"In exchange, Your Highness?"

"You gave Mandible a flute. What do you bring me?"

"Nothing. I thought you would want the dragons to live?"

"Oh, I do. It is an honour given to me from the Monks from the Upper Palate but tell me about this...Wizzy."

"Wizzy is a wisdom tooth given to me from my great, great, great times ten grandfather, Garth. A magician gave it to him. I believe at one time a magical giant panda gave it to you," she said bringing Wizzy out of the backpack for him to see.

"I recognize it now. I gave it to my court magician centuries ago. You call him Wizzy. That is a nice name. I don't suppose you would consider giving him to me to keep me company in my lonely eternal years?'

"Yes, give it to him, he's nothing but a pain in the...." Taddy Boy shouted eagerly.

"Your Imperial Highness," Holly interrupted. "As much as it pains me to miss his wise words, it would be my pleasure to return him to you. I hope you get the same enjoyment out of him as we have."

"Enjoyment! He just likes making us look dumb," Taddy Boy said.

"Exactly," Holly whispered over her shoulder.

"Wisdom is the greatest gift," Wizzy said.

"But the gift of the gab is the most expensive," answered Taddy Boy.

"You are most gracious, dragon rider. I will treasure him forever," Chinny said as he received the tooth.

"I bet he won't. He'll throw it in the silver river in no time," Taddy sneered.

"You never know," Holly replied.

"Excuse me?" asked the emperor.

"Oh, you know, you never know how long forever is."

"Yes, that is true. Now, the Moon Pearl. With a wave of his hand, the two white cranes beautifully embroidered on his imperial yellow robe with their long beaks, necks, and legs, came alive and flew gracefully into the air.

"Wow, that was cool!" Holly exclaimed.

"I find it rather warm in here," Emperor Chinny Chin Chin said.

"No, I mean what great magic. They are beautiful birds."

"The crane is the prince of all feathered creatures. They are the symbol of longevity, purity, and peace."

"Well, they definitely helped him on the long life bit," Taddy Boy said.

"What are they for?" she asked as the birds flew up and roosted on the top of the pagoda sheltering the throne.

"They carry the spirit of the departed to the heavens but these are my guardians of the Moon Pearl. Come, I will show you."

The birds took flight and led them across several streams and islands until they were in the center of the pyramid. The birds continued to circle above as they climbed the steps of a temple-like pagoda with an open roof. Inside the temple was a large, ornately carved box made of white jade.

"Here we are. Placed here many centuries ago, this is the Box of Eternal Harmony."

Holly looked at each side. The first side a carved image of a crane with one leg raised and wings outstretched was beautifully etched.

"This crane is a symbol of longevity."

Holly went to the next side and the carving showed a graceful crane among peony flowers.

"This means prosperity."

The next side had cranes amongst lotus flowers.

"This means purity."

The next had a crane standing among chickens.

"This means the crane has unusual ability and not of the common world."

"Finally, she looked at the top of the box and imbedded in with pearls and gold was a splendid crane sitting upon a rock and looking at the sun.

"This means authority that sees all."

"Wow, I have never seen such graceful beauty. I assume the Moon Pearl is in the box."

"It is." With a wave of his hands the white jade sides of the box appeared to melt away and transform into more beautiful white cranes. Gracefully, each one took flight and joined the other two circling above revealing a large golden nest and a huge pearl nestled inside.

"How beautiful," was all Holly could say. Even Taddy Boy was, for once, speechless.

The birds started to circle faster and faster causing a swirl of air. The Moon Pearl began to rise out of the nest and appeared to float in mid-air.

"Now you must place the eggs in the nest. Do it quickly as the Dragon Moon is nearly upon us."

Holly placed the five eggs along with the pieces of petrified dragons nest into the huge aerie nest with branches made of gold. Then she stepped back in awe.

Once in place, the nest also started to rise. The birds circled faster and soared higher and higher up in the giant pyramid raising the Moon Pearl and the nest with them. Holly looked up and saw the tip of the pyramid start to open up and reveal the clear night sky lit by the full Dragon Moon.

"We must hurry. You must have the Ring of Myth at the peak of the pyramid when the moon reaches its zenith."

"Then we must move fast as the moon is almost in position."

"That means going back out to face the yellow-eyed rodents," Taddy Boy warned.

"I know, but we have to do it."

"My soldiers will hold them."

"I sure hope so," Holly said as she and the emperor ran over the bridges and streams making their way back to the pyramid entrance.

The slab opened as they approached and the noise of battle was fierce. The soldiers had indeed kept the bats at bay but many on both sides had been lost. T-Pick and Hip Hop slipped deep into the bottom of the backpack.

"There they are! Attack, attack!" shouted Ruthless Toothless Brutus.

Swarms of bats that had been circling the pyramid went into a steep dive toward Holly and the emperor.

With a wave of the emperor's hand, Fangor returned to full size and immediately fired a huge fireball at the attackers while the enamel archers fired more volleys of arrows. Holly fired another Push Spell then scampered up the side of the pyramid with the emperor. The soldiers closed ranks around them forming an armoured shell with their shields with spears poking out like a porcupine.

Holly wanted to jump on Fangor and fly up to the peak but knew she would be too exposed to the attack. As the bats bounced off the shields in waves or were impaled on spear tips, Holly stuck out Nova Cane and fired her Push Spell again and again. The vicious attackers reeled backwards on each burst of energy but soon returned and attacked again.

The emperor slipped on the steep earthen side causing the tortoise shell to falter for a second. The Head Hunter, seizing the opportunity, flew in between the gap in the shields and clamped onto Holly with his talons and tried to lift her. Six enamel soldiers turned with their spears and stabbed the giant bat all at once. He slumped to his death on the ground trodden under foot as the rest of the soldiers moved upward.

"We must keep going, Your Highness," Holly said, helping Chinny to his feet.

Squads of archers continually moved and positioned themselves to keep sending wave after wave of arrows into the black mass but the slobbering fanged fiends kept ferociously attacking. Queen Hali Tosis was struck in the wing forcing her to retreat.

"Where General Puss?" she demanded when she saw Ruthless Toothless Brutus with a smoldering wing resting in the trees.

"Popped like a zit by the dragon," Ruthless informed her.

"What about Generals Boil and Scab?"

"Same for Boil but Scab and the Red Gums are still attacking from the west."

"Send everyone after the dragon; it is our only hope."

"Good idea, my queen."

Fangor soared through the horde, blasting his dragon fire and causing swaths of bats to fall smouldering to the ground. Then he noticed all the gummies turn toward him and away from the pyramid. Realizing that the bats were after him and leaving Holly and the eggs alone, he turned to the north leading most of them away.

The porcupine shell of soldiers finally reached the summit. The four sides of the pyramids point were flat forming a four-pointed star around the nest and with moon pearl suspended above it. The cranes soared high above in the night sky, ignored by the gummies. The Dragon Moon was just at its crest when Holly managed to climb on the platform formed by one of the points and, with the remaining bats swirling around them, Holly pointed the Ring of Myth at the Moon Pearl. As before, a white light flashed a beam from the Dragon Moon, through the Ring of Myth and surged into the Moon Pearl.

Fangor continued flying away, knowing he was outmatched and alone but if it saved the eggs his life was worth it. Slowly, the bats started to cling on to his wings to bring him down. He fought ferociously blasting as many as he could but their weight was slowed him.

"We have him," hissed Brutus.

The bats gnawed him again and again as they clung to his body, weakening him even further. Tired, bitten, and unable to go on, he wheeled downward and landed in the sands of the Goblin Desert. The black mass teemed all over him trying to sink their teeth into his hardened scales. He closed his eyes to await his fate.

The Moon Pearl glowed brightly then radiated a beam of energy down onto the eggs. The enamel soldiers kept the bats away as each colourful egg started to shimmer as an aura of light encased it. For a long moment the eggs absorbed the life-giving force. Holly couldn't help but have tears in her eyes when the shells began to crack then burst open. A baby dragon emerged from each egg.

The first to open was another green dragon just like Fangor, then a copper one, a blue one, then a red. Finally, the last egg opened and a beautiful pure white dragon emerged causing Emperor Chinny Chin Chin to gasp.

"What is the matter, Your Imperial Highness?"

Breathless with awe, he replied, "That is an Imperial White Dragon, the most exalted of all dragons, leader of all dragon realms. His name will be Maxilla, the Eternal Dragon."

"Wow. That is so awesome. I can't wait until he meets Fangor." Looking around her she said, "By the way…where is Fangor?"

"I saw him leave with thousands of bats following him. That is why there are so few bats remaining here."

Fear swelled up inside her. "Which way did he go?"

"He flew north toward the Goblin Desert."

"There is no way he could hold off that many drooling gummies. We have to go after him. But how?"

"I have an idea," the emperor said.

Waving his arms over the newly hatched dragons, an aura radiated from his hands and surrounded each newborn. Instantly, they grew into full-sized dragons and hovered above the nest.

"Wow!" Holly said in amazement.

Seeing the remaining annoying bats, several of the young dragons tried testing their breath of fire. Burp, burp, cough, splutter…then all of a sudden, the ignition was explosive as huge fireballs belched from their gapping jaws, lighting up the night sky. Several remaining gummies flew too close and were reduced to ashes before they could escape. "These beauties can help," the emperor assured Holly.

"How did you do that?"

"As I told you, I am the Guardian of Dragons. Now Maxilla will take you to find Fangor. I hope for his sake it is not too late."

The great white dragon flew down, allowing Holly to jump on his back. With the other dragons following, Maxilla surged upward and headed north, leaving Emperor Chinny Chin Chin and his enamel soldiers to finish off the last of the drooling gummies.

"She is a true dragon rider," he said with admiration as he watched Holly guide Maxilla with ease.

With the mass of black, hairy gummies crawling all over him, Fangor's limp, exhausted body was nearly finished. He had made peace with the end of his life and hoped the other dragons were safe. He had done all he could.

Giggling to each other, Ruthless Toothless Brutus and Hali Tosis sat triumphantly on a nearby rock overlooking the thrashing black sea of gummies completely covering the downed dragon.

"See, see, I told you we would have our dragon!" Brutus said, salivating at the prospect of having all the dragon scales they would ever need for their nightmare dust.

"Yes, my lord," the queen replied. "But we lost so many of our faithful."

"No worries, my sweet, we will remember them when we celebrate later as we feast on dragon meat and drink blood wine."

Queen Hali Tosis was not quite sure.

Fangor stirred when he thought he heard a familiar sound off in the distance. At first, he dismissed it as wishful thinking or a memory from the past but then he heard it again as the sound became louder. He knew what it was. It was the sound of dragon wings. Re-energized with hope, he lifted his head.

Startled at Fangor's sudden movement, some of the gummies took flight like crows, only to resettle and continue to gnaw on the dragon's hide.

The fireball from five dragons firing all at once was enormous and took the revelling gummies by complete surprise. Thousands of bats that were trying to tear scales off of Fangor turned into cinders while others, trying to escape, were caught in mid-flight.

"Whaaaaaaat?" was all that Ruthless Toothless Brutus managed to scream when he too was singed beyond recognition by Maxilla's white fire. Burnt to a crisp, his blackened form fell into a pile of ashes.

Even with a wounded wing, Queen Hali Tosis with a quicker eye was able to fly off just in time thereby managing to escape into the night air.

"Where did they come from?" she screamed.

With five dragons attacking and with Holly riding the magnificent white dragon using her Fire Spell, Fangor was soon rid of the mangy parasites clinging to him. Damaged and scarred but with re-invigorated blood pumping through his veins, he roared back to life firing flaming missiles and mustered just enough strength to take flight once more.

"Yes!" Holly screamed, happy to see her old friend alive and flying once again.

"Flee my nasties, fleeeeeee!" screeched the escaping queen.

Now six huge dragons soared and circled in the sky. On each pass they fired their blasting furnace fireballs at the remainder of the fleeing bats who were now trying to make their escape across the Goblin Desert toward the Land of Plaque.

Several hunters along with the rag tag remains of a once formidable and tyrannical army helped Queen Hali Tosis along.

"No need to chase them," Holly said pulling back on the white dragon's neck. "It will be a long time before they are ever able to try that again."

"Whaddaya mean, no need?" shouted Taddy Boy, unable to restrain himself. "I don't want to go through this a third time. Let's go after those varmints and blast every one of them out of the sky, once and for all!"

"I think we need to look after our friend," Holly said, seeing Fangor slumped on a nearby rock, completely exhausted.

She jumped off her dragon and ran to him. Wrapping her arms around his large head, she sobbed, "Fangor, are you all right?"

> "My dear friend, Holly,
> Don't be so melancholy,
> I may have fought my last fight,
> But I am happy the dragons took flight.
> We did our best
> And finished our quest.
> Please wish King Mo-lar my last goodbye,
> As a new dragon will protect his hive."

"But, but I don't want to see you die," she wept.

> "Some things must be what they must be;
> I have lived long and now I am free.
> I will miss you, my dear friend,
> But all good things must sometime end."

Holly sobbed once more as Fangor slumped and rested his neck on the ground. His brilliant green skin faded into a morbid grey. His eyes stared blankly off into the distance as he exhaled his final breath.

"No, no, this can't be," Holly bawled. "No, no, no!"

Desperately, Holly dug into her knapsack and pulled out her *Beginners Magic* book and frantically flipped the pages searching for a Healing Spell or Restore Life Spell but none could be found. To heal took a much more experienced wizard than a magician's apprentice and she knew it. Miserably, she slumped down and cried uncontrollably.

"I am sorry about our friend, Holly," Taddy Boy said, trying to console her. T-Pick jumped onto her shoulder and tried to lick her tears away while Hip Hop gave her a hug, but Holly couldn't stop crying.

"Real friends are those who walk in when you are down and out," a familiar voice said.

Holly looked up with tears streaming down her face. "What? Who?" She thought she had heard Wizzy.

"Perhaps I can help, Holly."

She had not heard Emperor Chinny Chin Chin arrive on his war wagon accompanied by several of his Imperial Guard. He now stood before her with Wizzy in his hand.

"Will you give me the Ring of Myth?"

Trying to stop blubbering, Holly slipped it off her thumb and handed it to the emperor who put it on.

The emperor waved his arms and pointed the Ring of Myth up into the night sky then over Fangor. A glittering sprinkle of starlight showered down from the Dragon Moon, covering Fangor in a mystical golden dust. Under the shimmering powder, each open wound began to close and heal, new scales sprouted like blossoms, and his dull grey skin began to change colour back into resplendent green.

Holly watched in awe and anticipation then jumped with glee when Fangor sucked in a new gasp of air and blinked his eyes.

"Yes!' she shouted with Taddy Boy. "This is wonderful. You saved Fangor...but how?"

"I told you, I am the Guardian of all Dragons."

Holly looked up and for a moment she swore she saw the emperor's face appear to change into that of a dragon then return to human form.

"How do you think I live eternally?" the emperor asked. "I have the blood from the dragon mother running through my veins given to me by the sacred monks."

Fangor, now completely healed, stood once more and roared with new life.

"New life runs through my veins,
I am free from all death's chains.
My heart feels right as rain
To protect the tooth fairies once again."

He flapped his wings then joined the other dragons circling above. Like children, they frolicked together under the Dragon Moon sky.

CHAPTER TWENTY-FOUR

Home at Last

In the mountains north of Bicuspid, a great gathering of all the fairies was taking place upon the news of Holly, the human magician's apprentice, and the dragons' return.

"How can we thank-you, Holly, for what you have done?
You fought our battle and you have won.
Fangor is back safe and sound,
Your name will forever be renowned," said King Mo-lar excitedly to the cheering of the crowds in Fairyland.

"After all this time we can return,
to our own Fairylands that for so long we have yearned.
We cannot thank-you enough,
You are what legends are made of," said King Wisdom from the Northern Upperfangs as he rubbed noses with his blue dragon.

"With our own dragons to keep us safe and warm,
We will never fear the deadly swarm.
Children's teeth all around the world,

Will once again receive a nice new coin," said King Mungmouth from the western Toungies, sitting like a cowboy on the copper dragon.

"With the bravery of a Girl Scout,
You have returned the music to the South.
We are forever in your debt,
Come any time for a gumbo and Poke Sally banquet,"
said King Jeb from the Southern Backtooths playing a banjo while on the other green dragon.

"One again the sacred dragon in the east shall live,
A great honour to receive the gift you give.
As a child so young,
Your name will forever be enshrined in our tongue,"
said King Toothhurty from the Eastern Palates bowing in respect with all of the other fairies from the Eastern Palates. Even the red dragon gracefully dipped his head.

"Your Highnesses, I thank you for all of your kind words but don't forget my dear friend Fangor, and my faithful friends, Taddy Boy, T-Pick, and Hip Hop." She gave Fangor a stroke behind the ear and Taddy Boy a big hug that made his heart glow a bright red. T-Pick rapped a beat while Hip Hop danced in circles. "We also had a lot of help along the way."

"Of your modesty, Garth would be proud.
You stand out in every crowd.
Because of what you did was of such magnitude,
We would like to give you a token of our gratitude.
Name anything that is in our power,
On you these gifts we will shower," said King Molar before the roaring crowd.

"Yes! Ask for a gazillion dollars from the Rainbow Pot of Gold! Or, or a new house, or a doughnuts for life..." Taddy Boy immediately suggested.

"Thank-you, King Mo-lar, but I really don't need anything."

"What? What? Noooo, get something for me, maybe a new fur, or, or..."

"That would be nice for Taddy Boy. I would like to come and visit now and then. I would like to see you all and, of course, Fangor."

Taddy Boy instantly changed into a brand new teddy bear, became quite quiet and glowed in his new fur.

> "Of course, my dear friend
> Any time, any when.
> But there must be something we can do,
> Something special just for you."

"Well...I think I am in a lot of trouble at home. My dad will be really mad with me being away so long. The phone ran out of battery so I couldn't keep calling him."

All the kings gathered around King Mo-lar to discuss the problem until finally they broke their huddle. King Mo-lar said,

> "I think we have found a solution
> To save a lot of time and confusion.
> King Dentin will take you back to the castle
> Where you will find no hassle
> Remember this is not good bye.
> Just call and we'll reply."

Just as before, when she had first come to Fairyland, King Dentin and the butterflies flurried around Holly and whisked her away back to the Bicuspid castle and placed her in the throne room of King Overbite.

"Welcome back, Holly," said the ghostly image of Garth standing next to spirits of King Overbite and Queen Pearly White.

"Oh, Great-grandpa times ten, it is so good to see you again. I have been on such an adventure."

"Nearly got us killed…I mean, more than once. You know, lots and lots of times," interrupted Taddy Boy.

"Yes, I have heard all about it. You were a brave girl and well deserving of being a Magician Level One.

"What about me? I was there all the way just like I was with you. Don't I get a title?" Taddy Boy asked sadly.

"Yes, I believe you do," said Queen Pearly White. "From this day forward you will be known as the Royal Companion and Fuzzy Comforter."

"Fuzzy Comforter! What am I, a blanket?"

"No, Taddy Boy, you are my best friend," Holly assured him as she gave him a heart-glowing hug.

"Okay, I like that; that means more to me," he sighed.

"Oh, and thank-you, Great-grandpa," Holly said absentmindedly. Then realizing what he had said, she looked up. "Magician?"

"Yes, little one. You have earned the right to call yourself a Magician…Level One, mind you, but Magician all the same."

"Thank-you, Great-grandpa. I will study hard so if I am ever needed maybe I can help again."

"Now hold on there. Don't think you are going to con me into another one of your 'adventures'," Taddy protested. "No sir, never again. Two is plenty for a stuffed teddy bear. Anyways, I wouldn't want to spoil my new coat."

"Okay, Taddy Boy, I've got the picture. I'll just leave you home with my little brother who likes using you like a football. You would like that, wouldn't you?"

"Well, let's not be too hasty…" he said, reconsidering.

"Thank-you for returning my queen," said a smiling King Overbite. "If it wasn't for you and your friends, I would never have seen her again."

"You're welcome, my lord."

SMAAASH!

A missile of some sort crashed through the window.
THWANGGGGG!

The surfboard reverberated in the high back of the king's throne.

"Hey dudes and dudettes," shouted the dripping wet, baggy-shorts-wearing Poseidon, heaving his board out. "What's happnin'?"

"My son! You too have returned," cried Queen Pearly White. "Now all my wishes have come true. I too will forever be in your debt," she said to Holly. "You have brought me back to my true love *and* my son."

"You are welcome, Your Majesty."

"Holly, because of you, our job is done here and we must leave," said Garth.

"What? You can't leave. Not now. I need you," Holly pleaded.

"Leave we must. We have roamed this earth for far too long and because of you we can now rest peacefully. You are now the Magician of Bicuspid to protect Fairyland."

"But how?"

"You will find all you need in my workshop. King Dentin will guide you and be your friend."

A bright white light appeared in mid-air, forming a doorway. Garth, King Overbite, and Queen Pearly White gave one last wave, walked toward it, and were slowly swallowed up in its beams.

"Good-bye, Grandpa Garth," Holly said sadly. "Good-bye King Overbite, and Queen Pearly White," she said waving back.

"See ya, Mom. See ya, Pops," called Poseidon.

Once the three had passed through the light, it faded and then disappeared.

"Well, that was cool, dude, but I gotta hit the surf. Nice to see ya again, Hodad." In an instant Poseidon had gone out the window, riding his board on a waterspout back to the Root Canal.

"Wow, is that it?" said Taddy Boy in the now silent room.

"I guess so," Holly said, shrugging her shoulders.

King Dentin softly landed on her shoulder.

"Well, at least you're still here."

Just then she heard a noise outside the door. The door swung open and there stood her dad and the custodian.

"There you are, young miss. We have been looking for you all morning. How did you get in here? We just left."

Caught off guard, Holly stammered a reply. "I, I came in from the other way. Did you see..." she said, pointing in the direction of Poseidon's exit.

"See what? Didn't see a thing. Heard a ghost though."

"But, but...oh well, you'd never believe me anyway."

"All morning?" questioned Taddy Boy.

"That's right. He said 'all morning'." She paused. "The Fairy Kings," she whispered. "They must have turned back time, at least for us humans anyway."

"That's right," Mr. Johnson said. "It's time we got you home. Your mother is worried sick about you."

"But Dad, we came to find out what the note meant and..."

Annoyed, he interrupted. "I don't want to hear anymore about that note from the tooth fairies. Because there are no tooth fairies!"

"But Dad, there *are* tooth fairies."

"Sure, we'll see about that," he said holding her hand and guiding her out of the castle entrance.

"But Dad…"

"No buts, just get into the car, young lady. Let's get you home." He put her bicycle into the trunk and slammed it shut.

Once on their way, he asked, "Where did you get that hat and that stick stuffed in your waist?"

"In the castle."

"What's with the funny looking feather?"

"Oh, that's Quill. He's my…"

"You shouldn't be touching stuff in there. Don't you know that it's a historical site? I don't want you ever going there alone ever again."

"Don't say anything," Taddy Boy cautioned. "We know that won't happen."

Before she could answer, Mr. Johnson slammed on the brakes. "Whoa, what is that?" he shouted, seeing the chameleon and praying mantis on Holly's shoulder.

"Those are my friends, T-Pick and Hip Hop."

"You kids pick up the darnedest things as pets. That thing won't give you warts, or something worse, will it?"

"No, Dad. He's cool."

"Yo, yo, old man,

Can you understand?

I'm no ordinary amphibian,

I'm a chameleon

I'm dapper,

I'm a rapper,

I'm the music man, man. Yo," T-Pick sang his beat box as Hip Hop danced.

"What the dickens…?"

"Don't worry Dad. They're cool."

"Okay, I guess. Do you know you also have a monarch butterfly on your hat?"

"He's my friend, too."

Offended that he hadn't been noticed, Taddy Boy complained, "Hey, he didn't notice my new threads."

"Give him time," sighed Holly.

A news report blurted out from the radio:

"The mysterious bats have all left the area of Bicuspid. No one really knows where they came from or where they went but scientists think they were a new breed on a rare migration."

"That's good to hear," said Mr. Johnson.

"Further studies will be made but for now, they won't be pestering the citizens of Bicuspid and the night curfews have been lifted," the reporter continued.

"What a relief," Mr. Johnson added.

"Coincidentally, the local hospitals also report a huge decrease in citizens seeking severe headache remedies."

"It sure is nice to be home," sighed Taddy Boy.

"None of the kids in school are going to believe our adventure."

"Wait till they get a load of Nova Cane," Taddy Boy said.

"That should knock 'em right out," Holly said as they both doubled over with laughter.

"What's so funny?" Mr. Johnson asked.

THE END

ABOUT THE AUTHORS

BRUCE KILBY

Born in Woodstock, Ontario Canada was formally educated in England, returning to the West coast of British Columbia in 1966. He now resides in Langley, B.C.

A long time songwriter and short story author, Bruce's wrote his first children's novel, *The Legend of the Tooth Fairy* with Ken Johnson. Bruce is also the author of *The Witch of Weasel Warren*.

Samples of Bruce Kilby's songs can be found at Firesidestoriespublishing.com

KEN JOHNSON

Ken Johnson was born in Vancouver, B.C. in 1951, and now resides in Cloverdale, B.C.

Ken discovered a passion for song writing in 1962 and continues today with his creative gift as a singer/song writer.

The Secret of the Eternal Dragon is the sequel to *The Legend of the Tooth Fairy* and is Ken's second attempt of taking a step beyond the comfort zone of song writing.

For many years, Ken has co-written songs with Bruce Kilby. Ken knew that Bruce was gifted with a great imagination and when asked, Bruce agreed to partner in this endeavour.

About the Artists

Jisoo Shin - Illustrator

Jisoo Shin was born and raised in Surrey, B.C. and is currently a student at the University of British Columbia studying French with plans to work as a teacher in the future. Jisoo continues to practice art in her free time; it being a lifelong passion of hers. She specializes in traditional line work and digital cell shading.

Elizabeth Yuan - Cover Artist

Elizabeth Yuan was raised in Coquitlam, BC, and is currently a high school senior pursuing art. She specializes in digital illustration and traditional painting.

Wendy Dewar Hughes - Book Designer

Wendy Dewar Hughes is an author, editor, artist, and designer. As well as helping authors write and publish their books, she creates programs to help creatives succeed. Wendy lives in British Columbia.
Her work can be found at
www.wendydewarhughes.com,
and www.summerbaypress.com.

Other Books by Bruce Kilby and Ken Johnson

This exciting adventure sequel continues in the modern day city of Bicuspid from the escapades of 800 years ago by the magician Garth described in The Legend of the Tooth Fairy by a magical teddy bear by the name of Taddy Boy.

Fangor, the last remaining dragon, has sensed dragon eggs have been unearthed in a place called Gumgolia and, driven by strong prehistoric survival instincts, wishes to bring them back to life. Holly, the unsuspecting young descendant of Garth, is summoned by the fairies to help them in a magical and dangerous journey through Brusha, Tonsilvania and the Land of Plaque. Once again the evil bats called the Drooling Gummies, under their Emperor Ruthless Toothless Brutus and his queen Hali Tosis, have returned to spread their Nightmare Dust, capture fairies and, at all costs, the last dragon. With the help from her friends Taddy Boy, T-Pick the chameleon, Hip Hop the Praying Mantis and several others along the way, Holly becomes a Dragon Rider and Magician's Apprentice in her quest to save the dragons and all the Fairylands.

BY BRUCE KILBY

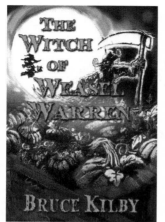

Late at night, Duke Skysquawker, a crow from the Northwoods Rookery, discovers weasels stealing pumpkins out of Farmer McSimmons' pumpkin patch. He reports the strange activity to his farm friends who realize they have to do something. Stranger, a relocated city raccoon, and his field mouse sidekick, Pronto, are sent to find out what is going on.

The two masked detectives discover that an evil witch and warlock have devious plans for this year's Halloween. Along with the Sugarplum Fairy, Quacks the Pig, Sneezer the Bloodhound, Gerome the Gnome, Patches the Scarecrow, and several of their other animal friends, they attempt to put a stop to the wicked plan of making Halloween evil once again.

The Witch of Weasel Warren is a fun fantasy escapade with plenty of scary moments and an exciting final battle between good and evil.